Aisling's Revelation

Vicki Wootton

Stargate Publishing

Aisling's Revelation

ISBN – eBook: 978-1-989149-04-1
ISBN - Print: 978-1-989149-05-8

Other books by this author

NOVELS

The Whisperer – The Children of Light Book 1
The Whisperer's Journey – The Children of Light Book 2
Where Have All the Young Girls Gone?
At War with Terror
Forbidden World
Reluctant Warriors
Fatal Harvest

NON-FICTION

Names of the World

Thank You

Terri Saya, Pauline Van Havere, Laurie Campbell, and Aubry Baptist for their keen eyes, favorable comments, and editing skills. I couldn't have done it without you.

I take sole responsibility for all errors, typos, and other follies not removed from this manuscript.

୫ଓଃ

Primary Characters

Elves

Aisling (pronounced *Eye-sling*)- Country farm girl

Irial (pronounced Eerial) - Elven envoy

Queen Fenella – Aisling's birth mother

Humans

Gran - Muirne Mac Roibín

Gran's friend - Aunty Patsy

Lena (pronounced *Layna*)

Korrigen (Pronounced korreeghen)

Domin (father/chief) Cragsil – leader of the northern Korrigen

Loamin (son) Cragsil – son of the Domin.

Momo (grandmother) Tilly – healer – mother of the Domin

Olgon – "the boy" son of Loamin Cragsil

Slaves

Lena – Aisling's friend
Master Gobrum – the slave master
Nápla – slave head cook

Dwarfs

Gyoka - leader of the dwarf warriors
Qurak – dwarf second in command

Dragons

Lord Felivar (Pronounced Fell-eevar) dragon leader
Jevtic (pronounced Yevtix) dragon monarch

1 – Aisling

Haven't ye finished those 'taties yet?" her grandmother said, her voice rising fretfully. "It's time to feed the birds and clean out the nests. And don't break any eggs today."

Aisling took a breath to answer, but gran hadn't finished her rant yet. She probably didn't expect her granddaughter to respond anyway. Aisling lifted the pot of peeled potatoes and put it on the hob of the stove, then she picked up a wooden bucket by the door and scraped the peelings off the table, adding them to the other scraps: stale bread crusts, vegetable waste, eggshells, tea leaves, nodding occasionally to her gran as she continued complaining.

"I swear, you get more absent in the head every day. I suppose it's your age. I don't know what you young-uns are coming to these days. I hope you're not mooning over some boy."

"All finished, Gran. I'm on my way." She bent to kiss her grandmother's cheek. "See you later."

She knew gran was in the doorway watching her as she walked around the side of the cottage to the fenced area where the hens lived. She sighed and closed the gate behind her, then threw the contents of the bucket across the ground, spreading them well so that all the poultry would have a chance to grab a morsel. Although most of the hens were already outside, pecking around the ground, this was the signal for the rest to leave their nests and join the feeding frenzy, leaving them free for her to collect the eggs.

After taking the eggs in the house, she returned and picked up a rake to clean up the dirty straw from the floor and nesting boxes. She didn't mind the work. It gave her an opportunity to think, something she did frequently when she was alone. Her grandmother called it lolly-gagging.

Today, Aisling was thinking about her grandmother. When she kissed her this morning, she'd realized that she had grown taller than gran. She's getting old, Aisling thought, recalling how gran walked with a limp and was always massaging her lower back. Gran complained about rheumatics and the corns on her feet, but she didn't let it interfere with her work. She just kept on slogging away. Today, she was weeding the vegetable garden. Tears came to Aisling's eyes when she realized she hadn't been as helpful or sympathetic as she should have.

I'll have to try harder, do things for her, carry heavy stuff so she doesn't strain her back. I don't know what I'd do if anything happened to her.

Aisling's father had been killed in a skirmish with some brigands who'd attacked the village when she was a baby. A few years later, her mother had wrapped up her little girl and left her with the parents of her father, and then she had left the village without telling anyone where she was going. Nothing had been heard of her since, although there was talk in the village of her going off with a traveller. Travellers were people who went around the countryside doing odd jobs, repairing equipment, buying and selling odds and ends. Most people thought of them as little better than thieves, maybe envying their independence.

She didn't remember either of her parents. Her whole life experience so far was with her grandparents. They were kind to her and provided all her needs, taught her all she knew, which was mostly how to run a small-holding. Her grandfather used to take his little donkey cart to the village market once a week, loaded with produce, eggs, milk and cheese, and sometimes, an animal or a few hens. In the warm months, she often went with him. Those were the happiest times in her life. He'd died when she was eleven years old after suffering from painful tumours for almost a year.

Before her grandfather died, they'd had a few cows and some sheep, in addition to the poultry, but that would have been too much work for an aging woman and a young girl to manage, so the remaining stock was sold, and they now eked out a living from the poultry, a small apple orchard, and the vegetable garden. They also kept some bee hives for honey.

Aisling spread some fresh straw in the nests and on the hen-house floor and then shovelled the waste into the composting box outside the fence.

I wonder how gran's doing. Maybe she needs some help. She put the tools away and went around the back of the cottage to the vegetable garden. A movement in the nearby trees caught her eye, but whatever it was had disappeared by the time she turned to look. She

3

shrugged. When she reached the vegetable garden, her grandmother was sitting on a tree stump resting her head against the hoe she was holding between her knees.

"I've finished, gran," she called as she opened the gate.

Her grandmother started and looked up at her, then she tried to raise herself with the hoe for support. She looked a little confused at first, but quickly recovered, although she didn't answer Aisling.

Maybe she's embarrassed that I saw her resting. Poor gran. "Gran, would you like to go in the house and have some tea. I can do some hoeing if you like." She reached out for the hoe, which the old woman was still clinging to. "Here, give me that. I'll walk to the house with you. You must be tired, working in the hot sun."

Aisling put her arm out to support her gran and together they walked to the front of the cottage and went inside. "There, gran. It's a lot cooler in here. Sit down and I'll make some tea."

"I'm all right; don't fuss," her grandmother said irritably. However, she went over to her favourite chair and sat down, expelling a long breath. "Did you get the eggs in?" she asked.

"Of course I did. They're in the cold box with the others."

"Did you wash them first?"

Aisling felt a touch of irritation. "Yes," she replied. She dipped the iron kettle in the water drum to fill it and put it down hard on the stove top. *I've got to*

4

understand she's not feeling well and may be in pain.
That would make anyone irritable. It's not her fault.

"It looks as if the fire needs a few more logs," she
said and went outside to get some.

∽∾

Aisling was exhausted when she finally went to bed.
Her grandmother had fallen asleep after drinking her
tea and eating a scone, so she had been left with the
task of weeding the garden. After that she had done
some baking and cooked a meal for them. Gran had
seemed a bit dozy and kept dropping her food when
she tried to put it in her mouth. She became more and
more irritable as the evening wore on, so Aisling helped
her with her nightgown and tucked her into bed.

She had barely fallen asleep in her loft bedroom
when she heard a thud from downstairs where her
grandmother slept, followed by a long moaning groan.
She virtually slid down the ladder from the loft in her
haste to find out what had happened. Gran was lying on
the floor beside her trundle bed. She looked as if she
was trying to get up, but her body wasn't responding.

Aisling knelt on the floor beside her and tried to
roll her over, but this only made the old lady moan
louder. She moved her head and mumbled in a garbled
attempt to speak but couldn't say anything that made
sense to her granddaughter. "I don't understand what
you're saying, gran. I want to help you; you can't lie
there all night. Let me get you back in bed where you'll
be more comfortable."

Gran started to struggle as if she wanted to get up,
but something wasn't working properly. Aisling noted

5

that only one side of her body was moving while the other side seemed to be scrunched up as if it was shrinking. *This is no good,* she thought. *I'll have to move her whether she likes it or not.* She stood up and surveyed the situation, trying to plot the best way to move the old lady back onto her bed. *I'll have to turn her over, she decided. If I can get my arms under her, I might be able to lift her.* The bed wasn't high, barely knee-high from the floor. The hardest thing for her was changing her gran's wet nightgown.

Once her grandmother was lying back in her bed with the covers pulled up to her chin, Aisling noticed one side of her face was drooping, the same side as the inactive limbs. "It's all right, gran, I'll take care of you, don't worry." She squeezed her gran's right hand, the good hand, and felt some week pressure in response. "I'll go to the village in the morning to fetch the healer."

As she turned away to put the wet nightgown in the wash tub, Aisling thought she sensed a movement outside the window, a quick shadow that disappeared into the darkness. The rippled glass panes were hard to see through, so she couldn't be sure. It could have been a night bird. The windows were only designed to let in light, and there was nothing but candle light from inside at this time of night.

2 - The Stranger

೩೦೬

Aisling woke up with a start to see sunlight through the little round window of her loft. The cottage was eerily silent, although there was plenty of noise outside. It was chilly too. Usually the stove fire was lit by this time. She quickly sat up on the edge of her bed and changed into her work clothes, knee britches and a long tunic of coarse linen, and sandals for her feet. She needed to visit the outhouse, but first she had to check on gran. Her heart speeded up as she slid down the ladder, not knowing what to expect. It was the silence that frightened her the most. It could not bode well. She would have expected gran to be making some sort of sound, moaning, sighing, or snoring, not this silence.

She crept over to the alcove where her grandmother slept and knelt beside the bed. "Gran! Are you all right, gran?" she murmured. But her eyes told her she would not get an answer. The old woman's chest didn't rise and fall with breathing. Her eyes were staring sightlessly at the low ceiling and her skin was paler than she had ever seen it. Aisling touched her hand and found it was icy. She lowered her head onto the still body as tears sprang to her eyes. "Oh gran, I'm so sorry. I should have..." but what could she have done? She was fifteen years old with no experience of illness and

7

dying, apart from her grandfather's death. But that had happened over many months and was expected. This was so sudden and unexpected.

The pressure in her bladder brought her to her feet. She couldn't wait any longer and rushed out the door and across the yard to the outhouse. She walked slowly back to the house. *What am I going to do?* She stopped under the plum tree and wept into her hands, her shoulders moving in time to her sobs. *Oh, Gran! What will I do without you? There's so much work. I can't do it all by myself.*

The rooster crowed, reminding her that the poultry needed feeding, and the eggs...

Rustling in the trees startled her. She wiped her eyes with her sleeve and turned to look. It was a man. She wasn't sure if she should be afraid of him, so she just froze, staring at him as he looked back at her. He looked quite young and was very tall with long silver hair. His clothes were unusual, to her at any rate. He wore long, skin-hugging leggings and a knee-length tunic, both of a fine green material that she couldn't name. He carried a bow and sheath of arrows on his left shoulder.

Finally, he smiled at her; then she realized he was quite handsome in an alien sort of way. He took a step towards her with both hands up facing forward, then he ducked his head and said, "I'm Irial." His voice wasn't like those of other men. It sounded refined, almost musical.

Aisling was dumbfounded. She couldn't think what to say, so she just nodded.

"You don't need to be afraid, Aisling," Irial said, taking another step forward. "I know you're are passing through a difficult time in your life and I want to help you."

Finally, Aisling found her tongue. "How do you know my name?" she blurted, taking a step back towards the cottage door.

"I have been sent to overwatch you and keep you safe."

"Why? Who sent you?"

"My people have an interest in you, Aisling." He moved past her to the door and opened it. "Come on, there's a lot of work to be done and I'm going to help you." She followed him to the door but stayed on the doorstep. Irial turned and looked at her. "I know you have just lost your only kin and are feeling devastated right now. Let's take things one step at a time. You make some tea while I take care of the poultry. How does that sound?"

She wiped her eyes with the back of her hands. He sounded so sure of himself, but what did he want with her? *I'll find out, I suppose.* "All right, but what am I going to do about my gran?"

"What do you normally do when someone passes on?"

"When my grandad died, his friends came and buried him out back. Gran had to register it with the village clerk."

"Does she have any friends who could help bury her?"

Aisling automatically began to get a fire started to heat water for tea. "There's some old ladies she has tea with every week when she goes to the village to sell the eggs." Once the kindling caught, she added some small pieces of wood and a couple of thin logs.

"Do these friends have sons or husbands that could dig a resting place for her remains?"

He has a strange way of saying things, she thought. *He must be a foreigner.* "I suppose so," she replied with a tinge of guilt for not know much about her grandmother's life.

"May I sit down for a moment?" he asked. "I think you should as well. You need to eat something. We can talk while you are eating."

She nodded and pointed out a chair for him by the table. She was glad he was ready to talk. Now maybe she could find out what he wanted and where he was from, but it didn't turn out quite as she'd hoped. She poured her tea, offering him some, which he turned down. "Just water for me, thank you," he said.

Aisling toasted a couple of scones in front of the stove and spread them with butter and raspberry jam. Irial also declined the food.

Once they were settled, he started to talk. "Here's what we should do. You go into town and register the passing." He stood up suddenly and went over to her grandmother's body. After a moment, he came back and sat down. "I just wanted to make sure she was gone," he said. "When you've done that, find some of her friends and tell them about it. Do you think they would come to prepare the remains?"

"I don't know," she replied. "Maybe. When my grandad died, she did the preparations as you call it.

"Very well. While you are gone, I will take care of the livestock and anything else that needs to be done."

She frowned and took another bite of her scone.

"Don't worry," Irial said. "I'm not going to rob you."

Aisling felt her face turning red and she stammered, "I was ... wasn't, I mean I didn't think..."

"Don't worry about it," he said, getting up and going to the door. As he passed it, he picked up the scrap bucket. "I'm going to take care of the poultry now while you get ready to go."

He's taking over my life, she thought. *Who is he and what does he want with me?* But she was glad in a way. She felt too shaken and confused to think clearly and do everything by herself.

When she was ready to go, she went to the fence of the poultry yard and looked to see what he was doing. He put down the rake he'd been using in the hen house and came to join her.

Taking her hand, he turned, and his penetrating green eyes held her gaze. "I see you're ready to go." He turned and looked at the track that led to the laneway and then back at her. "This is very important, Aisling. Do not say a word about me to anyone. No one must know I am here. We would both be in peril if certain factions knew I had contacted you. It really could be a matter of life and death for both of us if word got out. Do you understand?" he squeezed her hand with his surprisingly smooth one and looked her in the eyes.

"I don't understand, Irial, but I will do as you ask, as long as you don't have ... I don't know how to say it."

"You mean as long as my intentions are honourable?" She nodded. "I swear it on the head of my

11

mother. My purpose is honourable and extremely beneficial to us and to you. All right?"

"All right. I swear I will not tell a soul. I must go now."

Irial was still holding onto her hand. He raised it to his lips and kissed it before he let her go.

Aisling felt a warm current flow through her as she walked down the lane to the village.

⇛⇚

Her mind was in turmoil by the time she reached the village. The mystery of Irial's appearance at the cottage vied with the sudden death of her grandmother for her attention. In her current state of mind, both these events had life-changing potentials for her. Why didn't he want her to reveal his presence? *I should be thinking about my poor gran, not some stranger,* Aisling scolded herself. *What am I going to do without her? How will I manage everything? Poor gran, why did you have to die?* Tears started pouring down her face. She had stuffed some cotton rags in her pocket before starting out, fearing this might happen; she pulled one out to wipe her face and blow her nose. I must think about what I need to do. Which was more important, registering gran's passing or telling her friends?

The village, Enisdale, looked almost deserted, as it usually did when it wasn't a market day. Most of the men and women would be working at this time of day in their gardens, workshops, and at their looms or bakeries. She waved to the blacksmith as she passed his open smithy, then she saw a familiar woman leave one of the shops and turn to walk the other way. It was one of gran's friends, so she broke into a run to catch up with her.

"Auntie Patsy," she called.

The woman stopped and looked around. "Aisling, what...?" As soon as she saw Aisling's red eyes, her expression changed to concern. "Is something wrong?"

Aisling stopped and wiped away another tear. "It's gran, auntie, she..." she stopped with a sob unable to continue.

Auntie Patsy was one of gran's closest friends. She put her basket of bread down on the doorstep next to her and put an arm around Aisling's shoulder.

"Has something happened to her?" Aisling nodded and sniffed back some tears. "Is she hurt? We should get the healer if..." Aisling shook her head, no. "Then what...?"

Aisling choked back a sob. "She's passed on," she managed to blurt before she was overtaken by a flood of tears.

"She's gone? Oh, you poor dear." The woman put her arms around Aisling and held her tight, then she picked up her basket. "Come on. We'll go to my house and have a cup of tea while you tell me all about it."

Aisling notice the glitter of unshed tears in Patsy's eyes as she turned to lead the way. Patsy's house was one in the middle of a row of small attached house around the corner from the main avenue.

Once they were sitting in Patsy's little parlour, with cups of hot tea and slices of freshly-baked bread with butter and strawberry jam, Patsy started the

13

conversation with the question: "What can I do to help?"

"I don't know what to do, Auntie; can you tell me?"

"Hmm. I suppose the first thing we need think about is..." she hesitated and swallowed some tea. "Taking care of her remains. I don't think you need to do it. I'll get some of her friends to prepare her and some of the men to dig the grave. I suppose you'll want it next to your grandad?"

Aisling nodded. "That would be good." She picked up a teaspoon and stirred some more honey into the tea, fearing another emotional outburst at the thought of what they were discussing. When she felt more composed, she added, "Do I have to register it today?"

"Don't you worry about that, I'll do it when I get back from the burial. When we finish our tea, I'll go and round up some of the girls and their menfolk. Do you want to wait here and rest? You could go with us in the cart, or would you rather go back now?" The girls she was referring to were the group of older women who were gran's friends.

"I want to go home," Aisling replied.

"All right. Do you want to take Rufus with you for company? He'd enjoy a nice run and I know he likes you."

Aisling was quite familiar with Auntie Patsy's old sheep dog. He was getting too old to round up sheep and stray cattle and now spent most of his time sunning himself on the back doorstep. Almost as if he could hear what they were saying, he gave a little yelp and scratched the door.

Patsy's kindness and reassurance made her feel a little better, although she still felt anxious about the approaching activity. She almost wished it was over. She knew she would be too tired to do any work by the time she reached home from lack of sleep and walking to the village and back.

Patsy and the dog followed her out into the street. "I almost forgot," Patsy said. "I expect you'll be wanting a memorial ceremony at the chapel?"

"I suppose so." Aisling yawned. "Sorry, I'm a bit tired. When does it have to be?"

"Not today, but sometime soon." She reached up and kissed Aisling on the cheek. "Now you go home and try to get some rest. And you be a good boy, Rufus, and take care of this girl!"

3 - Aisling alone

W hen she returned to the cottage, Irial was gone. She looked in the orchard, the poultry yard, and the garden, but the only sign he'd been there at all was the neatness of the henhouse, the clean tools and some clean dishes on the draining board in the kitchen.

Where could he have gone? she wondered. Although he'd disappeared, she still appreciated all he had done to help her. She looked in the cold cupboard and saw there were five or six new eggs in the egg tray, all immaculately clean, the way gran liked them. This reminded her that Gran's dead body was still on her little bed in the alcove off the kitchen. She walked over to the alcove to take another look at her beloved grandmother, but found he'd lain a sheet over her, whether to keep off the flies or... Did he think she wouldn't want to look at her?

Rufus was lying on the mat just inside the door, chin resting on his paws, watching her. He gave a little whine when she looked at him and a feeble tail-wag.

"Are you thirsty, boy? Let me get you some water." She took a pan from a hook on the wall and dipped it in the water barrel, gratified to see that Irial had filled it from the pump. She laid the pan down close to the dog's nose. After standing up and sniffing it, he took a few laps and settled down again on the doormat.

She leaned over him and looked outside. It was a little past midday. "I think I'm going to follow suit and take a nap, she told Rufus. "There's nothing urgent that needs to be done." She climbed the ladder slowly, almost too exhausted to pull herself up, and flopped down on her cot.

Rufus's excited barking woke Aisling some time later. She could hear the rattle of a cart navigating the uneven surface of the footpath and the sound of voices as it screeched to a halt near the cottage. She sighed and sat up, wishing it was all over.

She heard a woman's voice below her in the kitchen. "Here she is," she called to her companions.

"Where's the girl?" another woman asked.

"Shh, she's probably resting, poor child." That was Auntie Patsy.

I'd better go down and talk to them. She stood up and straightened her clothes, which were all wrinkled from being slept in. *I can't worry about that now.*

She climbed carefully down the ladder and turned to face everyone. There were four women, 'the girls', in the kitchen all looking towards the alcove. She recognized all of them as women who had been to the cottage a few times to visit gran. When they heard the ladder creak, they all turned to face her. "Hello," she said timidly.

"We didn't mean to wake you," one of them said. Aisling thought her name was Mavis, or something like that.

"Don't worry," she said to the group. "I was already awake. Thank you for coming, aunties. Is there anything I can do to help?"

Aunty Patsy came over and gave her a one-arm hug. "Did you get any rest?" Aisling nodded. "Well if you really want to help, how about putting on the kettle for some tea? Then you can go out and talk to the boys about where to dig. We'll get started while you're doing that."

Aisling was glad for an excuse to go outside. She didn't want to see what they were doing with her grandmother.

Aunty Patsy called her to the table that had been carried outside and placed in the shade of a tree. *It's almost like a picnic,* she thought. The women had brought some small cakes, and the men a keg of apple cider, taking bites and sips while they rested for a few moments. The men were not exactly jovial, but neither were they mournful. Respectful was the word that came to Aisling's mind.

It was after sundown when Muirne Mac Roibín was finally laid to rest wrapped in one of her finest linen sheets. Someone had lit a small bonfire a few paces away from the grave where everyone stood silently with their last thoughts of their friend. Auntie Mavis's husband, who was a lay preacher at the chapel, led them in a prayer for her soul.

Soon after, the friends returned to their homes in the village. Before she left, Aunty Patsy admonished Rufus, "you keep watch over Aisling while she's sleeping."

෨෭

Aisling was awoken the next morning by one of Rufus's friendly barks, which was discernible from his warning barks by its tone. Warning and defensive barks were deeper and more frantic, ending with growls, but when he was welcoming a friend, it was shorter and more high-pitched, excited. She could picture him wagging his tail and trying to jump up and lick the person he was greeting.

I wonder who that could be, she thought as she rolled off her cot and put on her slippers. It was no use trying to see anything from the little window above the cot. All she would see would be light and some colours. *It's probably one of the people who were helping last night. Maybe they want to take him home.* She wrapped a shawl around her shoulders over her nightgown and climbed down the ladder. As she reached the bottom, the cottage door opened to reveal a tall figure silhouetted against the daylight.

Her heartbeat began to race. "Irial?" she asked tentatively.

"It is I," he replied.

His voice was so beguiling, it sent a quiver through her body. *I hope he didn't notice.*

"Do you mind if I come in?

"Yes ... I mean no, I don't mind." *What's wrong with me?* "Come in and sit down. I'll make some tea." *Now I sound like gran.*

"I'll do that while you get ready to go out."

She nodded and went back up the ladder. *This is very strange,* she thought as she splashed some water

19

on her face and wiped it with a cotton cloth. *What does he mean, go out?* She didn't know how to handle this and there was no one to guide her. She could hear him rattling around in the kitchen as she replaced her nightgown with a clean pair of britches and a tunic.

When she returned to the kitchen, she saw the table laid for breakfast just as gran used to do it. a dish of butter and jars of honey and home-made jam on the table with knives and spoons, a pot of tea in the centre. Irial was holding slices of bread on a toasting fork against the bars of the stove.

He turned around and smiled at her. "Almost ready. We have a lot of work to do, so I thought we'd save the scrambled eggs until it's done. Here's your toast." He slid the two slices of toast onto a plate and laid it before her.

"Thank you," she said, blushing. "Are you going to have something?"

"Just tea," he replied, pulling out a chair and sitting opposite her.

After pouring her tea and adding some honey, she buttered the toast and smeared some jam over it. "What do you mean, we have a lot of work to do?"

"I want to talk with you, but first we have to take care of the livestock and water the garden. I thought after that's finished, we could have something to eat and go for a walk."

"Oh," was the best response she could come up with.

"By the way," Irial said, "where did the dog come from?"

"One of my aunties left him here as a sort of watch dog. His name is Rufus."

"Is that because of his orange fur?"

"I suppose so. When I heard him bark this morning, he sounded so friendly, I thought Auntie Patsy had come to take him home."

"He's a very intelligent dog," Irial said. "He knows who's a friend and who's a foe."

ॐॐ

Once all the chores were done, they cleaned up and had a meal of eggs scrambled with sautéed vegetables from the garden before leaving for their walk.

"Why do you want to talk outside?" Aisling asked as they climbed the slope towards the woods.

"Several reasons," Irial replied as they set off up the hill towards the woods. "One, I have a lot to tell you and I don't want to be interrupted, and two, we can pick some mushrooms and berries. Besides, I find the woods both restful and invigorating" He looked at her and smiled. "How do you feel?" he added.

Aisling frowned. Nobody had ever asked her that before and she wasn't sure how to answer. Should she tell the absolute truth, or the polite truth? How do you tell the difference? "I am sad because my gran has gone." He nodded. Was that the total truth? She had a feeling there was more, for one thing, she felt excited, but should she tell him that?

"Anything else?" he prompted.

"I don't know why, but I feel excited, as if something unexpected is going to happen."

"Are you happy?"

Vicki Wootton

She looked at him. He looked as if this was an important question. *Am I happy,* she thought. To her surprise, she realized she was, even though she was mourning the loss of her beloved guardian and only family she knew. Aisling nodded.

"Good," Irial said, taking her hand to help her over the stile that led them out of the meadow and into the woods. "Now we can talk. You must have many questions about me and why I'm here.

4 – Revelation

☙❧

First, I should tell you who and what I am. You already know my name. I'm an elven messenger and I've come to bring you home."

Aisling froze. She reached out to a tree for support, as cold shivers shot through her body. She moved her lips, trying to formulate a response, but nothing came out. He reached for her, but she shook him off. "Don't …."

She looked at him in terror. What was he talking about? What did he mean, home? This was her home. This is where her mother and father and her whole family had lived all their lives. She slid down the tree trunk and rested her head in her hands with her elbows on her knees. She's heard the folklore about the *wee-folk* all her life, the fairies and elves who stole infants from their cradles and took them away.

Irial stood a few steps away, leaning against another tree, watching her. She peered up at him through her fingers. There was nothing 'wee' about him, and she was no infant in a cradle.

She looked at Rufus who was lying on the ground between them. Surely, he would protect her if she were in danger, but he'd been quite friendly with the elf.

"What do you want with me?" she asked in a dull voice. "Did you put a magic spell on my dog? Are you going to steal me away now that I have no family?"

"No, I did not put a spell on Rufus." Hearing his name, the dog slapped his tail against the ground. "I am not bent on kidnapping you. You are free not to go with me if that is your wish. If you would trust me for a moment, I will explain everything."

I suppose I could at least hear what he has to say. But she was still wary. "All right, tell me."

He straightened up and reached for her hand to help her up, but she brushed it away. "Let's walk while we talk," he said.

She sighed and pushed herself up off the ground.

"First I want you to show me your ears."

"What? What are you talking about?" she pressed her hands over her ears.

"All right but look at mine." He brushed his silvery hair back revealing one of his ears. "See the shape?" his ear came to a slight point at the upper edge, not enough to look grotesque, but noticeably different from the people she knew. "That's what elven ears look like. Does it look familiar?"

A chilling wave enveloped her. She put her fingers through her golden hair and gasped as she felt the same points. *Why didn't I ever notice this before? Why didn't someone point it out to me?* Surely other children would have mocked her for being different. She realized that her ears were always concealed by her hair and in chilly weather, she wore hoods. When she had tried to braid her hair like other girls, her grandmother had stopped her. "Leave your hair alone," she'd say. "You want to be proud of having such pretty hair and not try to hide it away in silly plaits." Come to think of it, her grandmother always wore bonnets that covered her ears.

"Was my gran one of you?" she asked.

"She wasn't, but she was a wonderful guardian for you. When our people became aware that she was about to leave this realm, I was sent to bring you home."

"Why didn't she tell me? What about my mother and father?"

"Your mother was, but not the man she married. He really was your grandmother's son. It was decided that it would be best if you didn't know about your mother, then you wouldn't inadvertently let something slip."

"But why couldn't we all have stayed in Fairyland or whatever you call it. Why did we have to live here?"

"We call our home the Realm of Light, or just The Realm. Leán, the elf who you knew as mother, was the one who abducted you and brought you here to live. There are dark forces who may have influenced her decision to bring you to the Mid Realm. She probably thought she was doing the right thing, saving you from being killed by them if they found a way to get at you."

"I don't understand," Aisling said. "Why would the dark forces want to kill me? And who are they?"

"Are you getting thirsty? There's a stream up ahead where we can get some water and sit down while I tell you the whole story."

After all the climbing, they were now going downhill. They reached a grassy dell which sloped down to the stream and was surrounded by trees. She scooped up some cold water in her palm and drank it, then dipped in for another mouthful. Irial was sitting on a grassy bank when she turned around. She was still sceptical about his story—for that's how she thought of it—a fairy tale. *I'm too old for fairy tales*, she thought, but she shrugged her shoulders and sat on the grass an arm's length away from him. *At least it's entertaining.*

She looked at him as if to say, 'go on'.

"Let me tell you a bit about your people first," he said. "The people who live in the Realm of Light have magic abilities, and that is the only thing that differentiates us from those who call themselves 'normal' people, other than our ears, and have longer lives. Sadly, we elves are not very fertile. You rarely see a couple with more than one child, and that child is very precious, especially where an heir is vital to a powerful family.

"Elves aren't the only people who live in the realm; it's a world like this one." He moved his hand in an arc that encompassed their current location. "There are good folks and bad folks. We have our royalty and governments, and on occasion there are disagreements and conflicts, especially between the light people and the dark. There are several types of elven people as well. For example, I'm a silver elf, and you are a golden elf."

"What other colours are there? How do you tell the difference?"

"The Golden elves are usually royalty, the rulers. The silver, like me, are the ones who assist the golden. Then there are the green elves who have an affinity with plant life, and the blues with an affinity with water, the indigos who generally deal with weather. There are also two rare types, black and red. We don't see many of those as they live away from the inhabited centres. The black elves generally live in caves in the mountains and have an affinity for minerals, which they remove from the rocks. The red elves deal with fire.

"As for the differences, the way you can tell them apart is by their appearance, mostly eye and hair colour. I, for example have silver hair and green eyes, while your hair is golden, and your eyes are green, but with a touch of amber."

"Does that mean I'm royalty?" She felt silly asking this but went along with it because that's just how it happened in fairy tales.

"It does, and that's the crux of the matter. It's the reason you were brought to live here and not told anything about your origins."

"But what about my mother and father? Surely they weren't elves."

"The people you think of as your mother and father were your guardians. Your real parents are the King and Queen of Lycea, one of the northern realms. The woman you thought of as your mother is a distant cousin of your real mother, and your adoptive father was the real son of your grandmother, Eithne. Oh, before you go on believing that your mother abandoned you, she did not. Leán was recalled to Lycea when your stepfather Cathán, was killed. The woman you know as Auntie Patsy was the person who circulated the story that she'd run off with a traveller to cover her sudden disappearance."

Aisling look down at her hands which squirmed together in her lap. She found it hard to believe what Irial was telling her but couldn't think of a way to discover if it was true, what question to ask for proof. It was too complicated for her to take in.

She saw Rufus at the stream, lapping up some water. When he'd finished, he shook himself before coming over and resting his chin on her lap.

"Can we go home now? I mean *this* home."

"In a while. We're waiting for someone. It won't be long." He stood up. "Let's go and look for mushrooms. There are lots around here."

Aisling stood and patted Rufus on the head. At least he was something familiar.

"Who are you waiting for?" she asked Irial as they set off down the bank of the stream.

"She's my partner on this mission. We were both chosen by your parents to escort you back home. Ráona has been surveying the route we have planned to make sure it's safe."

They were finding lots of mushrooms to fill the basket she'd brought. "What if I don't want to go?" she asked.

He straightened up and looked at her. A mixture of emotions crossed his face before he answered. "I think you would be very ill-advised to stay here. You would be in peril now that your main guardian is gone. The enemy will find you sooner or later."

"Who is this mysterious enemy?" Aisling was getting tired of hearing these implications that she was in danger.

"Have you heard of the Korrigen?" he asked.

"No, what are they?"

"They're a clan of little people, some sort of cross between an elf and a gnome. They appeared in our realm a few centuries ago from across the sea. They've been spreading throughout the Realm at a frightening rate. There's conflict everywhere they decide to settle. They seem to be incapable of negotiating or reasonable discussion and are very belligerent when challenged.

"About sixteen years ago, they decided to start a settlement in Lycea, commandeering some of our best farmland and killing a lot of livestock. This led to an open war. We knew we had to drive them off before they took over the whole country. Korrigans have some magic powers that make them hard to engage with. They are not very big—the largest are about your size— but they move like lightening. There was a battle on the border where they'd been destroying farmer's crops and killing livestock, so we went to challenge them. The moment we reached them, most of them disappeared into holes in the ground, but we caught a few. Unfortunately, one of the casualties was their leader's son."

"What do you mean, holes in the ground?"

"Oh, they are the entrances to their cave systems. Sometimes they burrow into a hillside to make temporary dens if there are no natural caves around. They seem to prefer to live underground."

They were interrupted by movement in the trees. With a look of recognition, Irial stood up. "Ah, here you are." Aisling looked behind and saw a tall, slender woman. She rose to her feet and joined them. "This is my partner, Ráona."

Ráona held out both her hands towards Aisling. "It's an honour to meet you, your highness."

The greeting shocked Aisling. What did it mean? She looked to Irial for an answer.

He laughed. "You'll have to get used to that, your highness."

"But ...." She wanted to say she was just an ordinary country girl, not royalty, but after what Irial had told her, she didn't know what she was. Unless they were making fun of her....

Ráona put her arm across Aisling's shoulder. "You'll get used to it, my lady. You are the daughter of a king; that makes you a princess."

Aisling bent to pick up the basket of mushrooms. "Can we go home now?" She was determined not to be taken in by this pair, until she was convinced they were telling the truth. Farm girls didn't just turn into princesses overnight, except in fairy tales.

Irial looked at the tree shadows. "Yes, it is getting late. You must be hungry."

When they left the trees and were preparing to climb over the stile, Ráona noticed a horse tied to the fence by the cottage. "There's someone there," she said.

"Will you go and see who it is?" Irial said. "We don't want anyone to see us, apart from your Auntie Patsy. If it's her, wave to us and we'll join you, otherwise, we'll wait here until whoever it is departs."

Aisling started off down the hill with Rufus leading the way, tail wagging, uttering little yips as he ran. When she got closer, Aisling recognized Auntie Patsy's little filly from the white patch on its forehead. She turned and nodded to the two elves, but they didn't come out of their hiding place. *They must want me to make sure it is her.*

Aunty Patsy came around the corner of the cottage as Aisling reached the front door. "I wondered where you were," Patsy said.

"I just went up the hill to pick some mushrooms." She showed the basket to Patsy.

"Good to see you keeping busy. I know how you must miss your gran, and it wouldn't be good for you to sit around moping. Shall we go inside and have a cup of tea?"

Before Aisling shut the cottage door, she waved to the elves.

"I see you have company," Auntie Patsy commented. "Let me get some water for the tea. They may want to join us"

Aisling looked at her with raised eyebrows. "Do you know them?"

"I know of them." Patsy filled a kettle from the water barrel and put it on the hob while Aisling added some kindling and a few logs to the dying fire. "Your gran told me they might come for you one day, but I'd hoped it would be later rather than sooner."

31

They sat around the table drinking tea and eating buttered scones. "Do you know what they've told me, auntie?"

"Eithne only told me you were someone special. I don't think she wanted anyone to know too much about you because you might be in danger if certain bodies found out you were here." She looked at the two elves as they came in through the door. "So it's true then?" she said to them.

Irial nodded and smiled at her. "Sit down," she said to the elves. "I agree with you about the timing. We'd hoped she could stay here longer, but...."

"She could come and live with me," Patsy said.

"There are compelling reasons for her to return home as soon as possible," Irial said. "It's very thoughtful of you to offer, though."

They all talk about me as if I have no say in what happens to me. "Can't I decide for myself?" she said. "Don't I have any rights?"

"We'll talk about it later," he replied.

"How do I know that you aren't the ones gran was afraid of?"

Aunty Patsy stood up. "I think I should be going, it will be dark soon." She looked at the two elves. "I have a feeling we can trust you, but if she comes to any harm..."

"I assure you, good lady, she will be safer in our care. I am going to tell you something that should convince you. Come outside."

Patsy followed him across the yard to her horse, where they stopped and had a short conversation. He then took something out of his pocket and showed it to her. Whatever it was, she smiled when she saw it. He untied the horse's reins and helped her into the saddle. She waved and smiled at Aisling and trotted away. As she went down the path to the road, she whistled to Rufus and he fell in beside her.

Aisling and Ráona cleared up the dishes and then the three of them walked around the holding and saw that the poultry were shut safely in their pen for the night.

"I wonder why she took Rufus," Aisling said. "And what did you show her?"

"Because you won't need him any longer. We'll be leaving tomorrow. Let's go back inside and talk about it."

5 – Leaving home

ॐ✥

This is what I showed her." He showed her a glass oval with the likeness of a woman imprinted on it.

"Who is it?" Aisling asked. "She's beautiful."

"That's your mother, Queen Fenella of Lycea."

Aisling felt goose bumps rising on her arms. Was this real? "May I see it?" She held out a shaking hand to receive the picture and held it near one of the lanterns. As she looked at it closely, her eyes filled with tears.

"Does that remind you of anyone?" Ráona asked.

"I don't know; she looks a bit familiar, though."

"Auntie Patsy recognised her instantly," Irial said. "That's what convinced her."

"I was astounded when I saw you sitting by the stream." Ráona said. "Your resemblance to the queen is startling. That's how you will look in a few years,"

"How old was she when it was painted?"

"It was a year before you were born, so she would have had a hundred and eighteen years."

"A hundred and ... *years*? That's so old, but she looks so young."

"Actually, she's quite young for an elf. We are a long-lived people. There are several elves in Lycea who have almost reached a thousand."

Aisling held up the plaque. "Can I keep this?" she asked Irial.

"It would be better if I kept it until we're in Lycea. In case we meet any obstructions. It could be used to confirm your identity."

She took a last look at the portrait and gave it back to him.

"You said we are leaving tomorrow. I can't just leave everything. What about the poultry and the garden?"

"I made arrangements for Patsy to take care of everything. She'll send her two sons out to pack up everything that needs to be moved and take it to Enisdale. Her son is betrothed, so he might live here after they are wed. I'm sure they will take care of everything. I scanned her while she was here, and I sensed she's an honest and honourable person. She also said she has a notarised document from your grandmother leaving her in charge if you should leave," Irial added.

"Can you tell when someone is not truthful? Aisling asked.

"Yes. That is one of our skills."

"You will have to develop your own skills now," Ráona said.

"What do you mean?" she asked.

"We don't know what your skills are but be assured, you have some. We'll have to test you and help you bring them out."

Aisling yawned. "I hope you don't mind if I go to bed. I'm very tired."

"Of course not," Ráona said. "We'll stay on watch down here. We have a lot to do tomorrow."

Aisling lay in bed but didn't fall asleep immediately. There was still some light outside, and a blackbird still sent a few chirps from the old oak tree. She imagined it was a mother bird calling home her fledglings and smiled.

As the light faded, she realized this was probably the last time she would sleep in this place. A tear ran down the side of her face and came to rest in her ear. She wiped it away with the sleeve of her nightgown and closed her eyes. No sound came from the kitchen and she wondered if they were still there. Maybe they'd gone outside.

She turned over onto her other side and closed her eyes but sleep still didn't come. There was so much churning around in her mind; first gran dying, then the strange appearance of the two elves and the story they'd told her. A princess? How can I be a princess? I'm just a humble farm girl. Fairy tales....

The rooster crowed his morning welcome from the roof of the nesting pen, warning Aisling that it was time to get up. She awoke with a feeling of apprehension as she recalled the events of yesterday. Going to the chest where she kept her clothes, she wondered what she should wear. What do you wear when you're leaving home for good? She lifted out a linen tunic that her gran had lovingly washed and ironed. Holding it to her nose, she imagined she could smell the sunlight in which it had dried. *Poor gran; I'll miss you so much.*

Maybe I should ask Ráona. She put the shawl around her shoulders and went to the top of the ladder. She couldn't hear anything from the kitchen, so she climbed down and looked around. *Maybe it had all been a dream. I'll just do what I'd do on a normal day.* She noticed the fire under the stove was stoked and the kettle stood on the hob. So much for the dream theory. Some bowls and spoons had been laid on the table and a cooking pot stood on the hob where it was being kept warm but not cooking.

She heard voices approaching the door, a male and a female. And stood still, waiting for them to enter. When the door opened, Ráona entered first, carrying a bowl of fresh eggs. "Welcome the day," she said.

"Welcome the day," Aisling repeated, although to her this day was less than welcome.

"We've made some porridge," Irial said, kicking off his boots outside the door. "Did you sleep well your ... I mean Aisling?"

Once more she was overcome by a feeling of unreality. Two elves had taken over her gran's kitchen and made porridge for her breakfast after telling her she was a princess. No one would believe a story like that, but they acted as if it was the most normal thing in the world. "Fine," she replied. She turned to Ráona. "Are we really leaving?" she asked. "What if I don't want to go?"

Ráona came to her and put an arm over her shoulder. "There is a reason we are in such haste," she said. "Come and sit down; I'll give you a bowl of porridge. What do you like on it?"

"What? Oh, the porridge. Honey and cream please."

"I'll get started on the eggs," Irial said.

"What are you going to do with the eggs?" Aisling asked.

"We're going to boil them hard and take them with us. It's one of the most efficient ways to carry food on a long journey because they're not too heavy. We can pick wild plants and fruit as we go. There are plenty of streams and pools for drinking water."

Aisling finished her porridge and picked up her tea. "What were you going to tell me?" she asked Ráona.

"Ah yes. The reason we are in haste. The king, your father, is ill. Even the most skilled healers seem to be unable to cure him. They suspect he may be the victim of a Korrigen curse. His greatest wish is to see his daughter before he departs for the Elysian Plain."

Aisling put down her cup and wiped the back of her hand across her mouth while she thought about this information. This was becoming more and more complicated. *They have a good story,* she thought, *an answer for everything.* "What's his name?

"Briartach. King Briartach of Lycea," Ráona replied. "Would you like to see what he looks like?"

"You have a picture of him as well?"

Ráona shook her head. "Something more real than a painted likeness." She glanced at Irial who nodded in response to her unvoiced query. "I will have to put my hands on your head to do this," she explained. "Are you ready?"

Her hands rested lightly on Aisling's head and before long, she began to feel dizzy. Everything seemed to swirl around for a moment and then coalesced into a garden. A man resting on a long chair shaded by the vines of a pergola. As they drew closer to him, he blinked once and closed his eyes. He was dressed in a long white robe trimmed with gold, matching the gold rings on his fingers and the medallion on his chest. He looked very emaciated, his cheeks sunken and the hands lying across his abdomen were wrinkled, with prominent blue veins on the backs.

He opened his eyes and smiled when a shadow fell over him. A woman with golden hair leaned over and kissed him. Suddenly the scene faded, and they were back in the cottage kitchen. "Was that the queen?" Aisling asked when Ráona removed her hands.

"It was," she replied.

"Are they really my mother and father?" she asked.

"They really are," Ráona replied. "And now, if your royal highness permits, we must pack up and leave."

Aisling fidgeted awkwardly on the chair for a moment, thinking about the newest episode in what she thought of as the fairy story. She stood up. "I don't know what to wear," she said. "Will you help me choose something suitable?"

She beckoned to Ráona and climbed the ladder. "I keep all my clean clothes in this chest," she said. "Shall I put it on the bed?"

The next several minutes were taken up by deciding what she would wear, and dressing. Ráona insisted she take some dark garments from her grandmother's clothes chest. "We'll be going through some dark places and it is best to wear something dark there."

They packed up some spare clothes and some comfortable boots and returned to the kitchen.

Everything had been wiped cleaned and put away. Irial had packed some bread, greens and salt along with the eggs in a cloth bag.

"Ready to go?" he asked them.

"Is it all right if I look around outside?" She was thinking this would be the last time—if their story was true—she would see her old home. She had tears in her eyes by the time they turned and started up the hill.

6 – The journey begins

୬୦୶ୄ

While we are walking," Irial said as they climbed the hill, "We would like to test you for gifts."

"What do you mean?" Aisling asked.

"Normally, all elves are blessed with gifts, but they are not usually awakened without some sort of stimulus. Take last night, for instance, when you asked Ráona about your father. She was able to awaken your gift of far-seeing."

"And it wasn't difficult," Ráona said. "I think you are a natural."

"What is far-seeing?"

"It's seeing things in another location," Irial replied. "The drawback in your case is that you have to be familiar with the place or person you want to contact. That's why Ráona linked you through her own mind. She knows the palace and the king and queen."

"That's amazing! are there many gifts?"

"All elves have at least two gifts which they inherit from their parents. Since you have been raised without those parental stimuli, your gifts are still dormant."

"But we do have some clues," Ráona said. "We know what gifts the king and queen have, so those would be the first things we would test for."

"Did they tell you to do this?" Aisling asked.

"Your mother suggested we might try," Irial replied.

Vicki Wootton

They climbed over the stile at the top of the slope and set off across the grass towards the woods.

"Is it a long way to Lycea?" Aisling asked.

"It's relative," Irial replied. "The Realm of Light is in another dimension, which means, we could be there now; it could be all around us, but we have to cross over to reach it. What we are seeking now is a portal through which we can cross.

Aisling pondered that for a moment. "I don't understand."

"Let me see if I can help you," Irial said. "Did your grandmother take you to chapel when you were growing up?"

"Yes, we used to go on special holy days."

"Did they teach you about angels?"

"Sometimes."

"I'm guessing you were taught that angels are all around us protecting us." Aisling nodded. "These angelic beings are here with us now, but we can't see them. That's because they are in a different dimension from us."

"But they can see us?"

"That's right. They have the power to be able to cross the boundaries at will. We elves can cross between our home dimension and the human dimension but because we are not sanctified beings, we must use special portals.

"Can you see angels?"

"No. They are only visible to beings who have special powers or gifts, but some of us are able to sense their presence."

They entered the woods and continued much deeper than Aisling and gran ever did to gather berries and nuts. The trail continued to climb, and the light seemed to be fading.

"It's getting spooky," Aisling said with a shudder. "Why is it so cold?"

"Maybe it's because it's going to rain," Ráona said with a smile. "Can't you smell it?"

Aisling took a deep breath. "Like wet leaves?" she asked.

"That's right, but don't worry, we'll find some shelter."

Aisling realized that Irial had gone ahead. He returned and led them to a clearing below some rocks and above a small stream. "This should be good. The rocks will shelter us if it rains." he said. "Are you still cold?" he asked Aisling.

She nodded, regretting she hadn't brought her sheepskin coat. "Can we light a fire?"

"It's best not to. It might draw the attention of our enemies. But we've got something you can use to keep warm." He rummaged through the bag he'd been carrying on his back and drew out a piece of folded cloth. "Wrap this around you," he said. It will keep in your body heat and shelter you from the rain."

Aisling took it, unable to imagine how such a flimsy thing could keep her warm, nevertheless, she unfolded the small pack, shook it out to its full size and wrapped it around her head and shoulders. After a few minutes, she started to feel warmer. She looked up and smiled at her two companions. "It's like magic."

43

Ráona smiled. "It's more science than magic. With the help of the fairies, we've discovered a way to adjust the molecules in the fabric to retain heat. It's much more useful than wearing heavy clothing when travelling."

Aisling was speechless after hearing this. It was too much for her to digest all at once—she didn't even know what *molecules* were—so she focused in on the most astonishing information. *Fairies? I thought elves were the same as fairies.*

"No, they're a completely different people," Ráona said.

How did she know what I was thinking? Oh, it's too much to think about for one day; I'll have to leave it until tomorrow. She yawned. "I think I'm going to sleep now." After the almost sleepless night and all the walking they'd done during the day, it didn't take her long to fall asleep this time.

The next morning, they continued their climb through the forest where coniferous trees now dominated the scenery and the air was decidedly colder. Aisling had folded the cover Arial had given her into shawl-size and wrapped it around her shoulders and body.

"What about finding out if I have any gifts?" Aisling asked when Irial had gone ahead.

"I'm sure you do. You've already revealed one, an important one. You've got far-seeing. Another vital gift is far hearing. Let's try it. What am I thinking about?"

"You want me to answer that?"

44

Ráona nodded. "Close your eyes and see if you can tell what I am thinking about. Give me your hand so you don't trip on anything."

Aisling closed her eyes and allowed Ráona to lead her, but she couldn't read her mind. "Relax your mind. Try not to think about anything."

After a few more minutes of letting her mind wander she felt something tickling on the edge of her awareness. "A bird?"

"Very good. What kind of bird?"

She closed her eyes again, but nothing else came. "I don't know."

"That's fine," Ráona said. "You just need to practice. See if you can find out what Irial is thinking."

"He's coming back," she said.

"Very good. A good way to practice this gift is becoming consciously aware of the life around you. There are hundreds of creatures out here. If you can become aware of them individually, feel what they are feeling, you'll be able to develop this gift rapidly."

"How's it going?" Irial said. He turned around and walked beside them and was silent for a moment.

Aisling felt uneasy, as if there was something dangerous nearby. "What's happening?" she asked. "I feel frightened."

"You can sense it. Good. You're developing good signs. You're right; there is something out there...." Irial moved his arm in an arc. "It might not be anything serious, but we must stay alert. What do you say?" he asked Ráona.

45

"It seems to be coming from over there," She pointed about thirty degrees to their right. I don't think it's a Korrigan. It might be one of their spies."

"You're sure there's only one?" Ráona shrugged. "I think I'll confront it." Irial said. He put his hand on the knife he carried in a sheath on his thigh and moved off the trail into the trees.

"Is confronting it dangerous?" Aisling asked, looking around nervously.

"It's a good idea, really. If he can do that without killing it, we might learn something about the enemy. Don't worry about Irial, he has many protective skills. That's why he was chosen for this mission."

They continued along the path which was becoming steeper. Ráona stopped after a while and stood with her head cocked to one side as if listening to something. Aisling heard a faint pop from somewhere nearby, then she heard someone pushing through the bush and moved closer to Ráona.

The bushes moved beside them and Irial appeared, shaking his head.

"No luck?" Ráona asked.

"No. just before I got to it, it disintegrated with a loud pop, like a punctured bladder."

"So you don't know what it was?"

"The only thing I got was that it was some sort of hairy animal about the size of a fox. Before it popped off, it radiated hostility and hatred. I'm wondering if it was some sort of golem."

"What's a golem," Aisling asked.

"It's a simulacrum, a creature that has been created by magic for a specific purpose. They're very rare, because not many can create them. It was probably sending back messages to its owner and was programmed to self-destruct when it was discovered."

"What are we going to do?" Ráona asked. "They must know where we are and the direction we are going."

"We'll have to try the other route. It's more difficult to reach, but even if they know about it, they may not have placed watchers there yet."

Aisling put her hand over her mouth and yawned.

Ráona put her arm around the girl's shoulder. "You're getting tired, aren't you?"

"A little bit," Aisling replied. "I'm hungry as well."

"There's a turn-off a little way ahead. Think you can make it?" Irial said. "We can sit down and have something to eat when we reach it. There's a spring as well."

Ráona held her hand as they continued to climb. Once they reached the intersection of the paths, she let go. "Let's find a cosy place to sit," she said.

They sat in a mossy place in front of the rock face of the mountain. Irial filled their water bags while Aisling and Ráona spread out some food on a clean cloth from Aisling's bag. The bread they'd brought was still fresh and the butter was soft. Added to some cooked eggs and fresh vegetables they'd picked from gran's garden before they left, it made a tasty meal.

"Are you sure it's the Korrigen that are looking for us?" Aisling asked.

"It has all the signs of them," Irial replied. "We can often tell who a person or a creature is by its aura, the light of its life. There are personal auras and species auras. The species aura is the easiest to read."

"Why is that?" she asked.

"It's more generalised," he replied. "For example, a flock of sheep has a specific aura that surrounds all of them. I think theirs is a yellowish green."

Ráona nodded. "They also have personal auras reflecting their feelings, if they are in pain, hungry, or contented. Animals are much less complicated and are easier to read than higher sentient beings."

"How do you read an aura?" Aisling asked.

"It's a gift," Irial said. "I only have a weak talent for it, but Ráona's is much stronger.

She turned to Ráona and asked, "can you tell how I feel right now?"

Ráona smiled. "You have such a mix of emotions, it's hard to sort them all out. That's understandable given what you're going through. I see sadness, excitement, fear. Fear dominates the other feelings. Do you want to talk about that?"

They are so kind, she thought. *Surely, I can trust them.* "It's … I guess it's because everything is changing so fast. I don't know what's going to happen to me. And those creatures …."

"The Korrigen?"

"Yes. Why do they want to hurt me? I haven't done anything to them."

Irial stood up and started to pack away the cloths and utensils from their meal. "We should be on our way; I want to get to the gate before nightfall." he said. "We can talk while we are walking."

Aisling and Ráona picked up their bags, brushed the moss off their clothes, and joined him on the path. "Remember I told you about the chief's son being killed in the battle?" Irial asked. Aisling nodded. "The clan chief wants revenge, and what better way to get it than to take the king's child?"

"But how do they know it's me? And how did they find me."

"That's what we would like to know."

"They may have been spying on us since we left the palace," Ráona said. "If they can create simulacra, they could have been close to us without our suspecting they were there."

"We know now, though," Irial added. "We can be on the alert for them now we have their signature." He turned to Aisling. "let us know if you sense anything that makes you feel uncomfortable, no matter how trivial."

Vicki Wootton

7 – The Gateway
⮜⮞

They failed to reach the Gateway before sundown as
Irial had hoped. They'd had to leave the soft, mossy
earth track they'd been following and veer left into the
mountains. The slope gradually became steeper with
more rock underfoot than earth. It was scattered with
loose stones that slid underfoot, so it was necessary to
walk carefully with eyes on the ground. As twilight
approached, it became too difficult even to see the
ground ahead.

"Let's stop here and make camp," Irial said. "The
ground shouldn't be too hard around the trees, and we
can spread some pine-needles for padding where we're
going to sleep."

They'd reached an area that was less slanting and
wider than the trail they'd been walking on. It was quite
dark by the time they settled down for the night, but
the two elves didn't want to start a fire that would be
visible leagues away. They'd each created a bubble of
light with which to illuminate the area enough to
arrange their bedding and distribute some food and
water.

Aisling had never slept out of doors before this
journey and was quite nervous, but she was too tired to
complain. Just as she pulled her cover around her

50

shoulders, the howl of a wolf startled her. Then another answered the first, and soon several more joined in, turning it into a chorus.

"Don't be afraid," Ráona said. "There are just talking to one another. They won't harm us."

"They are probably warning others about our presence in the area," Irial added. "They don't normally bother higher sentient creatures like us. They are very intelligent animals and have even been known to help people in trouble. Nevertheless, we are going to stand watch all night." He turned to Ráona. "I'll take first watch."

The following morning the air was hazy and quite cold, but a golden glow through the mist told them the sun's heat would soon clear the air.

"We'll have some more climbing today, and the trail will get steeper, but we don't have far to go now. Aisling looked up the trail as she put her bag on her shoulder. "It looks like snow up there," she commented. "How far away is that peak?"

"It's too far," Ráona replied. "It's many leagues away, but we're not going that far. We wouldn't be able to reach it from here either, even if we wanted to."

"Which way is the village? Can we see it from here?"

"No," Irial said. "It's behind the slope of this hill, over to the right. We were circling the mountain most of yesterday as we climbed higher."

He moved past her and led the way with Ráona behind them. It had been very cold when they started out, but now the sun was no longer veiled with mist, it became warmer. The labour of constantly climbing the hard path soon warmed everyone's blood. They

51

continued to climb after stopping for some water at a mountain stream and eating eggs with bread and butter.

They reached their destination by late afternoon.

"Here we are," Irial announced, holding his upright palm towards the wall of the mountain.

"Where's the gate?" Aisling asked. "I don't see anything but bare rock."

Irial held his hand out to her. She took it, still puzzled. He led her into a shallow alcove that looked like solid rock to her. "All right," he said. "Put your hand here." He indicated the left side of the alcove.

Aisling stepped forward and gingerly put her hand out. Instead of touching solid rock, her fingers went right through it, as if it wasn't there. She looked back at Irial and smiled. "It's magic!" she cried. "How does it work?"

"It's a spell of concealment. Anyone who looked this way would just see solid rock. You must know it's here, and even then, it's not easy to find. Most of us can sense it when we get close enough, but no one else would even guess it was there. Only elves and other magical beings can sense it and pass through the gate safely. Anyone else would just receive a shock and be thrown back, but in any case, this Gateway isn't used very much, and few people come this way."

"Shall we go in?" he said. He led the way through the Gateway into a chamber filled with a faint glow of light. There was no indication of the light's origin; it just permeated the whole chamber, almost like a luminous mist. Looking back, Aisling couldn't see any sign of the Gateway, just smooth rock like the rest of the room, however, she did sense that something was there, a sort of pulling sensation.

The walls were lined with wooden chests, at least twenty of them, all were fastened with gold-coloured metal hasps.

"These chests hold supplies for people returning from the Mid-Realm," Ráona said. She turned to Irial. "Do we need ... Oh bless me, what's that awful smell?"

Aisling's heart jumped a beat. She could smell it too; the stench of rotten meat.

"There's something dead in here," Irial said. "It's coming from over here, in one of these chests." He walked over to a chest and opened the lid, then shook his head and went to the next one. As he raised the lid, the smell permeated the whole cavern. Irial staggered backwards, dropping the cover. He looked at Ráona with tears in his eyes.

"What is it?" she asked apprehensively. She moved closer to him and put her hand on his arm.

Irial put his arms around her and held her tight. "It's Cathán," he replied, releasing her and wiping the back of his hand across his nose.

They both looked at Aisling who was cowering against the wall as far from the chest as she could get. She was shivering and rubbing her hands together for warmth. *I wish they would tell me what's happening.*

"We're sorry you had to be present for this," Ráona said. Aisling could see tears glittering in her eyes. "One of our friends has been killed and we must perform the rite of the departing. We must bring the body out and examine it before we do that to ascertain who was

53

responsible. If you like, you can go into another room while we do it."

"No, I'll stay," Aisling replied. "If I'm truly what you say I am, I should learn about elven customs. I can close my eyes if it's too...." She pulled a blanket out of her pack and put it on the floor of an alcove, still folded, then sat down on it leaning against the wall.

"Before we start, we should look in the other chests in case there's something else to deal with," Irial said.

The two elves split up and started opening the chests. Ráona took a blanket from one of them and held it under her arm.

An exclamation from Irial drew their attention. Aisling didn't hear what he said, but his meaning was clear. He was angered and disgusted by what he saw. The smell issuing from the trunk was excrement. "Damn them," he mumbled. "They've even added a message: 'We'll see you soon'!" he turned to Ráona. "I'll clean this up first, then we can start on Cathán. Let's pray we don't find anything else."

Aisling watched as he held his hands over the contaminated chest and uttered some words that induced a flash of light inside that cleared the smell of excrement, but the stench of a decaying body still hung in the air.

When they spread the blanket on the floor and started to remove the body, Aisling closed her eyes, although she couldn't avoid a glimpse of a head that had been severed from its body. She put her knees up and rested her head on her hands so that all she could look at was the floor.

"Oh, no!" Ráona sobbed, "Why, why did they need to...?"

"They're fiends from the underworld," Irial replied. He looked angry and disgusted.

Everyone was silent for a few minutes while the two elves continued the preparations, then Ráona called to Aisling. "We are going to start the ceremony now. Would you like to join us?"

When she looked up, she saw Irial and Ráona standing over a blanket wrapped bundle on the floor. They joined hands and started to sing. The music of their voices was so beautiful, it washed over her like a heavenly blessing—the way she imagined angels would sound—bringing tears to her eyes. She'd never heard anything like it before. The singing slowed, gradually tapering off as they backed away from the remains. The song suddenly rose in a crescendo that finished with a brilliant flash of light.

Temporarily blinded by the light, Aisling waited a few seconds before opening them and looking across the cavern. The two elves were standing still holding hands, their heads bowed. There was no sign of the body that had lain there moments ago. "What happened to the ... your friend?" she asked

"He's gone to the Fields of the Ancestors," Ráona replied.

"What are we going to do now?" Aisling asked. She realised something had changed now and they might have to make new plans.

"That's what we need to decide," Ráona replied.

8 – Change of plans

ॐॐ

Let's pack up some supplies and get out of here," Irial said, walking to one of the trunks and lifting the lid. "It looks as if they helped themselves to a lot of our stores; there's not much left. Don't take any foodstuffs; they may be poisoned."

"Why don't we poison all the food in case they come back?" Ráona suggested.

"I don't know." Irial replied. "What if one of our people comes for supplies?"

"We could leave a sign that only an elf could understand," she replied.

"We're going to close this Gateway when we get outside."

"A double lock?" she asked. "In case they come the other way and want to get out into the Mid-Realm.

"Of course," Irial replied. "We'll both do it, make sure it's strong enough to keep them out. Let's be on our way."

The trio had picked up some fresh blankets and clothes, plus some cooking utensils, a tent and five small knives. Now they were all packed into bags made of some strong material that Aisling hadn't seen before. They stood in front of the Gateway and took a last look around and then left the cavern.

"I wish I could go home," Aisling said as they started walking down the slope. She yearned to be in the warm little cottage with all the familiar trappings, safe from fear.

"I'm sorry, your highness, but I fear someone else will be living there now." Irial said. "I can understand how frightened and apprehensive you must be feeling after all that's happened, but there's no going back. You would not be safe in Enisdale now that the enemy knows where it is."

Ráona put her arm around Aisling's shoulder. "Don't worry, Princess, your parents chose us to bring you safely to your true home, because of our skills and experience."

Aisling nodded, but her brows were still furrowed with doubt. "Why are you calling me 'highness' and 'princess'? she asked.

"It is what you are, your highness," Ráona replied. "We want you to get used to the idea that you are an elven princess, not a human farm girl."

Despite what they said, Aisling still felt dubious. She didn't feel like a princess in her work boots and clothing that is worn by working farm girls. *I suppose I could think of them as travel clothes. It wouldn't be practical to go climbing mountains and crossing streams in silks and dainty slippers.* She looked at Ráona who was walking ahead. She was wearing short green tunic and darker green leggings, but something about the fabric made them look richer than her own undyed linen. Even her boots looked expensive, and they didn't seem to get dirty or scratched as hers did.

They walked down the slope from the Gate until mid-morning and the early mist had disappeared. Once they were among the trees they found a game trail running roughly northwest, but it meandered as animal trails usually do. They were following the edge of the mountains now, keeping them on their left. As soon as they reached a small rill burbling down the slope, Irial suggested they stop to rest and eat something.

"The food we brought from home won't last much longer," Aisling said as she spread a cloth on the ground. "What are we going to do then?"

"We'll have to hunt, I suppose," Irial replied. "Have you ever hunted for game?"

She shook her head. "I don't like killing things," she replied. "I had an awful time when gran killed the hens. She always wanted me to help her and I couldn't bear to see the poor creatures in such a panic. It was as if they knew what was coming. My grandad used to kill pigs and sheep as well, but I always ran and hid when I saw him sharpening his knives." She thought for a moment, looking at the knives they'd brought out to cut the cheese and the bread that had hardened. "Is that what these knives are for?"

Ráona looked at her and smiled. "You have the heart of a true elf," she said. "We hate killing our little brothers and sisters, but sometimes, like now, it is necessary, and we always do it with compassion. The knives have many purposes, self-defence, skinning and preparing game, cutting arrows and shaping bows, even for healing, sometimes."

"So if you have to kill an animal, how do you do it?"

"Normally, we use bows and arrows, and direct the arrows strait to the heart so the creature doesn't have to suffer a slow, painful death." Irial said. "We abhor the sort of traps mid-worlders use. They are so cruel."

Aisling nodded in agreement. "We could pick berries and nuts as well." she said. "And mushrooms. I love mushrooms with cheese."

"And there are edible roots we could look for too,"

"Now that we've settled how we are going to prevent starvation, we should be going," Irial said.

"Where are we going now?" Aisling asked Irial who was leading the way.

"The next Gateway is in the Canyon," he said. "It will take us a day or two to get there."

"Aren't you afraid the Korrigen might have found that one too?"

"There is a remote possibility they may have, but we have no choice in the matter. We have to get to the Realm."

"How many Gateways are there?"

"Hundreds. They're all over the world, but we are restricted to the ones close enough for us to reach on foot. I'd say there are probably a dozen within reach."

"We could be walking around for weeks at this rate," she replied.

"I hope not. I think they just followed us to the one we exited from and may not have found the others."

"They're in for a shock when they find it locked," Ráona said from behind.

"The thing that concerns me is the Network. Now that they've found the way in, they could come out anywhere," Irial said.

"What's the Network?" Aisling asked.

"All the Gateways are attached to one another through a tunnel system. Basically, you can enter anywhere you desire, and exit anywhere you please."

Aisling shuddered.

"Don't worry," Ráona said. "We'll clear them out. Other races are also threatened by these fiends and we will band together to extinguish them from the network."

"What others? Are they also magic?"

"Most of them are, one way or another."

"What are they like?"

"Some of them are just like us, but with different skills, but others—the Elemental Elves for example—can manipulate elements like fire, water, earth, and air. Those skills are very useful in maintaining the tunnels of the network."

"Are they all in your Realm?"

"Our Realm," Ráona corrected her. "Not all; many of them are from the Far Realm, but others are found in the Dark-Realm."

"What other kinds of beings are there, in your, I mean *our* Realm?"

"I think you would find the dragons interesting."

Aisling's eyes opened wider. "Dragons? Do they live near Lycea?" This was fascinating news for her, albeit a little frightening.

"Some of them, mostly the blue dragons. They live in the mountains several leagues from Lycea, but we see them in the skies quite frequently."

"Are they friendly or are they our enemies?"

"There used to be warfare between us, but we came to an agreement with them about fifteen hundred years ago. They sometimes help us with problems, fighting the Korrigen for example, but they can be quite temperamental. They are an arrogant people and require respect from anyone they deal with. If they feel they have been disrespected, they won't speak to us until they feel we have made amends, usually with expensive gifts."

Aisling's eyes lit up. "I can't wait to see them," she said. "If we can use the next Gateway, how long will it take us to reach Lycea?"

"Once we go through the gate, we could be there the next day."

The climb through the rocky terrain was exhausting, and with the trees becoming scarce, the temperature increased. The elves didn't appear to sweat, but their skin became very flushed.

"We should take a break," Ráona said, fanning her face with her hand. "And we need to find some water; my flask is almost empty."

While they were inside the other Gateway, they'd taken two water flasks each from the supply trunks. The material from which they were made was something new to Aisling. They had a pearly sheen, were flexible to touch, and weighed virtually nothing. Even filled with water, they were lighter than expected. They closed with soft corks and had corded fibre around the necks for carrying.

"Irial stopped and sniffed the air. He closed his eyes and concentrated for a moment. "There should be a stream a little farther up the trail. We can stop there and rest for a while. How are you doing?" he asked Aisling.

"I'm getting a bit tired," she replied. "And my feet are sore."

"You'll be able to cool them in the stream when we stop," Irial said. "It's not far now."

They turned a bend in the trail, veering towards the mountains, and heard the burbling and shushing of rapidly moving water ahead.

"How did you know it was here?" Aisling asked.

"It's an enhanced sense we have," he replied. "You may have such senses yourself. They just take practice. We begin training in early childhood. You can already sense danger, so it shouldn't be hard for you to activate some other senses."

It didn't take long for them to reach a wide stream flowing over and around the rocks in its path, throwing off white foam as it hit obstacles.

Aisling sat on a rock and removed her boots. She was developing blisters on both her heels and the soles of her feet.

"Come on," Ráona said. "Let's bathe them in the cold water for a while." She sat down and started to remove her own boots. "I'll have to see if we have any salve for your feet."

The sun was setting in front of the three travellers, dazzling them, as they scaled the trails higher into the mountain range. Eventually, the sun fell below the horizon, all but a single ray of light that shone through a narrow gap.

"Is that the canyon?" Aisling asked, pointing to the light.

"It is," Irial replied. "And we must hurry while there is still light enough to see where we are going."

Aisling felt as if she'd been walking forever. Her feet were numbed by the cold air now that the sun was down. It was the beginning of summer, but up here, it felt like the middle of winter with snow on the peaks and ice films on the rocky ground underfoot. Every breath she took produced a cloud of mist when she released it. When they reached the canyon, the final rays of sunlight were reflected on its north-facing wall, giving them enough illumination to see where they were going.

She could see why they called it the canyon; it was about the width of two men side by side with their arms stretched out, but the side walls were very high, unmeasurable from their point of view. "It looks as if a giant with a big axe chopped a groove in the mountain," she commented.

"That giant was the Ice King." Ráona said. "Every drop of moisture that fell into a crack in the rock turned to ice and expanded, widening it a tiny fraction more every year to make this groove. It took thousands of years to form."

Aisling was at a loss for words. She'd never heard anything like that before. The village school had given the children the most basic education for practical country living. They'd been taught how to read, and enough math to enable them to make calculations relative to their activities. The boys learned more manly skills like carpentry, animal husbandry, managing livestock, and so on, while girls learned how to cook, sew, and take care of a garden. She was silent for a few minutes and then asked, "do you think I'll be able to learn things like that when we get to Lycea?"

"I'm sure you will, your highness." Ráona replied with a smile. "You'll probably have your own private tutors."

Aisling gave her a suspicious look. *Is she making fun of me?* "Tutors? Are they like teachers?"

"They are."

Aisling was so tired, she was beginning to stagger as she walked. If they hadn't kept talking, she was afraid she might have fallen asleep on her feet.

Irial, who had been walking ahead, turned around and looked at her, when he realized how worn out she was, he opened his pack and felt around until he found a small vial of pink fluid. "Here, your highness, take a few sips of this." He removed the cap and held it out to her.

"What is it?" she asked, yawning."

"It's an energiser. It will give you enough energy to keep going until we reach the Gateway. He held out the vial again and this time, she took it. The fluid inside had a faint pink glow when she held it. She looked at him again. "How much?"

"Take a mouthful and see how you feel. "I'm sorry you've had to go through all this stress," he added. "If the other Gateway had not been exposed, we'd have been home before the next sunset."

Aisling put the tiny bottle to her lips and tilted it, allowing a small amount to fall into her mouth. She savoured for a moment, found it had a pleasant flavour, not unlike raspberries, and then swallowed it. She looked at Irial, who nodded, and took another sip, and then returned the vial.

She could already feel the lethargy draining away. She took a deep breath and continued walking with more energy. "I feel much better now," she said. "Is that stuff magic?"

"No," Ráona replied. "It's made from natural ingredients, although the apothecary may have added a tiny spell to make it work faster."

The three stayed close together when the sunlight finally disappeared. All they had now for illumination were the two glowing crystals carried by Irial and Ráona, one on either side of her. The upward slope continued for a while and then levelled out and began a slight downward tilt. A half-moon eventually appeared through the opening behind them.

"Ah, here we are." Irial moved to the wall on their left and put his hand against the rock face.

9 – Through the tunnels

&~&

Once inside the Gateway, the cavern was much like the previous one. Circular with smooth glowing walls, a row of trunks around one side. The main difference was the water fountain in the middle. There were also sanitary and bathing facilities inside cubicles across from the trunks. Irial and Ráona did a quick survey of the room to make sure there was no sign that the enemy had passed through recently.

"What shall we do first?" Irial asked. "Eat, sleep, or bathe?"

"All of those," Ráona said. "And I know what I'm going to go first." She went over to one of the trunks and took out two sheets of fluffy material. She beckoned to Aisling. "Come on, Princess," she said. "I'll show you how the facilities work. Bring something clean to put on when you've finished."

They both took some clean clothes from another trunk and carried them to the cubicles. The walls of the cubicles we translucent but not transparent. Ráona opened one of the doors. "Hang your clean clothes and the towel over there, away from the spray. You can turn on the water with this lever." She opened a small door in the back wall. "This is for if you need to relieve yourself." Inside was a small hollow stool which didn't look much different from the outhouse back home, except it was smoother, made of a finer material, and didn't smell as bad.

"Think you can manage, or do you want me to help you?"

The notion of someone helping her bathe didn't seem fitting to Aisling. Babies were bathed, but big girls washed themselves. "I'll be fine, thank you," she said. To her relief, Ráona left her alone.

While they had been bathing, Irial had thrown together a meal. Aisling didn't realize how hungry she was until she saw the food spread out on a clean cloth. There was fruit, cheese, some sweet bread and a delicious white drink that tasted faintly of almonds.

☙❧

Aisling felt disoriented for a moment when she woke up and saw the immaculate cavern with its rosy illuminated walls then, as things fell into place, her confusion changed to excitement. She had heard stories about heroes who went on great adventures and saw many wonders in their travels, but she never dreamed it could happen to her. This was turning into a real adventure, although she made no claims of heroism.

She sat up on the sleeping pad and looked for her companions. Irial was across the room humming to himself as he looked through the trunks, and Ráona was in one of the sanitary cubicles. *That's what I need.* She picked up her clean clothes and walked over to one of the empty booths.

"Joyful dawning," Irial said to her as she passed. "I hope you slept well."

67

"Good morning," she replied. "I slept very well."

When she returned from the refresher, they were sitting on the pads with a veritable feast spread out on the cloth. They'd eaten all the eggs and the other things they'd brought from the cottage and now had a selection of fruits and vegetables, breads and cheeses, looking as fresh as the day they were produced. There was also a drink with the creamy, nutty flavour she'd enjoyed the night before.

"Do you know what time it is?" she asked. Her former life had been guided by the time of day, time to feed the poultry and collect the eggs, time to water the garden or go to the village. She realized that she would have to make some adjustments now but didn't know what they would be, apart from waking and sleeping.

"It is probably dawn," Ráona said. "But it doesn't really matter while we are in the Gateway system."

After they finished eating, they packed up a few supplies and prepared to leave. Irial went to the wall marked by a circle of tiny holes opposite the entrance. When he laid his palm over the holes, an opening appeared and after they were through, it closed behind them. The tunnels on this side of the entrance cavern were the same grey rock as the mountain, unpolished and bare, although the ground under their feet was smooth. The lighting, a glow from the roof, followed them as they moved through.

"Are these natural caves or were they dug out?" Aisling asked. She knew about mines and digging for ore, but if these tunnels were as extensive as they said, they must have taken a lot of work.

"Some of each," Irial said. "Wherever possible, they used what was already there, caves and mines, but most of the work was done by the dwarfs."

"Dwarfs? You mean they are real? I thought they were just creatures from fairy-tales."

"They are very real," he replied. "They live in underground communities all over the Realm. They're Elementals whose major gift is the ability to work with the earth, shaping rock and collecting ores. They used to fight against our intrusions into their mines, trying to keep us from taking their treasures, but wise leaders from the Light Realm negotiated with them, showing them the benefits of trading for the things we both needed. They used to have terrible famines before the treaty, and now they have more access to food, seeds and domestic animals, things they had to steal from us before."

"So now they help you build tunnels," Aisling said. "Was that a long time ago?"

"Almost two thousand years."

"If the Korrigen are using the tunnels, can the dwarfs help you ... us fight them?"

"They do, but the little pests are very hard to catch, they just disappear when they sense danger."

"They are even worse for the dwarfs because they have started building underground dens in their territory and stealing children and anything else they can gain access to."

"That's awful," Aisling said. "I didn't realise it was so bad."

It was quite peaceful in the tunnels with only an occasional clinking noise from a distance. There were frequent intersections and turns along the way, marked by signs engraved in the rock that Aisling couldn't read. According to Ráona, they gave directions.

They had been walking for several hours when a commotion arose around a curve ahead of them: Screeches and grunts, the clang of metal against metal, and screams of pain.

The two elves froze for a moment, bracketing Aisling between them, then Irial said, "take the princess and go back; I'm going to see what's happening."

He drew his sword and crept silently to the bend. The noise seemed to be coming closer. They watched him peer around the corner and then move out of sight. "Come on," Ráona said, grasping her arm. "We have to keep you safe."

More screams and cries of rage followed them until they reached an intersection and turned the corner. Ráona stood, sword in hand, guarding the tunnel entrance while Aisling crouched against the wall behind her.

The racket seemed to be following them, coming closer every second. What had happened to Irial? Aisling was trembling in terror, trying to form herself into a tiny bundle. *I wish I could make myself invisible.*

Suddenly, Ráona gasped and Aisling saw a gout of blood spray out from her back as she collapsed on the ground. Seeing the blood spread into a pool around Ráona, she turned and ran, tears flowing from her eyes. She looked over her shoulder to see if she was being followed but didn't see anything. She took the knife out of her belt ... Irial had said it was for defence, but she wasn't sure if she would be able to use it.

Gasping for air was making her throat raw, but she kept on running, having no idea where she was going, only getting away from whatever was attacking them. Ráona was dead, she was sure—nobody could lose that much blood and still live—but what had happened to Irial? The sensation of danger was mounting, making her heart pound furiously. She knew there was something behind her but didn't know how to avoid it. Her only hope was that she would meet someone friendly who could help her.

The ground suddenly disappeared in front of her and she was falling, her body hitting rocky steps all the way down into oblivion.

10 – Captive
ॐॐ

The first thing Aisling became aware of was the awful smell. It was like a combination of rotting meat and the horrible weed that grew in the woods near the cottage … stinkweed they called it. When she tried to move her foot, an excruciating pain shot up her leg. The air was musty and the ground damp under her back. Her clothes were wet too; she must have wet herself. *Oh, Creator, what can I do? Please help me.*

She realized the muffled background noise was people talking. They seemed to be arguing about something because voices rose at intervals and were silenced by hard thumps on a wood surface.

She leaned back against the hard wall and closed her eyes. Her feeling of helplessness vied with the pain in her right leg for her attention, and there was nothing she could do about either of them. Seeing Ráona die like that had shaken her more than she realised. She put her head down and sobbed despairingly. *Poor Ráona, she was so nice, like a big sister and now…. She gave her life for me. If only I could do something, if I had some magic I could use.*

She scooted her bottom back against the wall to sit up straighter, as if that would make her think more effectively. The sound of voices had faded now and all she could hear was the faint cries of children playing. *Maybe it's not so bad after all if there are children down here. Who am I trying to fool?*

I have to think. What would be the most useful magic? She didn't really know much about magic, apart from what she'd read in fairy tales and the things Ráona and Irial had told her. They didn't say anything about how it worked or how to develop the skills. *The most useful ... healing would be good so that I could do something about this leg. I'm sure it's broken.* She sat without thinking for a few minutes, feeling her surroundings slipping away. After a while, it seemed as if something in her mind was spinning. Suddenly she felt a mental click, as if something had fallen into place.

Aisling tried to relax, hoping that might help. She put both hands on the injured leg and closed her eyes to concentrate on the pain. It might require a spell, but she didn't know what words to use, so she started as if it was a prayer. *Please, dear Lord, make this awful pain go away. Go away, go away, pain, go away!*

Soon, her leg began to feel numb. It felt a bit cooler as well, as if the inflammation was withdrawing. She scrunched her toes and found it didn't hurt as much as it had before. With a sigh, she rested her hands in her lap and thought about other things that might be useful. *I know! ... what did they call it? Far – something. I've got it, far-seeing! Maybe there's a skill for sending messages, far-sending. They did say something about being in extreme peril. Who should I send it to? The only magic person is Irial and I don't know if he's still alive.*

She began to concentrate on him, calling his name mentally. After a while, her head began to buzz. It was like being in a big cavern with hundreds of people all talking at once, their voices blending together, but she persisted. *Irial, Irial, can you hear me? I fell through the floor ... cold dark place ...people talking. Irial...!* She repeated it a few times but received no response from Irial.

Now that the pain in her leg had diminished slightly, Aisling began to feel drowsy and closed her eyes. She awoke with a start with no idea how long she had slept. She could feel terror approaching in the form of footsteps and mumbling voices, still arguing by the sound of them. They were coming for her. Her leg began to throb again and when she tried to move it, sharp pains flashed up her leg. Her heart pounded, and nausea clutched her stomach. *Oh, Lord Father, please help me!*

Dim, flickering lights lit up the tunnel as they came closer. She closed her eyes again. *I don't want to see them. Help me; I'm so scared.*

They stopped in front of her, still grunting to one another, then a voice said in her tongue, "Wake up Princess. Our leader wants to welcome you to our nest. Come on, stand up."

She couldn't resist opening a narrow gap between her eyelids. When she got her first glimpse of these creatures, she closed them again. They were horrible! The tallest of them would only have come up to her shoulders, but it was other features that repelled her. They were humanoid, with dark greyish green skin and matted black hair. Their reddish-brown eyes and the dark blue tongues were revolting. They were bare apart from the cloth that looked like animal skins that they wore around their waists.

"I can't stand up," she said, trying to sound contemptuous, but achieving only a frightened whine.

"What's wrong with you?" the speaker asked with a sneer. "Oh, I know you're a princess and feel you should be carried, but too bad, we haven't got a carriage, so you'll have to walk."

"My leg is broken!" she yelled, close to tears.

The creature looked down at her legs and kicked her right foot. Agonizing pain shot up her leg and throughout her body. She screamed, her eyes flooding with tears. He grunted and turned and spoke to one of his companions. Two of them went off at a run, back the way they had come.

"I have sent for a board to carry you, princess," the talkative one said.

Aisling glared at him. "Stop calling me princess. I'm not a princess, I'm just a village girl, a peasant."

"That's not what we heard," he replied with a sly wink at the other Korrigan.

I don't want to talk to this ugly monster. She leaned back against the wall and closed her eyes, as if that would shut him out. In truth, she was terrified, recalling what Irial had told her about the death of their leader's son and the leader's threat of revenge.

"Where are you taking me?" she asked, reluctantly. *Might as well see what I'm up against.*

"I thought I told you that already," he replied. "You are going to meet the chief."

"Is he your leader?"

"Of course he is; he's the chief."

"Why does he want to see me?"

He winked again at the other Korrigan. "You'll find out. He's really looking forward to meeting you. You should feel honoured." He looked down the tunnel. "Ah, here they are."

The two Korrigen came into view, carrying a long board on their shoulders. They laid it down on the ground next to her and looked at the spokesman for instructions. After he'd growled a few words at them, they prepared to lift her, two grabbing under her arms and two her feet. The moment the creature touched her foot, she let out a piercing screamed. She'd never imagined there could be such pain. The one who had touched her jumped back, startled. The spokesman growled at him. He approached again took hold of her other leg at the ankle. The spokesman came to her right side and put one arm under her thigh and the other under her knee. The moment they started to lift her, she fainted.

Aisling woke up in a dimly lighted cavern, lying on a pad. Her injured leg was throbbing painfully, almost beyond bearing. She realised that someone had tied a narrow board to it bound with strips of leather, otherwise, she couldn't feel any other changes made while she was unconscious.

The malodorous air was even stronger in this cavern than in the tunnel and it shamed her to realise that her bladder had released, adding ammonia to the mix. She looked around and saw the two candles on the floor near an opening that provided the lighting and sensed there was someone outside. Are they guarding me? As if I could run away with this leg. "Hey!" she called in a hoarse voice. Her throat was so dry, she could barely talk at all.

A head appeared and then one of the creatures came into the cavern and stood a body-length away, looking at her expectantly. Aisling was surprised to see it was a female. She was wearing the same little skirt as the men she had already met. *Perhaps she's here to look after me*, she thought. *I hope so.*

Aisling knew the female would probably not understand if she asked her anything, so she had to communicate with gestures. The most important thing right now was something to drink, preferable water. She pointed to her mouth and mimicked drinking and then cleared her throat, hoping that she would be understood. The little woman nodded and said something in her own language, then she left. She came back a few moments later with a clay bowl half filled with a milky liquid, behind her were two male Korrigen, one of which, by his attire, was someone important. In addition to his skirt, which had patterns around the bottom, he had ornamental rings on his arms, and a headdress of feathers on a leather band. The other man was the spokesperson she had already met. He was carrying a wooden stool which he placed on the floor a few foot lengths away from her and bowed to his superior.

"I am honoured to announce our revered leader, Domin Cragsil," he said. "I am Loamin Cragsil, son of Domin Cragsil, second to leader. The domin wants to talk to you."

I'm not talking to anyone until I drink something. Aisling looked at the woman holding the bowl, hoping it was something to drink. She cleared her throat for emphasis. The woman looked at the chief and said something in a low tone. When he replied, she knelt on the floor and handed the bowl to Aisling.

Aisling took a sip and screwed up her nose. It tasted truly awful, sour and slightly mouldy. Aisling looked at the loamin, assuming the first names were their titles. "What is this?" she asked.

"It is very nutritious," he replied. "Fermented donkey milk with some healing herbs."

"Could I have water?"

"Drink what you are given and be thankful we are feeding you at all," the Loamin snarled. "My father is trying to decide what to do with you now that we have you. If I had not spoken for you, you would not be alive. It still might come to that."

11 – Irial

Irial staggered as he entered the king's suite. The injuries he suffered in the fray with the Korrigen were slow to heal. He suspected they used some sort of poison in the missiles from their blow-pipes.

King Briartach was reclining in a chaise longue by the window. He looked almost as frail as Irial felt, pale and wasted, his golden hair lank and faded by his illness, but his golden eyes were still as alert as ever. Queen Fenella came to meet him as he approached, bowing as deeply as he was able, which amounted to a dip of his head. She looked as if she hadn't had much sleep recently.

"Come and sit down, Irial" she said, taking his arm and leading him to a wicker chair near her husband. She sat in a matching one facing the garden behind him.

The king nodded. "What have you got to report, my boy? "What happened?"

"I fear the tunnels have been invaded by the enemy, my lord. It seems they are making their homes in the underworld and sally forth whenever they want to attack us or need anything."

"What about our daughter?" he asked in a husky voice.

The queen snapped her fingers and said, "refreshment." Almost before the word was out, two fairies flew in with crystal drinking vessels and a full carafe, which they placed on a small agate table in the middle of the group. The first cup went to the king, who drank greedily, as if he was dehydrated. "Thank you, Tinellas, we can manage now." The two fairies chuckled in their high-pitched voices and flew away through the open window.

"My lord, I fear they have captured her. She still lives, but she broke her leg falling through the hole. She is in pain, but I suspect someone is looking after her because the pain fades for a while occasionally."

The king groaned. "How did you find out all this?" he asked.

"That's one piece of good news, my lord, it appears she has developed the power of far-sending. She called me and explained what had happened to her. Unfortunately, she didn't receive my response. I don't know why, but she did use far-hearing once with … with Ráona." It was hard for him to talk about Ráona. Thinking about her and how she died was too painful. He looked at the king and queen, his eyes filmed with tears. He and Ráona had worked together for almost a hundred years. *I miss you so much, Rannie.*

The royal couple looked at each other silently for a moment. "A terrible loss," the queen said. "We'll all miss her, but you most of all, I suspect." She poured some more lime water in her goblet and took a sip. "So you think our daughter still lives? How are we going to get her away from those fiends?"

The queen wiped a tear from the corner of her eye. It was painful enough having their only daughter stolen away to be raised by strangers in another realm, but at least the fosterers had been well chosen by her cousin. When they finally discovered her whereabouts, they were thankful she was being treated well. Now their only child was in the hands of a powerful enemy, and who knows what they would do to her? She reached over and took her husband's hand, giving it a comforting squeeze.

"That is what I want to consult you about. I agree that we need to know what their intentions are, but I think we should start making plans to rescue her. She's an amazingly intelligent young girl and we need to find a way of contacting her. The fact that the Korrigen chief is keeping her alive is promising. He may have got over the loss of his son by now and has other plans for her."

"That's still not very reassuring," King Briartach said. "The best outcome I see would be ransoming her, but they haven't sent a ransom message, or anything." He yawned and leaned his head back on his pillow.

"You tire, my lord. Would you like to postpone this until you've rested?" Irial said. He was not feeling too fit himself.

Briartach raised his head and glared at Irial. "This is too important for such trivia as resting. We have to make a plan."

"I beg your pardon your majesty." The king nodded. "I was going to suggest we initiate a conference of your most skilled councillors and come up with a plan of action."

"Done!" the king said. "You and Fenella get to work on it immediately." He whistled to summon a fairy. When the fairy appeared, he growled, "Send my healer." The fairy vanished like lightening.

"Let's go to my salon and put together a team," the queen said to Irial. She kissed her husband and squeezed his hand, then led Irial to another room in the royal suite. "I'm going to order some food to eat while we work on it. Do you have any medical needs?"

"I'd like my healing draft," he replied. "I should have brought it, but my mind was on more important things."

The words were barely out of his mouth when another fairy appeared with a small vial and set it on the table in front of him.

"How is your healing progressing?" Fenella asked.

"Quite well," he replied. "We've identified the poison and now we have a way to fight it." He held up the vial.

Three fairies flitted around the room, setting the table, arranging dishes and giggling. *I wonder what they find so funny,* Irial thought. Fairies had been around since long before his birth, but they were still unfathomable to most elves. They were the one species whose minds were closed to them.

They probably know more about us than we know about ourselves, he thought. One of them flew by his head, chortled and ruffled his hair.

According to historic records, the little creatures had originally infiltrated elven society and become voluntary workers filling all sorts of useful niches. They were efficient and fast, appearing and vanishing at will. Although they understood the elven language, they rarely had anything to say. Irial speculated that the giggling and chortling was their speech.

Although Irial and the queen chose four other people to form a committee, he still doubted it would be much help in rescuing Aisling, or even keeping her alive long enough to be rescued.

"We must find a way to contact her," he said.

"We'll just have to keep trying," one of the older committee members said.

"Could we send someone down there?" another suggested.

"The only people who can get around in the underworld are the dwarfs."

"Well I think we should bring them in on this. They have more to lose with those fiends loose in their habitat." Róisín, the woman who suggested this was an interspecies diplomat.

"Yes, I think we should do that immediately," the queen said. "Could you take care of that, Róisín?"

A fairy flew into the room through the open window. He alighted on the floor and touched the queen's hand. He issued a few chirps which no one understood. Queen Fenella smiled. "Thank you for that information, Innes. Would you like to join our group? It would be very helpful in rescuing the princess."

She turned to the other committee members and explained. "Innes said that fairies can enter the Underworld without detection. The only drawback is that they have to enter and leave very quickly because the environment down there is toxic to them."

"How much time would they have?" Irial asked.

Innes touched her hand again. "Innes tells me they have twenty breaths."

"That's not much time, and we certainly don't want them to be harmed," Róisín said.

Fenella and Innes had another brief discussion. "They would have more time if there was someone with them who could tell them Aisling's exact location."

The queen looked at Irial. "I think you should rest; you look exhausted," she said. "We'll take care of the immediate tasks. Róisín can contact the dwarfs and set them in motion while I report to my husband."

"I want to help; it's my responsibility." Irial couldn't resist the urge to rub his abdomen where the pain was worst.

"You're no good to us or anyone if you are not fit. Now, go and rest! I'll send our healer to your quarters to give you some healing therapy."

"I'm so sorry, your majesty." Irial stood up carefully, reluctant to use his abdominal muscles where the worst injury was. After bowing his head to the queen, he shuffled out of the room. He was now glad Queen Fenella had insisted on him having quarters on the royal family's level where he would be close. Now that he was alone, he folded his arms over his stomach and bent forward, relieving some of the pressure. Normally, he would have been able to heal himself, but the poison on the darts blocked his self-healing power, and he had to rely on a healer and medicine."

As he walked to his rooms, Irial's thoughts turned to the battle in the tunnels. When he'd turned the bend in the tunnel to see what was causing the commotion, the tunnel was empty, or was it? The lights had been dimmed, so he couldn't see much. He smelled a powerful scent in the air that spelled danger, but he had no idea what was causing it. He had crept forward cautiously, keeping close to the wall. As he got used to the dim lighting, he could see lumps scattered over the floor, the bodies of several dwarfs, lying in pools of orange blood. A terrified scream echoed through the tunnel from behind him. He turned back and ran, fearing Aisling and Ráona had been attacked. He'd barely taken two steps when something pierced his back, knocking him to his knees. After that, he didn't remember anything until some elves had found him and brought him to the palace. It was while they were carrying him out that he received Aisling's message. He didn't find out about Ráona until later. *Oh, blessed Lord, please watch over our sister, Aisling,* he prayed as he pushed aside the curtain and entered his room.

12 – Aisling in the Underworld
≈◦≪

The passage of time was meaningless to Aisling. Korrigen came and went randomly. Once she'd been visited by some children who stood around and stared at her as if she were a dangerous animal until a little boy ran forward and kicked her broken leg. When she screamed in pain, the others joined in and, screeching delightedly as they kicked various parts of her body. Eventually she'd lost consciousness.

She learned that the little woman who was taking care of her was called Tilly and she was the domin's healer. Judging by her withered breasts, she must have been quite old. Aisling also discovered that Tilly understood her language.

"Why are you helping me?" she asked her one day. "I thought the Domin was going to kill me."

"I talk him," Tilly replied. "My son has evil temper and not think when make threat. He sad, losing son, but I say you not kill him."

"So he's not going to kill me?"

The old woman nodded her head, "Not."

"So what will he do with me?"

"You walk good, you be slave."

After that conversation, she became even more depressed. What good was it to be kept alive as a slave?

Surely, they will find a way to rescue me, if they know where I am. But do they know? I'll have to try to send another message. Pray Irial is alive. She lay back on the damp, smelly mattress, closed her eyes and concentrated. She tried to far-send several times before giving up. This time, she'd received a lot of eerie crackling noise mixed in with a moaning like wind blowing across the top of a chimney. It's no good, she sighed.

Tilly had told her to exercise her leg, stretch and bend it. But it hurt too much. She moved down the pad so that she was lying flat and tried to lift her right foot. After raising it a few finger breadths, she lowered it gently back to the mattress. *It's no good; I can't do it.* She closed her eyes. *This is so boring, she thought, just lying here doing nothing. Even working as a slave is preferable to this.* Tears flowed down her face. *I wish I'd never left our little cottage. I wish gran hadn't died. We were happy there before all this stupid mess started. And Ráona would still be alive.* She sobbed as if her heart would break. *Maybe Irial had been killed as well and that's why he doesn't answer.*

Aisling didn't know how long she'd been asleep when the commotion began outside her prison cell. There was much racing around, people shouting orders, crashes and bumps of things being moved around. *Maybe they've come to rescue me,* she thought hopefully. *But there would be screaming and ... oh what's the use?*

Four Korrigen males came into her cell carrying a contraption made of leather attached to poles. They dropped the thing beside her sleeping pad and one of them babbled something to her, gesticulating with his hands. Receiving no response from her, he shrugged and signalled to the other three. The four of them surrounded her and each grabbed one of her limbs and started to lift her. The pain from her leg was so agonizing, she screamed. The one holding her injured leg dropped it as if it had burned him, leaving the other three to drag her onto the skins.

Tilly came rushing in and started scolding them. All four fell to their knees and bent their heads. If she hadn't been in so much pain, Aisling might have laughed. They looked terrified, as if they expected to be executed on the spot. After she had finished ranting at them, she pointed to the opening and they crawled outside on their knees.

"Fools," she said, shaking her head. "But what you expect from slaves." She raised Aisling's head with one arm and thrust out a stone vessel with the other hand. "Drink!"

Aisling took it and looked inside. It was the same foul-smelling liquid she had been fed twice a day, but she drank it, trying not to breathe in its putrid odour. As least it gave her some minor relief from the constant pain, and Tilly had told her it would help her bones to mend.

"What's all the commotion? Has something happened?" Aisling asked.

"We move," she replied. "How you feel now?"

"A bit better," Aisling said. *Not much better*, she thought. She wanted to keep on the good side of the old woman; her life might depend on it. "Where are you going?"

"We!" Tilly said. "You go more safer place."

"Why?"

"Too many questions, girl. You may be princess, but to us you no better than slave." She shouted something outside and the four slaves returned. After giving them another tongue-lashing, she left.

I don't feel like a princess, she thought. At least it would lessen the boredom. Maybe someone has been poking around, looking for me. And it might make us easier to find it we're on the move. There must be other creatures around to see us.

The four slaves gingerly picked up the makeshift stretcher by the poles and carried it out into the tunnel, watching her closely for any sign of pain. Tilly had them completely intimidated. What if they really would kill the slaves if they didn't handle her carefully?

This was the first she'd been out of the cell in she didn't know how long. It felt to Aisling like months. She had almost become accustomed to the putrid smell, but she was still reluctant to open her mouth when she breathed. The thought of that foulness entering her mouth was nauseating. As far as she could tell, they were moving in the opposite direction, away from the place she'd fallen. That would make it harder for the elves to track her.

"What happened to you?" a soft voice said near her left ear.

She glanced to the side and saw the slave girl was looking straight ahead. "I fell through a hole in the tunnel," she whispered back. *I'll have to remember her, she thought. She might be able to help me.*

The apparent leader of the four slaves looked over his shoulder and snarled at the female slave. The girl said something to him in Korrigen, and that seemed to satisfy him.

As the pain in her leg faded, Aisling started to feel drowsy. She yawned and closed her eyes. She was awakened periodically by Tilly to take more medicine and some gruel, but she dozed off almost as soon as she'd finished eating the rank-tasting mush that served as food. She had no idea where she was, apart from the fact that she was still a captive. One time she woke up and saw sunlight and smelled the fragrance of growing things, but whatever they were using to drug her didn't permit her to enjoy the fragrance for long.

When Aisling awoke for the last time, she found herself surrounded by rock walls, apart from a small opening that admitted a little light. It might have been natural light because it didn't flicker like oil lights. She found herself lying on a raised pallet covered with a greasy, rancid-smelling blanket. She managed to raise herself into a sitting position with her good foot on the ground and the injured one sticking straight out on the splint. She took a deep breath and realized that the awful stink was absent; the air was fresh with just a trace of rock dust. *If we are this close to the open air, I might have a chance to escape. But my leg has to mend first.*

She heard voices approaching and recognized Tilly with two males. Tilly came into the cave first. "Good, you sit up. Now need exercise."

"Can she walk?" the Domin asked.

"Soon," she replied, then the three of them held a short discussion.

"My son say no try to escape, try to send talk to friends, you die."

"And she make exercise," her grandson added.

Aisling nodded, not raising her eyes from her hands nesting in her lap.

"You understand?" the Domin snarled.

She turned her head sideway and squinted at him. "Yes." She could hardly bear to look at them.

After the two males left, Tilly knelt on the ground and untied the leather thongs holding the splint in place. Supporting her foot with one hand, she used the other to remove the splint and set it aside. She raised the leg and then lowered it until it touched the ground. Although Aisling's whole body clenched, ready for more pain, it was a lot less painful than she'd expected.

The old woman looked up at her and grinned, showing several missing teeth. "It good, no?"

"Yes, it feels a bit better. When will I be able to walk on it?"

"Soon. Need exercise. I show you. You do this." Tilly went through a routine of movements, all of which hurt to some degree, but the most painful was bending her knee.

"Thank you for taking care of me, Tilly." She thought for a moment. Maybe this was a good time to

91

Vicki Wootton

get some more information. "I notice that the lower leg is bent. Will it always be like that?"

"Yes, daughter. Sad, I say."

Tears stung Aisling's eyes. *I'll be a cripple for the rest of my life.* Another question struck her. "I can't believe my leg healed so fast. How long have I been here ...? I mean with you?" she didn't want to emphasize her status as a prisoner by saying captive.

Tilly patted her hand. "It is one moon and half."

"Will I still need the splints?"

"No, child. Not need. You move careful."

Aisling wanted to hug the old woman who had treated her with such kindness but was uncertain of the of reaction she would get.

"Tilly, did they move here so that my friends couldn't find me?"

Tilly scowled and pursed her lips. "I no say." She rose to her knees and stood up, then picked up the leather thongs and splints. "I send food," she said as she left the cave.

Aisling raised her good leg onto the pallet and then cautiously lifted the other one up. She then scooted back to lean against the wall. *I must think now, plan what to do, if there is anything I can do. Moving out of the underground could be a good thing or a disastrous one, depending on how things work here. And that's what I don't know.*

Maybe I failed to reach Irial because we were underground. Will they know when I'm trying to communicate? she thought about that for a moment. When the Domin made that threat, was he just trying to scare her, or did they really have a way to tell what she's doing? *I'll have to try,* she decided. Once again, she thought about the options spend the rest of her life here with these creatures or risk her life to get away from them. The answer was obvious.

13 – Action at the palace
༼ঔঔ৸

The king of Lycea was still very weak. Queen Fenella was beginning to believe that the only thing that would cure him would be the presence of his daughter.

"Is he feeling any better?" Irial asked her.

Fenella shook her head sadly. "The only positive thing is that he's not getting any worse. His condition seems to be stable."

"Talking about me again?"

They turned their heads and saw the king standing in the doorway supporting himself with an ivory staff. Irial jumped up and bowed, then went to his side and offered his arm.

"I can manage," Briartach said irritably. "I'll never get any better if people keep doing everything for me."

"You are probably correct, my love." The queen put some cushions on one of the wicker lounging chairs. "Come and sit with us. We were talking about the results of our search for Aisling."

"What's the progress so far? It's been more than a moon and we're no closer to finding her."

"The dwarfs tried to locate her in the underground, but..." She turned to Róisín. "Would you like to tell us what happened?" she asked.

"We contacted the local dwarf engineer, Godwil, and told him of our dilemma. His team spread out from the point where Ráona was lost. They used their sonar ability to locate the area where the rock had been altered. They believed the princess had fallen through a hole. It looked as if it had been a staircase, but they'd filled it in after she fell."

The king scowled. "How can they make a hole that big without anyone knowing about it?"

"Maybe they have the ability to change matter and move it with mind control. They also had a spell that made it undetectable to the eye, something like the way we camouflage the Gateways."

"Can dwarfs do that?" King Briartach asked.

"They can, your majesty. It's the skill that makes them such great engineers."

"Poor Aisling. She must have been terrified," Queen Fenella said reaching for her husband's hand.

Innes chirped and flew onto the arm of Fenella's chair. He put his hand on her head and twittered a long stream of information to her. "Thank you, Innes," she said when he'd finished. She turned to the others. "He says that the dwarf made a hole near the place where our daughter disappeared, and he went down to the underworld level, but the air down there was so bad he had to withdraw after three breaths, but he did find out one piece of information. Apparently, she was injured when she fell and is being take care of by a Korrigan female."

By the time she finished speaking, she had tears in her eyes. She looked at her husband whose eyebrows were drawn together with anger. She stroked his hand on the chair arm and then squeezed it. "She lives, my love. There is hope."

"All I can think of is finding the worst way possible we can punish them for this. My hatred for them is burning me up inside."

Fenella leaned closer and whispered in his ear, "Don't, my love. You're only hurting yourself."

Another fairy flew in through the window and landed on the table in front of them. This time, Irial took the message. His heart sank. This was the worst news possible. He had to tell the king and queen but dreaded doing so.

"What is it, Irial?" the queen asked. "Not more bad news, surely."

Irial cleared his throat. "They've gone," he said. "The whole clan, or whatever they call themselves, has packed up and moved out of the Underworld."

The four elves and the fairy exchanged glances. This was very bad news. There was no telling where the princess was now.

The king, whose face was even paler than before was the first to say something. "How could they get away without someone seeing them?"

"Apparently, they chose a good time," Irial replied. "They left during the sleep cycle of the dwarfs in that area and killed any dwarf they encountered on the way." They also planted false trails to confuse anybody trying to follow them. One thing we do know is that they have left the Underworld and are now either in the Mid-world, or the World of light, which would be better for Princess Aisling."

The queen clapped her hand once and said "refreshment." A few seconds later, a small team of fairies flew in to serve them drinks and snacks."

"We've got to find them," the King said needlessly. "I want everyone we can spare working on this. Irial and Róisín, get to work on it. We need the dwarfs in on it too, and Innis, can you round up as many of your people as can be spared to help us?

Innis touched Irial, who was closest and twitted.

"He says he will contact Queen Máira immediately." The fairy had flown out of the window before he'd even finished speaking.

"I just had a thought," Irial said. "Now that she is out of the tunnels, Princess Aisling might be able to contact me."

"You're the only person she can contact, so be alert," the queen said.

"Do you think she would be able to contact you or his majesty? Given your intimate relationship to her, that might be possible."

"Only if she thinks of it," Fenella replied. "She didn't even know we were her parents until recently."

14 – Aisling's new home

❧❦

Aisling was walking and could even leave her cave, but not alone. At first, Tilly walked with her so that she could encourage her to keep using the injured leg and assess her fitness. Before many days had passed, she was walking without help and her escort changed to female slaves.

One day, the slave who'd spoken to her in her own language was her escort. They walked through the tunnels of the massive cave the Korrigen had adopted as their home. "Why don't we ever go outside?" Aisling asked her after they'd turned left, deeper into the tunnel.

"Orders," Not a satisfactory answer.

Aisling tried again. "Where are we?"

This time the slave gave another one-word answer. "Mountains."

Aisling smiled. This was like a game, see who could give the shortest answer. "What can I call you?"

"Lena."

Aisling nodded. All right, she thought; how can I get her talking?

"Where are you from?" she asked.

"Stop! No more," Lena said angrily. "You cannot pick me to pieces."

That got her talking, Aisling thought. *She doesn't like talking about herself, so she may be embarrassed about her past. Or maybe it is too painful. Poor woman.*

"I'm sorry, Lena. Forgive me for prying. I would like us to be friends."

Lena nodded and pointed ahead.

After they had finished a circuit through the tunnels, Lena took her back to her cave. Before she left, she squeezed Aisling's hand.

Aisling sat down on her pallet and massaged her aching leg. She was gratified by the progress of the healing, although disappointed that she walked with a limp. It puzzled her why the Korrigen had given her such good care. *Maybe they are going to ransom me,* she thought hopefully, there was a greater chance if she was healthy.

She heard feet shuffling along the floor outside. Expecting someone bringing her some food, she stood up and went to the opening just in time to meet Tilly.

"Here, I bring you food," the old woman said. She handed the bowl to Aisling and went over to the pallet, sighing in relief as she sat down. "Being old, me."

"I'm sorry, Tilly. Couldn't you send someone to bring it?"

"No. I talk to you."

Aisling crouched down on the ground and put the bowl in her lap. The food was improving since they left the tunnels. Sometimes the soup-like mixture contained a few shreds of meat and some vegetables, although it was still mainly boiled grain and water. She picked up the wooden spoon and took a mouthful.

Tilly watched her for a moment and then spoke. "They want person with your tongue to talk you," she said. She looked very tired.

Aisling nodded and swallowed the food in her mouth. *This must be important.* Her heart began to flutter, and an icy feeling wrapped around her stomach. *Dear Lord, what now?*

"You move now," Tilly said. "Go to slave cavern. Work."

"But...," Aisling started to say.

The old woman wagged her finger at her. "No 'but'. You go."

Aisling had lost her appetite. She put the half empty bowl on the floor. There was nothing she could do. She was a prisoner and they were in charge.

Tilly stood up. "Take that," she said, indicating the food bowl. "I show new place you live. Come."

Before she had gone many steps, Tilly became breathless. Her feet became erratic, as if she had no energy to control them.

"Are you unwell?" Aisling asked.

"Old," Tilly replied.

Aisling remembered how suddenly her grandmother had deteriorated. One day she was working in the garden, the next, she was gone. *Unless I wasn't paying attention and didn't notice*, she thought. *Sometimes I was so wrapped up in myself, I didn't pay much attention to her. Poor gran, I took her for granted. I wish I had been more thoughtful. She was so good to me.*

She went closer to the old woman and held her elbow out. "Take my arm," she said.

Tilly looked at her arm and then up at her face. "You good girl," she said, linking her arm with Aislings'

"You have taken good care of me," Aisling replied. "If I can repay you in any way, I will."

As they walked slowly through the cave's meandering tunnels, they had to pause frequently so that Tilly could recover her breath.

They turned a corner and almost collided with Tilly's grandson. He looked over the situation, his grandmother being supported by a slave. "What's wrong, Momo? Are you ill?" He looked suspiciously at Aisling.

The two Korrigen held a brief conversation in their own language, then the grandson turned to Aisling. "Come," he said. "We take Momo to her grotto. I take you to slaves after." Apparently, he wanted to carry the old woman, but she refused. "She good," she said, squeezing Aisling's arm and nodding.

He sighed and said something to her, then he turned to Aisling. "She help you, you help her, yes?"

Does he mean just now, or all the time? "I don't know anything about healing," she said.

"She tell you," he said. That was about his limit with her language.

They went back the way they'd come and around another bend into a wider tunnel which, to her surprise, was lined with green plants lit up by small glowing balls that seemed to float in the air. A slave who had been tending the plants bowed and stepped into an alcove until they passed. A few steps past the garden, they came to a gap in the wall protected by a curtain of woven vines.

101

"Here is," the Loamin said, holding back the curtain.

Momo Tilly went straight for the knee-high pallet covered in clean white fur. She sat on the edge for a moment and then leaned back and pulled her legs up so that she was lying down. "Get thing for head," she said. Aisling looked around, hoping to see something that might serve as a pillow but, before she could act, Loamin went to one of the chests that lined one side of the bed and brought out a leather-covered pillow. Aisling lifted Tilly's shoulders while he placed it under her head. Tilly patted her hand and smiled at her.

Loamin asked her something and she shook her head. "You find medicine for me. He show you."

Aisling had to smile at the way she said it. She looked at Loaming for guidance. Bottles and jars lined some shelves opposite the bed; all labelled in a script that she couldn't understand. He looked back at his grandmother, who said a few words, after which, he picked a clay bottle and gave it to Aisling. "Does she want it in a cup?" she asked.

Eventually they worked out a dose and gave it to Tilly. She sipped it slowly, screwing up her mouth and nose at the taste. She gave the beaker back to Aisling, leaned back, and said in a sleepy voice, "you go now. I call, you come."

The loamin squeezed the old woman's hand and kissed her on the forehead, making obvious how much he loved her.

The slave quarters seemed very chaotic to Aisling. There was a wide, oddly-shaped central cavern surrounded by openings into smaller rooms that served a variety of functions. Loamin looked around until he spotted Lena and beckoned her over. "This Lena. She talk you," he said by way of introduction.

"Hello Lena," Aisling said.

Lena nodded and looked at Loamin for instructions."

She listened to him for a moment, nodding her head frequently. "As you say, my lord," she said when he'd finished.

Lena took Aisling by the arm and led her into one of the side rooms which was empty. "You must be very careful," she said. "Don't give anyone the impression that you are up to something. Most of these people—she waved her hand in the direction of the central cavern—will do anything to get the upper hand. That means they will spy on you and report real or imaginary infractions to the masters." While she was talking, she kept glancing at the entrance and spoke in a low voice. "You probably won't understand a word most of the other slaves say, but you'll learn. You should learn how to say conciliatory things like 'excuse me, I'm sorry,' and 'whatever you say', you get the idea. Oh, and 'can I help you with that?' is useful too.

Lena took her arm. "That's it for the laundry," she said. "Next, I'll show you the ...oh, good day Master Gobrum.

"What are you doing?" He was tall for a Korrigan, but his excessive breadth made him look almost cubic in shape.

"This is the new slave. The Loamin asked me to show her around. Is there something you need me to do?"

He grunted and glared at Aisling. "So you're the princess, are you?"

Aisling looked at Lena for guidance. "Answer him," she said.

"If it please you, master, I am not a princess." She was careful to keep her eyes focused on the ground.

"So, you're calling our leader a liar, are you?" She glanced up and away quickly. His low forehead was puckered into deep ridges and his mouth twisted in anger.

"No master. If he says I am it is true." *That didn't come out very well.* "I must have misunderstood you. I hope you will forgive me, master."

"Come with me," he growled, "You too," he added to Lena.

They followed him out into the central cavern and turned into another side room. It looked like some sort of office or control room with shelves of books and supplies, and several smooth boards with writing on them. "I have to find something for you to do," he said to Aisling. "I hear you're an elf princess, so I don't suppose you're used to hard work." He glared at her. "Well, I've got news for you; you're going to have to learn if you want to survive here."

Aisling was shocked by his vehemence. Why did he hate her? She hadn't done anything to deserve it. She raised her hand tentatively. "What?" he snarled. "And don't try to do any of your Elvin magic on me either. or you'll end up in the pit."

Aisling straightened her shoulders and looked him in the eyes, which were level with her own. "Please master, may I say something?" she asked.

Again, "what?"

Aisling glanced at Lena and then back at the slave master. "Before I came here, master, I worked as a farm girl. I know about taking care of animals, gardening, cooking, doing laundry, and sewing."

He looked at her for a moment, glanced at Lena and back at her. "I've never heard of a princess who could do all those things. How did you learn all that?"

"I wasn't a princess, master. I lived with my grandmother and she taught me how to run a small-holding like hers. We worked together."

"So what are you doing here? Are you a liar as well?"

"My grandmother died, and then two elves came and took me away."

He scowled at her. "You had better be telling the truth. And you will have to prove yourself."

Another Korrigan came into the room. He didn't look like a slave; he had a weapon tucked into the top of his leather skirt. He spoke urgently to the Slave master in their own language and Master turned to Aisling. "The Momo Tilly wants to see you, Go with him!"

He shoved Lena in the back. "Go with them to translate. And come straight back when you're finished.

Aisling was relieved that Lena was coming with her. She was tired of trying to make herself understood by these creatures. "What do you think he will have me doing?" she asked Lena.

105

"Probably the kitchen. We're always ..."

The escort poked them both in the back and spoke sharply to Lena, who turned to Aisling and put her finger across her lips.

Momo Tilly was sitting on the edge of her bed drinking something from a stone vessel. Aisling followed Lena's example and bowed to the old woman. Tilly waved the Korrigan away with the back of her hand. When he was gone, she pointed to some stools near the entrance.

"Sit," she said. "Closer. Your leg hurt?"

"A little bit," Aisling admitted. "I've been standing a long time, Momo."

The old woman rocked back and forth on the cot for a moment, humming to herself. "You work for me," she said finally. "I need helper. I teach this." She gestured towards the pots of living plants and shelves of bottles and jars.

For the first time since her capture, Aisling felt, if not happy, at least relieved. The fear and anxiety had diminished slightly, for the moment, at least. She still wanted to get away from this place. "Thank you Momo," she said. "I hope ... I hope I will please you."

Momo Tilly smiled, and then she started to cough, a wet, bubbly sort of cough. When she had recovered, she said something to Lena in her own tongue. Lena stood up and beckoned to Aisling. "She wants a potion for her cough," Lena explained. She went to a shelf on the right of the entrance and picked up one of the bottles which she held up for Momo's approval. When the old woman nodded, she crossed the room and poured a little of the green fluid into her cup. "Water," Momo Tilly said hoarsely, Aisling looked around and saw a stone water jar on the floor. She used a dipper to scoop some up and added it to the medicine.

Once she finished, Tilly passed the stone vessel to Lena, drew her feet up onto the bed and leaned back against the pillow. "That better."

"Are you ill, Momo?" Aisling asked. "I mean is it serious?" She didn't really know how to ask the question properly, or even if it was polite to ask at all.

Momo sighed and closed her eyes. "I old," she said. "Days falling away."

"I hope you get better soon," Aisling said.

"Giver bless you child. You good girl. You work for me?"

"I would like that very much," she replied. She looked at Lena who was taking in everything. "Could my friend help us as well. She understands your tongue better than I do."

Tilly said a few words to Lena who nodded her head and smiled.

"You go now," Tilly said. "I rest. She know the way."

The tunnels were very busy on the way back to the slave quarters. They had to endure being jostled, poked and kicked by the Korrigen they encountered all the way back. Many of the men and some of the females spat on them and uttered comments Aisling didn't understand, although by their tones it was obvious they were not friendly.

"You'll have to get used to that sort of thing," Lena told her, when they arrived at the slave quarters. "This is a busy time of day for them. It's shift-change and a mealtime."

"You mean they are workers?"

"Oh yes. This is a large community and they do everything you would do in a city. Many of the slaves work with them. They are the most abused of all the slaves who work in the mine and foundry. They don't last very long."

"What happens to them?"

"Mostly they get killed, in accidents or by the mine bosses."

This information soon dampened Aisling's mood. She'd been relieved when she left Momo Tilly's grotto, knowing she would be protected working for her.

"We'd better get you some clothes to wear," Lena said. "Come on, I'll show you where to get them." Most of the slaves she'd encountered so far seemed to wear the same clothes, the females wore sleeveless tunics of drab grey material that barely reached below their knees, and the men wore skirts of the same material.

They went into a long room off the central cavern that was lined with shelves and racks of folded garments. "The bathing facilities are through there," She indicated another opening. Both men and women milled around changing their clothes, entering and leaving the bathing room, and dumping the dirty garments in baskets. There was very little conversation, just get in and get out as fast as possible, mostly ignoring one another.

"Since you, or we, are to be working for the leaders, we must wear the tunics with the green bands, and we have to keep ourselves clean. Thank you for recommending me, by the way." Lena said. She laughed and leaned close to Aisling to whisper in her ear, "Old fatso is going to be furious about the old woman wanting both of us. He probably had all sorts of nasty things in mind for us to do. His favourite thing for people he dislikes is cleaning latrines. He'd get a lot of satisfaction out of having an elven princess doing that."

15 – The king's fate
❧⊱

Queen Fenella paced back and forth in the anteroom outside her husband's sleeping room, wringing her hands. The royal healers had been working with the king all night, but he was little improved over the previous day. He'd taken a turn for the worse around sunset, gasping for breath and moaning with pain.

"What in creation can be the matter with him?" she said.

Although he knew she was speaking rhetorically, the chief healer replied, "There are a number of possible explanations. It's tracking down the right one that is problematic. The way his symptoms keep changing is making it so difficult. We don't dare to try to treat all the different symptoms at once. As soon as we eradicate one, a different one presents itself. I and my assistant are convinced it's a spell, but one that brings on another attack as soon as we overcome the current one. We've never seen anything like it." The healer was a tall slender elf who now looked as concerned as Fenella had ever seen him in the hundred plus years he'd served them.

"So, do you have any ideas, anything at all?"

"Believe me, your majesty, I think of nothing else, night and day. The only thing that comes to mind—and my assistant agrees— is to consult the fairies. They have an older and more diverse knowledge of spell-craft than we do. I wouldn't be surprised if they could unravel this conundrum."

The queen saw that he was swaying on his feet, so she sat on one of the chairs. "Sit down, Andrel, you look worn out."

"You are most kind, your majesty. Thank you." The healer dipped his head in a shallow bow and sat down opposite her.

"I know how you feel," she said. "I remember when I took my training in healing, how much it takes of your own life-force. Let's just decide about the fairies, and then you should go and rest. Would you like me to contact Queen Máire, or should you deal with it?"

"Whatever you think is better," Andrel replied. He put his hand over his mouth to cover a yawn.

Fenella thought for a moment. "Here's what we will do," she said. "I'll take care of liaison with Queen Máire. We don't want the worlds to know how seriously ill the king is or our enemies will be down on us like a pack of wolves. If we do this through diplomatic channels, fewer will know." She stood up. "That's settled then. Now you go and rest. That's an order," she said with a smile.

16 – The trials of Aisling

Lena had brought a spare pallet over and laid it on the ground next to her own, amidst the grumbling and complaining of the surrounding slaves. "This is yours," she said.

Aisling was about to remove her shift when Lena stopped her. "Keep your clothes on."

"Why?"

Lena put her finger across her lips. "Whisper," she said. "If you have something to defend yourself with, it makes it harder for anyone to molest you. Tomorrow, I'll get you a spike."

"What do you mean?" Aisling asked. She was really worried now.

"You may have noticed that there are many male slaves in here. They think nothing of creeping up and trying to take advantage of you, especially someone as young and attractive as you."

"So, what do I do if one of them tries to...?" she couldn't bring herself to say it.

"If you don't have a weapon, scream as loud as you can and go for his eyes. There are other tricks, but, seeing how you're so young and innocent, I'll leave them unsaid."

"What if that doesn't work?"

"Keep screaming. Some of the other women may come to your aid. It pays to make friends. A group of friends you can count on could save your life."

"Do those men get into trouble for doing that to us, or trying to?"

"The mines. That's where they send trouble-makers. Another thing to keep in mind is that they also have friends who'll back them up."

"Why don't they split us up, so we have separate quarters?"

"I don't know. I suppose it's to keep us on edge. We can be easily cowed by always feeling that we're in danger and then we become easier to control." Lena yawned. "Let's get some sleep.

But that was easier to say than do. Aisling lay awake on the hard pallet, listening to the noises around the cavern. There was very little light, just a few lamps alight in the surrounding rooms where people were still working. In addition to the noises from the kitchen and laundry room there were the snores, coughs, grunts and sobs of the sleepers or would-be sleepers like herself to contend with. She did fall asleep eventually, although fear prevented her being totally relaxed.

A kick against her pallet woke her. "Wake up, princess," the slave-master growled. "Time to start work."

Aisling rubbed her eyes with her knuckles and yawned. She sat up and looked at the master's glowering face. "Has the Momo sent for me, master?" she asked timidly.

He smirked at her. "No, she hasn't. You work for me, and today you will be working in the kitchen since you are so proud of your cooking skills. Get up and get ready, now!" He turned and stormed across the cavern to his office.

She noticed that Lena had gone, already. She needed to relieve herself, so she rushed across to the clothes storage, hoping there would be nobody there. After sleeping in her clothes, she decided to get clean ones and chose a tunic with green stripes on the shoulders. She rushed out and made for the kitchen. When she entered the room, other slaves looked up from their work, chopping vegetables and meat, stirring big steaming pots, washing utensils and dishes. She didn't know what to do. Shouldn't there be someone in charge to show her? A large woman, not a Kerrigan, dropped the knife she'd been sharpening and came towards her. "What are you doing here? You want something? We can't work any faster, so whoever it is sent you will have to wait." She scowled at Aisling.

At least she was speaking a language Aisling could understand. "I'm sorry, mistress, the slave master told me to come here to work."

"He did, did he? I see. So why are you wearing the green?" She poked the green stripe on Aisling's shoulder. "Only the people serving the family can wear that."

"They told me to wear it yesterday. The Momo asked me to work for her."

"Well, what are you doing here?"

"The slave master told me to...."

"We'll see about that." She grabbed Aisling's arm and turned her towards the entrance, shouting over her shoulder. "You lot keep at it. They'll be here soon for their meals, and you know what happens if they're not ready."

She took Aisling to the master's office. "What's this then?" she yelled at him. "Does she work for me or does she work for the Momo?"

"What business is it of yours?" he growled back at her. "She goes where I send her, and I sent her to work in the kitchen."

"So why is she wearing the green?"

"She must have made a mistake and picked the wrong colour. She's only been here a day and you know how confused the new ones get." He sounded as if he was trying to pacify her.

He's scared of her, Aisling thought

"All right, girl, come with me. What's your name then?" she asked on their way back to the kitchen.

"Aisling, mistress."

"They call me Nápla. You sound like a good girl Aisling. Where'd you come from?"

"I've heard them call it the Mid-realm, a village called Enisdale."

"Are you the one they call 'the princess'," Nápla asked.

"Some of them do, but I'm just a simple country girl."

When they arrived back at the kitchen, Nápla looked around to make sure everything was in order and then she said to Aisling, "I've got an idea. Don't say anything about this to anyone, but I don't trust him, the so-called master. Let's do a test. When the Momo's tray is ready, you can take it to her and see what happens. If anyone tries to stop you, tell them I sent you. How does that sound?"

"It sounds good, but I don't think I can remember the way and I don't know the language to ask anyone."

"How did you get there yesterday?"

"Momo's grandson took us."

"Who's 'us'?"

"Me and Lena. She knows the way."

"Ah. I know her. Let me send for her." She called a young boy who was stacking clean dishes on a table. "Leon, go and bring Lena. She's probably in the sewing room."

"What shall I do now?" Aisling asked.

"Well, for one thing, you can wash your hands. I've heard the Momo's not feeling well so we want to keep everything that goes to her clean. Over there." She pointed to one of the tubs by the wall.

By the time Lena arrived, the Momo's tray was ready. "You carry the tray and Aisling can carry the bottle," Nápla said to Lena. "She needs someone to show her the way to the Momo's grotto."

"How did you swing that?" Lena asked when they were in the tunnel.

"The master told me to work in the kitchen, so I went there. When Nápla saw my green tunic, she asked me about it, so I told her about the Momo. She took me to his den and ... it was so funny. He's scared of her, you know?'

"I know. Everyone is, but the woman has a heart of gold. She only confronts the ones who treat us badly.

She is quite fearless, isn't she? They're probably afraid she'll poison their food."

"Would she do that?" Aisling asked.

"I wouldn't put it past her. A few of those brutes have complained about tummy troubles."

"Why do the Korrigen allow it?"

"Probably because it keeps a balance of power among the slaves, so they don't have to keep intervening over every disagreement. In truth, the department heads have more power than the slave master, that's what make him so grumpy all the time. You want to be careful with him. What happened this morning will really burn a hole in him and he'll take it out on you."

"I wish I didn't have to go back there. I was all right in my own little cave. I wasn't happy, but at least I wasn't terrified all the time."

"Let's see what Momo Tilly says, but don't tell her what happened with the slave master. People who carry tales to the Korrigen sometimes end up with their throats slit."

When they arrived at the Momo's grotto, Lena shook the curtain in the entrance. "We're here with your meal, Momo Tilly."

The curtain was pulled back by a tiny Korrigen woman wearing an elaborately decorated skirt of pale leather and a headband with brightly coloured feathers.

The two slaves bowed to her and entered the grotto to find Momo still reclining on the bed, but she was awake. "Put it over there," she instructed them, indicating a small table an arm's length from the bed."

When Tilly tried to sit up, the girl rushed to her side, uttering a few words; the only one Aisling understood was 'Momo'.

"I can manage," the old woman said, flicking her hand at the girl. With a bit of grunting and pauses for breath, she managed to manoeuvre herself into sitting position on the side of the bed. The girl stood near, anxiously ringing her hands. "Bring it closer," Momo ordered and the girl moved the table to where she could reach it.

"Good," the old lady said.

"Is there anything else, Momo Tilly?" Aisling asked.

"Yes. I have work for you. But first I eat." The young girl poured some liquid out of the bottle Aisling had carried. "This wife of grandson. Her name is Glady but say Loamini Glady. My son say I need person here with me always. I not need … how you say? Nurse-girl?"

"Nursemaid," Lena said. She bowed to Glady and said, "Loamini Glady."

The girl answered with a tremulous smile. "You name?" Her voice was barely audible.

"I'm Lena, and my friend is Aisling."

"She have bad leg?"

"I did, but Momo Tilly made it better," Aisling said.

"You go now, my good Loamini." Momo Tilly said. "They stay, work for me."

"We both stay?" Aisling asked.

"Why not? She know what I speak."

Aisling exchanged a smile with Lena. "What can we do for you?" she asked.

Tilly gave Lena a rundown of tasks that needed doing. "She wants us to water the plants." Lena pointed to the fountain in the far wall. "And then she wants us to start sorting out and cleaning those shelves. Before I do, I should take her dishes back to the kitchen and advise the slave master."

Lena went to the fountain and filled a tin container with water. She handed the first one to Aisling and filled another for herself. Tilly watched them as they moved to water the plants, intervening with more instructions.

"She says don't use too much water on them," Lena translated.

After Lena had gone to return the dishes, Tilly asked Aisling to help her wash herself and don some clean clothes. "Now we walk," The old lady stood up, took Aisling's arm and headed for the curtain. Outside in the tunnel, she turned them in a direction Aisling hadn't been before. The tunnel was wider and the ground smoother. There were hangings on the walls by some of the curtained doorways, and engravings running along at eye level.

"Is this where your family lives?" Aisling asked.

Tilly nodded. "My sons, my grandchilds, all my family."

A baby began to cry somewhere close by and after a few seconds, another joined in. "We go see," the old woman said, beaming. She led the way to an opening that was not curtained and entered.

Two young females were there trying to sooth and clean up two babies, one barely larger than a kitten and the other a bit bigger. Tilly was ecstatic. She let go of

Aisling's arm and started cooing over the infants and babbling to their mothers. She wanted to hold one of the babies, but the mother held it tight and said something to her, after which, the mother sat on a stool and started feeding him. This was the larger of the two and obviously a boy. The mother of the smaller child, a baby girl, already had her daughter at her breast.

Momo Tilly chatted for a while with the two mothers, and then turned to Aisling. "We go back now. I rest."

They had no sooner returned to Tilly's grotto than an irate Domin Cragsil turned up.

He ranted at his mother, obviously very upset about something while she listened with her back straight and chin up until he'd finished having his say and then she took her turn. Momo's response sounded gentler and more persuasive, than her son's, although she ended on a firm note as if berating him about his behaviour. As he was leaving, he glared at the two slaves and said something that sounded like an order.

"My son have fear," the old woman said. "I rest now. First give water."

Lena asked Tilly something in her own language and Tilly laughed. Lena put her hand out to help the old woman to a commode on the wall opposite the fountain.

"I was confused about 'give water'," Lena explained.

"I sleep now," Momo told them. "You go eat."

"Do you want us to return?" Aisling asked, hoping the answer would be affirmative.

"You come back later. Much work."

On their way back to the slave quarters, Aisling asked Lena what the Korrigan leader was so angry about. "He was upset about his mother taking you to the nursery. He said only special slaves were allowed in family quarters. He is afraid of giving slaves knowledge they could use against them." The two women squeezed back against the wall as a group of Korrigen guards passed by, although it wasn't wide enough for them to avoid being man-handled by them as they passed. Both women had to fold their arms over their breasts.

"Pigs," Lena muttered after they passed. "I don't know why the chieftain is so concerned; there are plenty of guards, too many if you ask me."

Aisling realized how true that was. She had been so used to living near the family quarters, she barely noticed them now.

"How did it go when you took the tray back?" she asked.

"Oh, Nápla was delighted, but I thought the chief would have a fit. There's not much he could do about a directive from the royal family."

They had to squeeze past another group of Korrigen who were standing in the middle of the tunnel talking. This time they had to endure having their bottoms pinched as they went by.

"Oh, one more thing, the chief said we have to do our 'regular work' when we return from the Momo's. I suppose that means you report to the kitchen and I to the sewing room."

"Do they ever order women to their quarters to … I don't know how to say it … use them?

121

"There are many ways to describe that," Lena said bitterly. "Molest, have sex, and several cruder expressions, but the answer is, yes, they do. They're like dogs, wanting to screw anything with a hole in it."

"Isn't there any way to protect oneself?"

"Not without getting hurt, although I heard that putting some mustard inside turns them off. They don't like to get their precious little tails burned. But you can't walk around with mustard inside you all the time."

"Has it happened to you?"

"It did, once. I laughed out loud when I saw his tiny little tail and he lost his desire. I got a thorough beating and couldn't walk for a few days, but it was worth it."

Now Aisling had another reason to be terrified. *What am I going to do? I don't know if I can hold out much longer.* She'd been meaning to attempt another contact with the elves but hadn't found an opportunity since they'd moved to this new location. *I'm really going to have to try, tonight.*

17 – Fairies to the rescue
⤜⤛

Two fairies arrived at the royal palace of Lycea the day after their help had been invited. Soon the royal bedroom was filled with the fluttering and chirping of the two healers as they assessed the king's condition. Although they only came up to the waist of elves, they were a force to be reckoned with. With Queen Fenella, the king's healer, and the palace fairy, Innes, overseeing them, they went about their task with gusto.

After what seemed like hours, although was probably only minutes, they reached a conclusion. Seeing that the king was exhausted, Fenella suggested that they retire to the ante-room. "Have you found the cause of the king's illness?" she asked through Innes.

There was a brief conference between the three fairies, and then Innes put his hand on the queen's shoulder and relayed their conclusion. "Healer Andrel was correct in suspecting a spell. This one is very complex because it contains several triggers as well as some blocking effects. Now that they've identified the triggers and blockers, it should not be difficult to remove the spell, from his majesty."

"What a relief!" the queen said. "I feared we were losing him. I wonder who could have concocted such a spell. I'm sure the Korrigen are not capable of such a skill."

Innes relayed the question to the fairy healers and, after listening to their explanation, transmitted it to the queen. "Dark fairies?" she exclaimed. "I thought they'd been driven from this realm."

"They were," Innes replied. "They settled in the lands of the Korrigen. It seems they have brought them back with them."

"That is dire news indeed," Fenella said. "However, we should be talking about how to cure the king. What recommendations have the healers for us?"

"They suggest we remove all the triggers from his majesty's diet. They will stay until the spell is destroyed, which might take a few days."

"You mentioned blockers," she replied. "How do they affect the treatment?"

"The blockers are set to prevent medicines working to improve his health. They will give us a list of items that must be removed from his majesty's diet in order to facilitate healing. They may also have to do some casting as the spell is removed, just to make sure it's completely obliterated."

"Will he always have to avoid those items, or will that only be until he is healed?"

"The ban will only be temporary."

The queen stood up. "I'm going to explain all this to my husband. Andrel, would you like to join me? After he's rested and taken some refreshment, they will return to start working on his healing. Oh, and would you mind explaining to the fairy staff which foods to avoid? Thank you, everyone."

ℰ∙ℛ

Irial poked his head into the royal family room and looked around. As no one was there, he went and looked in the anti-room to the royal sleeping chambers and saw the king and queen watching the sunset through the open window. He knocked gently on the doorpost.

"Oh, it's you. Come and join us Irial." The queen pointed to one of the bamboo chairs.

Irial went closer and bowed to the king. He'd heard about the fairy healers early in the day and was hoping to see him looking fitter, but the king still looked haggard, although there was a gleam in his eyes that Irial hadn't seen in a long time. "Your majesty; I trust you are feeling better."

"As a matter of fact, I am, but it's going to take a bit longer to return to my full strength. Sit down, boy, so I don't have to crane my neck to look at you." Once Irial was seated, he continued, "did you know I'm not allowed to eat some of my favourite foods? I don't know how I'm going to live without mangos and coconuts, not to mention onions and carrots. According to the fairy healers, they're triggers to this cursed spell that's been giving me so much trouble."

"It is fortunate that it can be treated, your majesty." Irial said. "I'm looking forward to a sparring match as soon as you regain your strength."

Queen Fenella looked as if she was anxious to know the reason for his visit, so Irial turned his attention to her. "You'll be happy to know that we have a clue to the whereabouts of your daughter."

125

Fenella put her hand over her heart. "Oh, that *is* good news. How did you find her? Will it take long to rescue her?"

"It was the dwarfs who tracked them down," Irial replied. 'They have tribes in all the mountains, in all three realms and, as you know, they move around quite a bit. One of the tribes noticed much activity in one of the remote mountains in the Mid-Realm and, after a bit of discrete snooping, they realized that the population had grown significantly recently."

"Do we have a Door close to it?" King Briartach asked.

"Not very close. We'd have to travel overland for many leagues."

"When will you leave?" The queen asked, her expression fluctuating between delight and anxiety.

"We've had a team on standby ever since I returned, so all we need to do now is supply ourselves and leave. We could be on our way by the morrow."

"Take everything you need," the king said, "and all the creatures willing to join you. We will not stint on expenses or resources to get her back." He knuckled the corner of his eye and took the queen's hand with his other.

18 – Moving day

෨ඁ෴

It was strange to be living inside a mountain with no natural light changes and still talk about day and night. It was more like lights on or lights out with no guarantee that the time coincided with the outside world, but she'd become used to it now.

Aisling and Lena went straight to the kitchen when they reached the slave quarters. "You're a pair of busy little bees, aren't you?" Nápla greeted them. "Are you hungry?"

She sent them to sit at a table in the corner while she filled two bowls and two mugs. "There you are," she said, placing them firmly on the table. "Tell me what you've been doing. She pulled out a spare stool and sat down with them, calling over her shoulder to a couple of kitchen hands, "When you've finished that, wipe down the work areas and then you can go."

She listened to Aisling and Lena's rundown of their work for the Momo and the problems they have with the Korrigen in the passages.

"I've got something you can use to protect yourselves. Wait here while I find some." She got up and went over to a shelf that contained bottles and jars of various spices and herbs. She brought over a small jar that contained a yellowish paste. "Here, smell this," she said, removing the stopper."

127

"Ugh, my Lord, that is the worst smell I've ever…. What is it?"

"It's something we use to render bones. It loses its smell when it's cooked. I could give you a little bit each. Keep it in your pocket and open the top if they give you any trouble. They won't just walk away, they'll run." She ended with a hearty laugh.

"What's going on in here?" It was the master looking more disgruntled than ever. "You two should be working."

"They've got to eat," Nápla said. "Momo gave them a break, but she wants them to come back when they've finished."

"Have you put a spell on her or something?" he asked Aisling. "I know you elves and your tricks."

Aisling looked at the other two women for guidance, but they left her to answer for herself. She knew she shouldn't do anything to antagonise him. "I'm sorry, master, I don't know how to do spells. She asked us to work for her." She kept her head bowed.

"Why? Why you?" she asked, "and why does she want her as well?"

Lena chose to answer this time. "The old Momo is unwell, and she needs help. She wants me there to interpret for her, so she can tell Aisling what to do."

He banged is fist down on the table. "Damned elves." He stalked away with his fists clenched.

"What have elves got to do with this?" Aisling said.

"He's just upset because someone is overriding his authority. It would have been better if someone in the royal family had told him directly that you'd been reassigned."

When Aisling and Lena went back to Momo's grotto, they were surprised that the tunnels were almost empty of Korrigen. "Something must be going on," Lena said. "they're usually swarming all over this area, not that I'm sorry for their absence."

Momo Tilly was awake when they returned. Lena explained to her the problem they were having with the slave master. "It's not that we want to give him trouble, but we think his authority is being overridden."

"I understand," Tilly said to Lena in here own language. "Maybe I should send one of the junior grandsons to explain to him that I want you here."

"He thinks I have put a spell on you," Aisling said, looking at the old woman from under her eyelashes.

Momo Tilly laughed and shook her head. "You do spells?"

"No, my lady," Aisling said, alarmed. "I don't know anything about magic."

Tilly nodded and said something to Lena which made her beam.

"She says she is going to find a little cave for us to sleep in close to the grotto."

"That would be wonderful! Thank you Momo."

"You be with me," the Momo replied.

"She's really taken a liking to you," Lena commented when they were getting ready to sleep in their new quarters.

"Maybe she thinks of me as a child. She is obviously very fond of children. I can't think of anything else."

"It's more than that," Lena replied. "I think it's your air of vulnerability. She feels you're an innocent victim. You have good manners, you don't complain but take everything in your stride."

"It's nice of you to say that," Aisling said. "but I'm scared all the time."

The two girls settled down on their pallets and pulled up the fur covers. "I'm curious about something," Aisling said.

"Go on."

"I find it hard to believe that the whole Korrigen tribe moved from the tunnels to this new place and created all the facilities here in such a short time."

"You're right; they didn't. This is their main home site. Only a few of them moved to the tunnels. Once they'd captured you, they came home."

"You weren't in the tunnels, were you," Aisling asked.

"No. They'd only kidnapped me a few months earlier. "I'm tired from all that running around. Let's go to sleep."

She doesn't want to talk about it, Aisling thought. "Sleep well," she said. *I'd like to hear more about her, though. She sounds like an educated person, not a peasant like me.*

෨෬

One morning, Aishling was woken by an unusual amount of noise in the passages, Aisling thought they were being attacked. She sat up, her heart pounding.

Could it be...? If only they had found her and come to rescue her.

Lena came in, out of breath. "Phew! They're going mad out there."

"What's happening?"

"They're moving again. Don't ask me why," Lena replied, shattering Aisling's hopes.

"Where were you?"

"The Momo sent for one of us to go to the kitchen and get her food, so I thought I'd let you sleep a while and go alone."

"Is she all right?"

"She seems to be a bit stronger this morning."

"How do we get our food? Do we still have to go to the slave kitchen?"

"I'm afraid so, but it won't be for long. They're taking us with them."

"Why?"

"It probably has something to do with you," Lena said. "Something must have happened to scare them off. Maybe Momo knows."

When they arrived at the grotto, Momo was embroiled in a shouting match with her son. Aisling didn't understand what they were saying, but it was easy to tell they were in a contest of wills. Finally, the Domin stomped out, and from her smile, she could tell who had won.

The old woman explained to Lena in her own language, and Lena related it to Aisling. "The Domin doesn't want her travelling. He says she is too weak, and it will kill her, but she says if she goes you go too.

She must really see something in you if she's willing to risk her life to be near you."

"Why are we leaving, Momo Tilly?" Aisling asked the old woman.

After a brief discussion, Lena explained. "They captured a spy last night, a dwarf. They tortured him and found out that the elves know where we are. They killed the spy, of course."

"Do you think they will drug me again as they did when they brought me here?"

"Time to work," Momo Tilly said. "Much work. We pack."

All Momo's concoctions and ingredients had to be packed carefully in trunks and baskets, which took the whole day. Momo's son and grandson looked in from time to time to harass them about wasting time. Momo usually responded by asking them if the sun had set yet, to which they were forced to admit, not yet.

Lena translated the exchange

"So why hurry?"

"You have to eat and rest before we go," the Domin said. "I'm not having you collapsing when we should be making haste."

"I have my girls to take care of me, and I know you will provide me with a litter, so stop worrying, my son."

"Another thing, I won't allow you to be alone with those two..." he glared at Aisling and Lena ... "from now on, I want someone from the family to stay with you and keep an eye on them." He left abruptly, not giving his mother a chance to give her opinion.

It was impossible for her two slaves to reach the slave quarters and retrieve some food. The tunnels and passages were buzzing like an overturned ants' nest, so Momo Tilly sent two of the family bodyguards in their place. Despite their short stature, they would be able to bully their way through.

When the bodyguards returned, they were accompanied by Momo's granddaughter, the daughter of her only daughter. While Aisling and Lena relieved the guards of the trays, Momo and the girl greeted each other affectionately.

"This my good girl, Glowyn. She go with us." She kissed the girl on the cheek. "Now we eat."

When the time came for them to depart, two guards arrived with a large basket-weave chair with long poles attached to the sides. The seat inside was padded with furs. When one of the guards tried to help her up into the seat she brushed his hand aside. Whatever she said to him left him looking contrite and humiliated, but she soon cheered him up with a few more words. "He good boy," she said to Aisling as she made herself comfortable.

Four of these young men picked up the poles front and back and lifted it off the ground, and then joined the throng in the passageway. It was obvious they wanted to go faster than the crowd, but there was no room to pass. A short time into the journey, Momo's son appeared. He spoke to his mother first and glared at Aisling. "See trouble you make!"

Aisling didn't know what to say, so she just nodded. *He's acting as if I made him kidnap me. It's not my fault.*

The Domin bellowed down the tunnel and the other travellers moved to the sides and let him and his mother pass. The three young women were forced to run to keep up.

The route they were taking seemed to be leading them deeper into the mountain. "I don't know why they insisted on leaving at sunset," Aisling said to Lena. "It's not as if we're going overland."

"Maybe we will be eventually," Lena replied. "I wonder if she knows." Lena caught up with the Momo's litter and asked her. Tilly shook her head."

"She says she doesn't know," Lena said.

After running for what seemed like hours, Aisling's leg started to ache. She began to limp and couldn't keep up the pace of everyone else. It was stuffy and hot in the tunnels and the air was filled with fumes from the torches used to light the way. Finally, she stopped and leaned against the wall, coughing and panting for breath, with sweat soaking her tunic and running down her face. A few moments later, Lena came back.

"What's the matter?" she said. "Are you in pain?"

"I just can't keep up, my leg hurts."

"Is that the one that was broken?"

Aisling nodded, tears filling her eyes. Lena hugged her. "I'll see what I can do," she said. "You rest here while I talk to Momo."

Aisling slid down to the floor and rested her forehead on her knees. Someone trod on one of her feet and she opened her eyes to see who it was. "Nápla! Is everybody moving?"

"Looks like it," the kitchen manager replied. "It's going to take days to get everything set up again in a new place. What happened to you?"

"It's my leg," Aisling said. "It was broken when they kidnapped me and Momo Tilly has helped to heal it, but it still hurts a lot when I walk too long. And we had to run to keep up with the leaders."

"Let me see if I can help you; stand up!"

Aisling struggled to her feet, wincing when she put her right foot on the floor. She noticed that Nápla was watching people going past, most of whom were slaves and many of them were burdened with heavy packs. "Andrin," she called to a muscular young lad. "Come over here, you too, Shindy."

The two young men looked like Mid-Realmers. They came over obediently. What do you need, boss?" Andrin asked.

"Put those packs down. You're going to carry this young lady and you are going to be very careful with her. She has a bad leg and it's hurting."

Aisling was surprised at this and very uncomfortable. "It's all right, Nápla, I can walk now I've had a rest." To demonstrate she put her weight on the right foot and her knee caved in, almost making her lose her balance.

"You can walk, can you? All right boys let's get to work. First, I'll show you how to carry her. Shindy, you take the top. Stand behind her and grasp her arms like this." she demonstrated by putting her hands under Aislings arms and grasping both her forearms. "That way, you'll get a good grip without causing discomfort. Now, let's see you do it!"

Both Aisling and the boy felt awkward at first, but by the time they were ready to move, she was satisfied. Andrin had taken her legs, handling her right leg gently. Aisling was surprised to see Nápla pick up both boys' packs and shoulder them.

They had barely gone a dozen steps when they met Lena with one of the royal bodyguards. "Nápla, I see you came to the rescue. Thank you." She said something to the guard and he grunted a reply, shaking his head.

"He's a bit put out by your intervention and doesn't know how to handle the situation."

"Tell him he can carry these packs," Nápla replied with a laugh. "Seriously, let me speak to him."

Nápla bowed to the guard and gave him a spiel, with much nodding and gesturing to the people involved. He grunted and replied.

"He says he has been ordered to take care of the princess, so I told him the best way was to get some slaves to carry her."

The guard grunted something to Lena and pointed ahead. Once they were on the move again, Lena walked beside Aisling. "Momo gave me some medicine for you. She says to drink all of it and the pain will go away."

19 – New quarters
❧

The Chief called a stop when they arrived at a cavern big enough to accommodate the slaves and subordinate Korrigen. He and his family with all their retainers went ahead to the next cavern where they set up a rest area. Servants and slaves went about spreading pillows and pallets, while another group prepared refreshment for everyone.

Momo Tilly insisted on having Aisling and Lena with her, but gave her granddaughter leave to sit with her parents and siblings. She said something to Lena and Nápla, grinning at Aisling.

"What did she say?" Aisling asked.

"Just that it was fortunate that Nápla turned up with her two boys. Now she has three extra cooks and burden-carriers. She also said she will try to get a carrying chair for you."

All the pallets were lined up along the wall, some of them with privacy screens. It didn't take long for everyone to fall asleep, but the moment Aisling finally started to drift off, a massive rumbling noise came from down the tunnel they'd just been traveling.

None of the Korrigen seemed surprised or alarmed, so Aisling figured they'd expected it. But what did it mean?

ଛଠଙ

"They blew up the mine so that no one could follow us," Lena explained once they were on the move again. "They knew that the elves were coming to rescue you."

"What do they want with me? That's what I don't understand. I must have something they want to make them go to all this trouble."

"Do you want me to ask Momo?"

Aisling sighed. "I don't know. It might be something so awful, I would be better off not knowing."

"The only thing I can think of right now is...."

"Don't please," Aisling begged, although she was starting to develop a suspicion herself, and was terrified it might be true.

The tunnel was now uphill, and she was glad the Domin had agreed to allow her to be carried, although she suspected that Momo might have had a hand in that. Her carrier was not as comfortable as Momo's. It was more like a stretcher, a piece of tanned hide attached to a couple of poles. She couldn't sit up but was forced to either lie on her back and look at the roof, of lie on her stomach and lift her head to see where they were going. Not that there was anything worth seeing either way and holding her head up gave her a pain in her neck. She finally settled on her side, and eventually fell asleep.

৯◦৯

She is back in Enisdale with her grandmother. They are sitting at the kitchen table eating their supper when they hear a noise outside. It sounds as if a sharp wind had blown up and is tossing things around out there.

138

They peer through the window, but everything looks calm and peaceful. "Goblins," her grandmother says, dropping the window curtain.

'Goblins' was how they explained any mysterious event.

They return to the table and finish their tea. Gran is just about to start clearing the table when something hard and heavy hits the door. Before Gran could stop her, she opens the door to see what it is. She is pushed aside by a swarm of little dark creatures. As they surge through the kitchen, she tries to hide behind the open door. She sees one of them grab a sharp knife off the table and drive it into her grandmother's chest. The old woman falls to the floor without a sound, blood pouring from the wound. Aisling screams. She is frozen with terror and tears stream down her face.

The creatures turn their attention to her. "Hello princess," the largest one says, his flabby lips stretched across his face. "You're com...."

She awoke with a start, gasping for air, panting. Aisling used her palms to brushed tears from her cheeks.

She looked around. She was still in the tunnel, still surrounded by little dark people. She looked at the man behind her. "I want to walk," she said, sitting up and preparing to slide off the stretcher.

He shrugged his shoulders and stood still while she got her feet on the ground. Once she was walking on her own, he and his partner rolled up the stretcher and continued up the slope. Aisling heard them laughing as they disappeared around a bend. *So what if they were laughing at me? It's not my problem.* But she wondered if they knew something she didn't know? She shivered, remembering the dream, and went to join Lena and Nápla who were walking with Momo Tilly's carry-chair.

"Feeling better?" Lena asked.

"Much better. I had a little sleep, but I think I have Momo's potion to thank that my leg isn't hurting so much." She bowed to the old woman who grinned at her in reply.

As they climbed higher in the tunnel, the air cooled down and was fresher. Eventually, they turned a bend and saw the faintest hint of natural light in the distance. Rounding another bend, they saw an opening. Although it was night time, the moon gave some illumination, enough to see some details like trees and rocks, as well of a hint of snow on mountains.

They were brought to a halt in a wide cavern well before they reached the exit.

Lena led Aisling and Nápla to a space by the wall, away from the Korrigan, where they could talk in privacy.

"The chief wants us to wait while they check outside to see if it is safe to leave," Lena translated. She held out her forefinger to Aisling who hooked it with her own, and they both closed their eyes making a wish.

"What was that about?" Nápla asked.

"We were just making a wish," Aisling said.

"What sort of the wish? Is it magic?"

"No," Lena replied. "I was wishing it wasn't safe out there."

"I was wishing we would be rescued," Aisling said.

One of the Korrigen menials came over and gave them an order. "They want us to prepare some food," Nápla informed them. She stood up with a groan. "I'm getting too old for all this traipsing around."

When Nápla saw the place chosen, she said, "it won't be a hot meal, I can tell you that. There's no way we could light a fire in this little space." She and Aisling sorted through a pile of boxes and sacks while Lena went searching for utensils and dishes.

"This stuff must have been brought here earlier," Nápla said. "You have to give them credit for efficiency. They seem to have been preparing for this a while. Let's hope it's not rotted or been raided by rats."

Eventually, they were able to provide a snack for the people in the cavern, mostly the royal family and its retainers. It was mostly dried vegetables and fruit with some hard cheese and biscuits. The only thing they had to drink was water, much to the dismay of family members, but what could they do?"

When they were finally able to sit down again, they took their snacks over to a place away from the Korrigen, but they kept their voices low as they talked.

"Are you from the Mid-Realm too?" Aisling asked Nápla. She'd long been intrigued by Nápla's brown skin and her size. She was twice the height of the average Korrigan.

"I am, yes. But not the icy northlands. My people live in Glendonia, the tropical climes."

"If it's not a rude question, how did you get caught up with these fiends?" Lena asked

"Same way you did probably. We were working in the coconut groves, my two daughters and my spouse.

141

They came out of nowhere and before we knew what was happening, they had us bound up and helpless."

"What happened to your family?" Aisling asked.

"I'd rather not go into that if you don't mind." Nápla's eyes were glistening with tears.

Aisling felt guilty about stirring up Nápla's unhappy memories. She put her hand on the big woman's arm. "I'm sorry, Nápla" she said. "I've been told that I should think before I speak, but my tongue doesn't cooperate sometimes."

"It's all right, child." She patted Aisling's hand. "What about you" How did you end up here?"

Aisling told them about her grandmother's death and the elves coming to take her 'home'. "There's something that really frightens me about these creatures. I don't understand why they are being so nice to me. According to the elves, they had vowed to kill me because my 'real' father had killed the leader's son." Aisling twisted her hands together. "I have this terrible fear, it's something that came to me when I was thinking about what has happened and I'm wondering...."

"What is it child? You know you can trust us and we will tell you the truth if we know it."

At that moment, Aisling glanced across the cavern and saw Momo Tilly looking at her. *Does she know what we're talking about?* she wondered. *Is she in on whatever they're planning for me and being nice because I'm....* She couldn't finish the thought. "Never mind," she said to her two companions. "I'll ask you some other time."

Nápla yawned. "It's all right, child. We should try to sleep. It will probably take a while for them to finish looking around outside."

Aisling couldn't sleep with so much churning around in her mind. She wondered what had happened to Nápla's family. Especially the fate of her daughters, which tied in with Aislings fears. *Maybe I shouldn't have brought it up after all. She seems to have suffered enough, and it will only hurt her more to remind her of it. What I should be doing is trying to communicate now that we are almost out of the mountain.*

She leaned back and closed her eyes then took a few deep breaths in hope of relaxing enough to be effective. She knew she had the ability, now she had the opportunity to put it into action. *Now, what should I tell him?* She was targeting Irial because he was the only one she knew, the only one alive, that is. Place, scenery outside the caves, what else? Her own situation.

She concentrated on Irial. This is Aisling. I'm all right, we are near the entrance to the caves. Outside I can see trees and mountains and snow. All she felt was a sort of sleepiness, someone trying to wake up, then, Aisling? Is that really you? Tell me again, quickly. She started to repeat the information but was suddenly cut off by a slap across her face that sent her head crashing into the wall.

When she regained consciousness, she was lying on a pallet next to the one on which Momo Tilly was sitting.

Vicki Wootton

20 – Irial's exploration
ஒ‐௸

Irial sat up and shook his head, trying to wake his mind enough to assess the information from Aisling. The good news was her claim that she has not been harmed, but the sudden ending was ominous. He could hear her thoughts clearly enough, and from her mind, he could visualize her surroundings. He felt there was something amiss with one of her legs, but worse than that was the blow to her head and the pain of it colliding with the rockface. She'd been knocked unconscious, so it must have been a heavy strike.

He rolled out of his bedding and stood up to stretch. It was a freezing cold morning with a cloudy sky that threatened precipitation of some sort or another. He went deeper into the woods to do the necessities and collect some dry windfall branches to light a fire. Back at the camp site, he raked over the previous fire and laid a new one, lighting the twigs with a flick of his fingers, adding a few small branches, and then he went to fill the water bags.

All this activity gave him time to think about what he'd learned from Aisling. When he had last seen her, she had been in perfect health, but now he's sensed that she was afraid of something in addition to the injury to her leg—he wondered what caused that—and

144

the savage blow to her head while they were still in contact. *I should send a message to the palace,* he decided. *They need to be informed. Now that the Korrigen are moving, we'll have to change our rescue plans.*

The rest of his team was awake now, moving around unpacking rations and feeding the fire with more logs. "I've got water for the tea," he told them, tossing one of the water bags to Cathal, one of the Elven warriors. There were ten elven warriors in the team along with twenty-two Dwarven military, and a whole flock of fairies they called Tinellas. The Tinellas were good for surveying because of their ability to become invisible, in addition to their fighting skills.

When everything was ready, they sat down to eat their dawn meal and discuss plans. "We have a problem," Irial started. "The Korrigen have vacated the mine we were aiming for and have blown up that section of the mine behind them, so we won't be able to get to them that way."

"How did you learn that?" one of the dwarfs asked.

"The princess contacted me. She was able to reach me because they are close to an outside exit. They are planning to go overland to another site."

"How is the princess?" Euna, an elven healer, asked.

"She seems to be fine apart from the fact that she is terrified about something. All I could see in her mind was the image of a young Korrigan male. While we were communicating, something or someone struck her head, ending our discussion. I fear she may be injured by this blow, so it is imperative we find her as quickly as we can, but before we do, we must locate them. We

145

don't have time to circle around the whole mountain, so we'll have to find other means."

"One of the fairies alighted by his shoulder. He touched Irial's arm and related a suggestion. "Why not use the dragons? They can fly much higher than we can and have very keen eyesight."

"Areilt suggests we send for some dragons to look for them. I think it is a good idea, although I am reluctant to bring them into the Mid-Realm for fear they'll scare the population and start a panic."

"But I think our mission is important enough to take a chance," Piarus, Irial's second in command, said.

"I'll contact the palace and see what the king has to say," Irial replied. He stood up and went into the trees to sit down by the stream that ran down from the mountain. He still had the picture in his mind of the scenery outside the place where they were resting.

When he returned, the others were packing up ready to move out.

"Our instructions are to reconnoitre the area and see if we can find any further information with which to identify the tunnel exit. Queen Fenella will contact Grand Dragon Jevtic and ask for his assistance. I hope he's in a good mood. Appeasing him is not an easy task."

The others laughed. The dragons were notorious for their temperamental personalities. They were usually willing to help the other races if the project offered them some entertainment or other reward. They were easily bored and spent a lot of time sleeping, when they weren't playing hazardous games with one another, which often resulted in setting forests afire.

"Let's go reconnoitre," Irial said, picking up his pack and bedroll. He beckoned to the fairy leader, Davina who hopped over and touched his arm. He relayed some instructions to her and then spoke to the dwarfs. "We'll stay together, but you should lead, being more familiar with this sort of terrain. We'll set up camp closer to the place we were aiming for now that they've evacuated that tunnel."

21 – Aisling awakes

ॐ∽ॐ

When Aisling tried to sit up, the pain in her neck was excruciating. She couldn't turn her head sideways; when she tried to move it, she became dizzy.

"Neck hurt, yes?" Momo said. "head hurt?"

"I ...." Aisling was about to shake her head but reconsidered when a jolt of pain erupted. "Bad headache. Very bad pain." She watched the old woman for a moment, trying to gage her mood, then closed her eyes. It hurt too much to keep them open.

The Momo seemed to have mixed feelings—anger and concern—but it was just a flash, so she couldn't be sure. *Is she angry with me?* she wondered, *or with whoever hit me? But she did seem concerned.* Aisling was beginning to suspect that everything that had happened to her since she'd been with the Korrigen was part of a conspiracy against her and her real parents, and Momo Tilly was just as much part of it as her son, the chief. *She's probably more concerned about their plan failing than about me.*

She heard a movement from the pallet next to her and cracked open an eye to see. Momo was standing up. She came over to Aisling's pallet and touched her arm. "I find help for pain," the old woman said. "No move head!" That sounded like an order to Aisling. *I couldn't if I wanted to, she thought.*

Momo Tilly stood laboriously using her cane for support. She went to one of the storage baskets and rummaged through the contents until she found what she needed. She shouted to someone nearby and stood waiting until a young male Korrigan came running with a container of water. She took it from him and patted his cheek. She said something to him which, from the tone of her voice, sounded affectionate.

"He son of Loamin," she said. "Good boy. You like?"

What's she talking about. She thinks I should like him just because she does? But a cold hollow opened around her stomach. "I don't know him," she replied.

"You will," Tilly said. "He nice boy." She opened one of the packages she'd withdrawn from the basket and poured a small amount into one of the stone beakers, then she added some water, stirred it with her finger and brought it over to Aisling. "You drink. Pain go."

How can I drink if I can't raise my head? "Can't move," she said. I wish Lena was here. *I wonder where she's gone.*

"Wait," The old woman said. she turned around and opened another basket and this time sorted the contents gently until she found what she was looking for. She held it up to show Aisling what looked like a piece of straw and then put it in the beaker. "Now you drink!" she said, putting the straw to Aisling's mouth.

Aisling sucked the straw and her mouth filled with a very bitter potion. She screwed up her face and shuddered. "It tastes awful," she sputtered.

"You drink all! No pain."

149

Aisling managed to get most of it down and, to her relief, the pain did start to fade. After a while, she began to feel lethargic. Sounds of people talking drifted in and out of her awareness, but the hum of activity never completely disappeared. She was aware of people moving around her pallet and when someone accidentally bumped into it, she felt the shock vibrate through her body. Eventually, she fell asleep.

A click in her neck and a sudden sharp pain woke her. Someone was holding her head with both hands, one on each side. Tilly's voice spoke to someone and the hands were removed. The other person, a male voice, and Tilly were discussing something, but she couldn't understand a word they were saying. She opened her eyes a crack and peered between her eyelids. Momo was sitting on her pallet, and the man, a Korrigan wearing a red cape over his shoulders, was kneeling on the ground. She couldn't remember ever seeing him before.

Aisling groaned and tried to move her head but realized there was a stiff collar around her neck and it wouldn't budge. "Momo," she murmured. The old woman and the man turned their attention on her.

Tears ran down her face when she realized the fur cover underneath her was soaked, and she couldn't move, and she was hungry, too. "I want Lena. I do not understand what is happening to me. Where is she?"

There was more discussion between the two Korrigen, and then the chief arrived and an argument ensued between him and his mother. The Domin stalked away with an angry retort, followed by the one with the red cape.

The old lady came and looked at her, stroking her hand as she spoke. "Lena come," she said. "No cry. We make better."

Lena arrived with some clean clothes and an empty bowl. She was accompanied by another female slave carrying a tray of food. Lena had a brief conversation with the Momo. The old woman shook her head, and then she nodded and stood up. She pointed to her own pallet, and then shouted to a passing Korrigan woman.

They transferred her to Momo Tilly's pallet and began to take care of her. The old woman stood over them, watching every move as the two women washed her and put on clean clothes.

When a female slave arrived with some clean furs for the pallet, the two slaves changed the bedding and left, taking away the wet furs.

Momo Tilly told Lena that she should encourage Aisling to get up and walk if she could. She managed the three steps from the old woman's pallet to her own but was too exhausted to go any further. "I just want to go back to sleep," she said. "But I'm so hungry."

"Can you sit up long enough to eat and drink something." That was Lena's voice.

Aisling was about to nod her head but remembered how it had felt last time she tried. "I'll try" she said. "I need something to get rid of the taste of that horrid medicine she gave me."

To Aisling's dismay, Momo Tilly insisted she drink some more medicine before she lay down, but this time, Lena managed to slip something sweet into the mixture.

151

ෙ෧

When Aisling opened her eyes again, she saw it was night and all she could see was the moonlight on the trees and mountains outside the tunnel. A cold wind was gusting in from outside. She turned onto her side, trying not to jar her head, and looked around to see if anyone else was awake. Momo was snoring on her pallet, warmly wrapped in furs, and Lena was sleeping on a pallet behind her own.

"Lena!" she whispered. She felt guilty waking her friend but there were so many things she wanted to know.

"I'm here," a soft voice replied. "Do you need something?"

"I need to use the bucket." The slaves had spread cylindrical buckets around the perimeter of the cavern for the convenience of the royal family and its menials. Although they were covered when not in use, the smell still pervaded the cavern if they were not emptied frequently. They'd even put screens in front of them to protect the privacy of the users.

"Let me help you get up," Lena said.

Aisling crossed to the nearest convenience, leaning on Lena, and squatted over it. Fortunately for her the buckets were low to suit the height of the Korrigen.

As they walked back to their pallets, Aisling whispered, "Is it safe to talk? I have so many questions, things I need to know. I keep waking up, worrying about things."

"We can try. I'll move my pallet a bit closer," Lena said.

Aisling managed to lie on her other side so that she was facing Lena this time. "I ... I don't know how to say it. I'm really scared about something, a suspicion I have."

"Just say it," Lena said. she reached out and held Aisling's hand. "Putting something into words doesn't make it real. It's just what you feel. Try."

"I think I might know why they are being nice to me," Aisling said. "Do ... can Korrigen mate with other ... humans and elves?"

"Is that what you're afraid of?"

"I think they might want to use me like that ...with one of their young ... you know."

"Oh, Mercy. What makes you think that?"

"It's the way the Momo treats me, almost like family, and yesterday, there was a boy here and she kept praising him and saying he was a good boy." Aisling freed her hand to wipe away her tears, trying not to sob out loud.

"To answer your question, yes, they can. The slave master for example. His mother was raped by one or maybe several of them and he was the result. That's why he's so angry all the time. He hates them for what he did to his mother."

"Oh Lord above, save me." Aisling wiped away more tears. "I'd kill myself first," she said.

22 – The Dragons arrive

ॐॐ

Early in the afternoon the dwarfs found another entrance into the mountain. It hadn't been used in many years, possibly centuries, judging by the conditions. The ground was littered with heaps of bat guano, and farther in, they found a large cavern with stalactites hanging from the roof and shorter stalagmites popping up from the ground.

They came back and reported their find to Irial, who was helping his colleagues set up camp and prepare a meal. One of the elves had shot a large buck which was being prepared for roasting. They'd already done the ritual ceremony to appease the forest gods and request forgiveness from the deer whose life they had sacrificed.

They waited to discuss the dwarfs' discovery until everyone was sitting down, except the fairies who were flitting around performing their own rituals in the trees.

"Do you want us to keep searching this new cave?" the dwarf leader asked.

"I think it would be a good idea. They might change their minds about using that exit now they suspect Princess Aisling was communicating with us. There's a chance this new cave might connect with the one they're in."

"We'll set off as soon as we can pack some equipment and food for the journey," The dwarf said. "You said that the princess was cut off violently when you were communicating. Do you know if she is all right?"

"I can't communicate with her, but I sense her life. I don't dare try to probe any further for fear of what they might do to her. The thing that I'm most concerned about, apart from rescuing her of course, is what she is so afraid of. She obviously knows something is afoot, but I can't think what it is, and that's what is keeping me awake at night."

A message came from the Palace later that evening. The master dragon had agreed to send five of their younger dragons, partly because it would be a good exercise for their training and partly because they thought it might be fun to roast a few Korrigen. They were on their way and would arrive before dawn.

Irial had little rest that night. He lay awake for hours, worrying about what was happening to Princess Aisling. He sent out periodic probes, hoping to contact her but, apart from her life signs, he was unable to reach her conscious mind. *She must be sleeping,* he concluded. *But whatever had cut her off while we were in contact must have been a severe blow to have made her lose consciousness. I pray we are in time to save her.*

He fell asleep eventually because the next thing he was aware of was the sound of leathery wings flapping. He rolled over and sat up, rubbing the sleep from his eyes, and looked around. It was still dark, but he was able to see the dark outline of a large creature with glowing eyes a few lengths away. The dragons had arrived.

"We are here," the one sitting nearby said in dragon-tongue. "What we do?" he ended by blowing out a smoky breath.

It was not easy to understand dragon-tongue, but Irial knew enough to be able to interpret some of the blows, whistles, and tooth-gnashing, although he wasn't able to replicate it himself because elves didn't have the mouth-parts.

Irial stood up and stretched. He'd have to be careful with his communication because the dragons could be quite touchy and took offense at the least misspoken word. Irial bowed to the creature and pursed his lips to blow out some air, but he could never reproduce the smoky mass the dragons could. "You are very welcome, brother dragon. We are honoured by your presence this day," he said in Elvish tongue, knowing that dragons would understand. He suspected they were taught other tongues while still unhatched.

Resting on the ground, the creature towered over him. It was about three times his height and the length from tail to nose was the length of ten elves. Its glowing eyes were an orangey-gold colour and its scales looked silvery pink in the dawn light, although he knew that in daylight, they would look blue-grey.

"We are trying to rescue the elven princess who is being held by the Korrigen in that mountain." He pointed needlessly to the nearby mountain range. The dragon blew a small breath, his tail twitching, a sure sign that he was getting impatient. "I apologize, honourable friend. We know they are close to an opening in the mountain and would like you to fly around and try to find them."

The dragon blew out some more air. "We sisters and brothers."

"Pardon my error," Irial said with another bow. He looked up and saw the other four perched on the sides of the mountain, blowing pink-tinted smoke. They really were impatient. "I know you are anxious to get started, so I'll finish quickly, and you can be on your way. Please send someone to advise us when you find the opening to the cave."

The dragon stood up and stretched his leathery wings. "We flame Korrigen."

Assuming that was a question, Irial replied. "Only Korrigen, no humans and no elves or fairies."

"Now we have fun." the dragon flapped his—or her—wings and took off to the join the rest of the team.

23 – On the move again
❦❦

Aisling felt a little better physically, although she still had a headache and a stiff neck. It was her emotions that were in a turmoil. The information she'd received from Lena during the night had only made her more frightened.

The Momo and the son of her grandson were sitting together on her pallet, watching her as she sat up. Momo's progeny had a gloating smirk on his face which sent a wave of nausea through her. She lay back and rolled over so her back was to the two Korrigen, and then she sat up again. She heard the pallet creak behind and the shuffling of the old woman's feet as she came around to confront her. "How you feel?" she asked.

"Fine," Aisling said. "Where's Lena?"

"She bring food."

"I need to…." She nodded her head towards one of the buckets and winced at the sudden jolt of pain in her neck.

"Boy help."

"No," she shrieked. "Don't let him touch me." she was so outraged at the suggestion tears pooled in her eyes.

"He nice boy. You like."

"No! keep him away from me. I don't like him!" She hauled herself up and walked slowly across the cavern to a bucket that was farther away.

When she returned, Lena was there with a food tray which she had set down on Aisling's pallet. There was another one on a stool next to Momo Tilly's pallet, but the old woman was ignoring it. She was watching Aisling, frowning, looking very upset. The boy was gone.

Lena had spread some furs on the ground for them to kneel on while they ate. "What was all that yelling about?" she asked.

Aisling told her about her run-in with Momo Tilly. "He gives me the creeps," she said. "He's always staring at me and smirking, as if he knows something they're not telling me."

"I feel a bit sorry for him. It's not fair the way they are manipulating him. I saw him walking back to his mother's place. He was in tears. I don't think he even understands what it's all about."

Aisling scooped up some of the mush they were serving as food and put it in her mouth, swallowing it quickly to avoid the taste. "I know I shouldn't blame him, but I wish they wouldn't keep pushing him at me. It's disgusting. I wish there was a way to stop it without hurting him. Do you know how old he is?"

"Not really, but he looks about your age. How old are you?"

"Fifteen," Aisling replied. "I wonder what date it is. My anniversary day is in the month of Long Days, so I might be sixteen by now."

"I would advise you to tell them you're fourteen if they inquire," Lena said. "The age for twining, as they call it, is sixteen. I'll try to find out how old the boy is. I think I could get that from his mother." Lena put the used bowls back on the tray ready to take them away. "I'll have a word with Momo about the boy. See if I can convince her that what they are doing is hurting him."

࿏

By the middle of day, it seems as if the whole population had gone into panic mode. Everyone was scrambling around, shouting orders, and packing everything away, ready to move.

"I wonder where they're taking us this time," Aisling said as she finished folding her bedding.

"I don't know, but it's not outside, I can tell you that. They wouldn't go out in daytime."

"Oh Lord, not another tunnel. I thought I was going to see the sky and some trees."

"Something must have happened to make them change their minds."

Korrigan warriors were packing the opening outside with rocks and anything else they could find. It wasn't long before the word 'dragons' was being passed around.

The royal family, preceded and followed by their most skilled warriors, started moving towards another tunnel that sloped down from the cavern. Tempers were short and the leaders, the chief and his son were on a rampage, berating their guards and lashing out at slaves with whips, which only made the chaos worse.

Aisling noticed family members and their menials glaring at her, as if everything was her fault. She tried to keep out of their way, but Momo Tilly insisted that they travel with her. Now she was in the middle of the conflict without any means of protection apart from reprimands from Momo when she noticed someone push Aisling or try to trip her.

I didn't ask them to bring me here. I'd rather be anywhere than in this stinking place. Once more despair threatened to overwhelm her. I don't think I can take much more of this. But what can I do? Her shoulders slumped, and she wrapped her arms around herself as she moved closer to the wall, hoping they would ignore her.

She felt a gentle tap on her shoulder. "How are you coping?" a friendly voice asked.

"Lena. Thank the Lord you've come. I think I'm losing my mind. What are you doing here?"

"They sent me to bring some food for the Momo, so I brought some for us as well." She held up two square baskets with cloth covers. "Wait while I give her this."

They walked close together, chewing strips of smoked meat and seeds. The variety of food stuffs had been declining for a while now and they were down to anything that had been preserved by smoking or drying. There was no fresh fruit or vegetables at all. Even cheese was a rare commodity reserved for the chief's family, leaving everyone else to subsist on whatever they could scrounge, which for some included rats.

"What's new?" Aisling asked. It was virtually impossible for her to get any information being tied to

161

Momo Tilly all the time, but Lena had been sent to help with food preparation and distribution, so she had access to most of the gossip and rumours in circulation.

Lena leaned closer and screened her mouth with her hand. "The slaves are getting close to revolting. They are being starved because we're running out of food and what little remains is going to the Korrigen."

"They must be getting weak," Aisling said. "What would happen if they did?"

"There would be mass slaughter, but it's hard to guess who would win. The Korrigen have weapons, but I'm not sure they'd be very effective in such close quarters against an angry mob."

"I get the feeling that everyone is blaming me for what is happening, especially the top families and their retainers. That's why I'm so scared."

When angry male voices approached them from behind, Aisling cowered against the walls. When they stopped beside her, she tried to hide behind Lena, her heart thudding. *What do they want?*

One of the royal bodyguards grabbed her arm and pulled her away from the wall. The other one was holding a narrow strip of leather which he tied around her wrists while the first held them together behind her back. "No!" she screamed, trying to break free. Momo Tilly, who had gone ahead on her carry-chair, turned back and reprimanded them, but the leader bowed and explained something to her which generated a scathing response.

The old woman urged her porters forward and hurried off down the sloping tunnel.

"What are you doing?" Aisling demanded but the two bodyguards didn't understand what she was saying. One of them slapped her face, throwing her head sideways. She screamed when the piercing pain from the previous blow flared again.

"Find out," she cried to Lena as they dragged her away down the tunnel.

"Momo!" Lena replied.

She hoped Lena was right. Would Momo Tilly help her this time? What had she done to deserve such treatment? *I'm just a little farm girl,* she thought as tears streamed down her face. *I haven't done anything wrong.* She thought about the rejection of the boy. Maybe they were going to enforce their plan to put the two of them together. *Or maybe they're going to punish me because everyone is blaming me for all this.*

Although she was a head taller than the two guards, they were strong and, despite her determination not to cooperate, they managed to drag her along at a determined pace. After rounding a couple of bends and turning into another tunnel, they caught up with Momo Tilly. As soon as they were level, Aisling called to her, "Help me Momo. Why are they doing this?"

"I see. I talk my son," she replied. She then snarled something at the two bodyguards. They bowed to her, still holding Aisling's arms in a bone-crushing grip, they replied with what sounded like an explanation. The old woman harrumphed and urged the porters to continue.

They reached the Family in a small cavern bisected by a tiny waterfall that had worked a groove across the

163

floor. Everyone was milling around, elbowing others out of their way, shouting complaints and accusations at one another, while children cried. It was a chaotic scene at the centre of which Domin Cragsil and his mother were having an intense argument. Momo was out of her carry-chair so she could stand face to face with her son. She poked him in the chest to emphasize her argument and shouted loud enough to overpower him. Momo was obviously experienced in handling recalcitrant sons.

Finally, the chief shouted something at her and turned away with a flap of his hand and a few angry words. He glared at Aisling as he passed. "You trouble!" he said.

Momo gave some instructions to the bodyguards, who untied the restraints and let her go. Aisling stood there, rubbing her wrists, while her head pounded, and her knees threatened to give way. She was afraid to raise her head and see all the accusing faces. She wiped away some tears with the back of her hand once some circulation was restored. *This is a nightmare,* she thought. Down deep, she knew she wouldn't have been safe even here.

Momo beckoned to her and she shuffled slowly across the floor towards the old woman. *Maybe she will protect me, she thought, but only if I do as she says, and I will not make friends with that boy.*

"You stay with me," Momo Tilly said. She signalled to one of the bodyguards and gave him a brief order. The guard nodded, looked at Aisling, and then stood by them. "He look you," she said. "You be good girl."

So now I have to have that ugly creature in my face all the time. "My head hurts where he hit me."

"I give medicine when stop."

"I need Lena. I don't understand." She knew she was whining but she felt she had a good reason.

Momo waved to one of the older children. The little girl ran over, eyes glowing with eagerness at being chosen. "Momo!" she cried, kissing the old woman's hand. Momo gave her some instructions, the only word of which Aisling understood was 'Lena'. The elder finished with a kiss and a pat on the head, and the girl ran back up the tunnel.

Aisling realized that the mob of Korrigen was on the move again. Whatever had caused the delay must have been resolved. Momo Tilly signalled to the porters to bring her carry-chair and they set off after the rest of the family.

The little girl returned after a while with Lena in tow. After thanking her and giving her a sweet from her pocket—probably dried fruit—Momo turned to Lena and spoke to her at length. Finally, Lena was free to talk to Aisling.

"She says that she and the bodyguard will not let you out of their sight from now on." Aisling scowled. "She thinks it's the only way to keep you safe. The whole tribe is fuming, blaming you for everything that's gone wrong since you arrived." She put a comforting hand on Aisling's shoulder and squeezed. "They think it's your fault that they've lost their home and their children are going hungry, everything."

Aisling sighed. "Do you think I will ever get out of here?"

Lena lowered her voice. "Don't look at them. To answer your question, I think you have a better chance now than you did in the old place."

"What's happening with the slaves?"

"They are really getting worked up because all the food is being kept for the Korrigen. They sent their warriors to confiscate everything and now they are cooking their own food, or their menials are. It's too bad we're stuck up here with them. I have a suspicion the whole slave population is going to march out of the opening we just left."

"But aren't they being guarded?"

"It seems to me that the slaves are past the point where they are afraid of Korrigen. They'll overrun them and take their weapons if they must. Hunger is a great motivator."

Aisling stopped and rested her hand against the wall to remove a piece of gravel from her sandal. Immediately, Momo's porters and the bodyguard stopped and watched her as she retied the laces and stood up.

Momo beckoned her. "What she say?" she asked, looking pointedly at Lena.

"I must stay close to you," Aisling replied.

"Long time talk."

"Oh, we were talking about our homes, where we come from, stuff like that." *I should ask Lena about that,* she thought. *She seems to be a learned person. I wonder what she did before she was captured.* "We miss our homes and our families," Aisling added to emphasize what they had lost because of the Korrigen.

The old woman scowled at Aisling and nodded to the porters to continue.

It was not long before the boy came to walk by Momo's side. She held his hand and murmured to him. The boy looked at Aisling and quickly averted his eyes when he saw she'd noticed. She dropped back a pace and really looked at him. If she could overcome her aversion for Korrigen, he didn't seem too bad. His skin was the same greenish grey as the rest of the tribe, but his hair was a bit lighter and less matted. The boy's body was trim and well-proportioned for his race and age. What was it she found so distasteful about him? He was a Korrigan, that's what. *I wonder what they call him. Maybe Lena knows.*

She walked closer to Lena. "What do they call the boy?" she asked.

"Why do you want to know that?"

"It's what you said the other day about him being a victim just like me."

"I'll find out if you like. Do you want me to?"

"All right. They might be a bit nicer to me if I'm nice to him, but there's no way he's going to touch me."

Lena strolled over to Momo's little group and started chatting with her and the boy. They flashed a look at Aisling and continued their conversation. By the time Lena turned away, Momo was smiling and the boy was looking at his feet.

"His name is Olgon," Lena said.

"That's not too bad, I suppose. What did he say when you asked him?"

"Just that he was sorry."

"For what?"

Vicki Wootton

Lena shrugged. "Maybe that you don't like him."

Aisling sighed. "I'll try to be nice," she said. She rubbed the side of her face. "My head hurts. Is there a bruise on my face?"

"It is a bit bruised. Why, what happened?"

"One of those brutes hit me, again. I still have pain from the first time." Aisling could no longer hold back the tears that ached to be released. "I can't take much more of this, Lena."

24 – Dragons and fairies and elves

❧

Irial and his team walked up the rocky path towards the opening that Aisling had identified for him and the dragons had verified. One of the fairies flew up and landed on his arm. He chirped something which Irial was able to interpret from the images he received through thought exchange when they touched.

"Did you go inside?" he asked.

"No. Bad men with weapons inside."

"What about the dragons?

"Too big. Only blow fire at them."

"That'll keep them pinned down for a while until we get there. "Any sign of the princess?"

"No sign of her near, but that she was there recently."

"Well, at least we know we're on the right track. Thank you, Bearnes." He was about to send the fairy on his way when he thought of something else. "Are the dragons giving you any trouble? I know when they get playful, they can be quite dangerous. They don't know their own strength sometimes."

"Or they don't care," Bearnes made the tinkling sound that served as a laugh. "We fly with a strong repel cover. They don't like it, so they keep away from us."

"I just thought of something that might be useful," Irial said. "Are you able to contact the nymphs from this realm?"

"If I know anything about nymphs, they are probably close by right now. They seem to follow us everywhere. They like to know what we're doing all the time."

"Do you think we could ask them to help us?"

"How?"

"They're so tiny, I thought they might be able to get into the caves without being noticed, especially if they didn't turn their lights on. What do you think?"

"I'll try."

Nymphs were tiny intelligent creatures about the size of an elf's little finger. Their magical gifts were limited to the ability to communicate with intelligent creatures anywhere, and their ability to create their own light. They were frequently used by fairies and other creatures as spies.

Within seconds, they were surrounded by a cloud of the sparkling little creatures. Their bodies were light brown with light green specks, and their wings were translucent.

Irial explained what they needed to do, which was basically to enter the caves and locate Aisling. Once they'd found her, they were to send a message to the fairies and Irial and stay with her so that they could report movement. "Do not risk your lives," Irial said. "If they see you and attack you, get out of there."

The response was a variegated humming that was almost like music. They turned away and followed Bearnes towards the caves.

❧

The leader of the dwarf team that was exploring inside the mine was called Gyoka and the second in command was Qurak. Both were short men compared with the elves with muscular shoulders and arms. All the dwarfs boasted bristly chin whiskers and had hairy arms and legs. They all wore thick leather aprons with shin and arm pads. The only difference between them was the tattoos on their cheeks; the leader had twin tattoos—crossed swords in red ink—and the second had only one. The rest of them just had tattoos of manhood in blue ink on their foreheads.

One of the subordinates sidled up to Qurak. "We've found an opening," he reported. "You can hear voices in the distance. I think we've found them. What shall we do now?"

"Good work! I'll have to consult Gyoka. Wait here, and don't do anything that will alert them to our presence." Qurak went around the corner to an indent in the wall where his leader was reclining on a pile of furs, groaning and massaging his stomach. He'd been having cramps and diarrhoea since he'd eaten a badly cooked rat several hours earlier.

"Sorry to disturb you, boss, but the men have found an opening with voices on the other side. They want to know what to do now."

Gyoka sat up and then rose to his feet with a groan. "I'll go and tell Irial. We have to get instructions from him before we make a move." He bent over with his hand on his stomach and let loose a cloud of foul-smelling air. "Ah that's better. Sorry about the smell but I had to let it go. Now, stay near the opening and keep watch. Don't try to enter the other area and keep quiet. We mustn't give away our presence. You go and stay with them. I'll be back soon. If anyone is hungry, he'll have to eat dry bread and salted meat. No cook fires."

25 – A radical solution

আ৶৶

Aisling slept for a while after the Momo gave her a potion for her headache. When she awoke she noticed the smell of roasting meat in the air. Sitting up, she saw many of the Korrigen were eating meat cooked in its juice from bowls. *I wonder where that came from,* she thought. *It smells like pork, but I haven't seen any pigs around here.* She rolled over and stood up.

Momo Tilly was sitting with the boy, Olgon, both stuffing the stew into their mouths and licking their fingers. "You want some?" Tilly asked.

Aisling looked around. It looked as if everyone was eating it. *Why not?* She stood up and was reaching across for the proffered bowl when a large body ploughed into her and screeched, "No! Don't touch it! It's … it's…." Nápla choked on a sob. Her face was wet with sweat and tears, crumpled with anguish."

Nápla pulled Aisling close to her sweat- soaked tunic and held her tight. "Don't eat it, girl." She broke off with a hiccough. "Don't touch it."

"Why" Aisling asked, pulling back. "It smells delicious."

A couple of bodyguards rushed over and grabbed Nápla, dragging her away to an empty space in the middle of the tunnel. "They're killing the slaves…."

Those were her last words, cut off as one of the guards slashed deeply into her throat.

Aisling screamed. She turned away from the appalling sight and threw herself face down on the fur pad she'd been sleeping on. *What did she mean?* Aisling wondered. *Killing the slaves.* A cloud of ice filled her insides as the unthinkable truth slowly dawned on her. The aroma of meat pervading the tunnel suddenly made her feel sick; her mouth filled with water and her stomach heaved as she bent over and vomited on the floor. When she'd finished, she sat back on the fur, wiping her mouth on her tunic. She risked opening her eyes a crack and looked around, avoiding the body lying on the floor. Everyone was frozen in place, glaring at her with unconcealed hatred, even Momo looked displeased.

Then she felt a gentle hand on her back and looked up. "Is it true?" she asked Lena. "Are they eating the slaves?"

Lena pulled a cloth from her belt. She knelt on the side away from the pool of vomit, and wiped Aisling's face. She turned around and spoke to Momo Tilly who was behind her and said something, then she turned back to Aisling. "I told her we would clean up the mess. They're leaving now; they only stop to eat. God-cursed cannibals," she added in a whisper. "Yes, they are cannibals."

Aisling rested her face in her hands, sobbing. "Merciful Father. I can't believe…." She wiped her eyes with Lena's cloth. "What are we going to do?" she asked.

"This is a very dangerous moment for us. We have to be very careful."

The Korrigen were hastening downhill along the tunnel, many of them not even bothering to take their belongings. Momo Tilly shrieked a command at them, beckoning with her hand.

"Develop a bad limp," Lena said.

Aisling stood up and let one of her knees fold. She rubbed it for a moment, groaning with pain, and tried another step, but pretended the leg wouldn't hold her weight. She leaned on Lena for support as she limped slowly down the tunnel.

"Very good," Lena said softly. "We don't want to go too far."

They heard shouts and screams coming closer behind them. They could hear steel hitting the stone walls. The commotion became more desperate, the closer they came. By now, all the Korrigen in the tunnel had disappeared in panic.

"We need to hide," Lena said. "If any of those animals find us, they'll kill us."

With all the rubble left on the floor by the fleeing Korrigen, they were able to create a hiding place by piling some of the larger pieces in front of a small recess and crouching behind it.

When the Korrigen rounded the corner, they were far too busy trying to save their own skins to worry about a couple of female slaves. They sped by and disappeared down the slope after their leaders. A few of them slowed to kick the blood-drenched body of poor Nápla as they passed before disappearing.

When the slaves appeared, still full of fury and vengeance, they were too weak and exhausted to continue the chase. Some of them hadn't eaten anything in days and the energy to retaliate was fired by their rage against the Korrigen. The leaders of the charge were all carrying Korrigan weapons they'd liberated from their original wielders in the mass attack.

They began to fall to the floor one by one, until the whole group was down, rubbing their eyes and yawning. "Somebody should keep watch. They might decide to come back," a dark-skinned man with a wounded eye said."

"Are you volunteering, Rafe?" one of the other men replied.

"Hey, I've only got one eye. That's a job for someone with good eyesight."

Lena pushed aside the rubble from her hiding place. "Don't worry, Rafe, I'll do watch for you."

"Lena! How did you get here?" Several heads raised from the floor when they heard the woman's voice.

"They asked me to translate for Aisling," Lena replied.

"You mean you've got the princess away from them?"

Aisling kicked aside a basket and stepped out into the open. "I wish you wouldn't call me that," she said. "I'm just a country girl from Enisdale."

"You're not planning to stay here, are you?" Lena said. "They'll be back as soon as they get organized."

"We know that," a fair-haired boy of about fifteen said. "I wish we had some water. I could drain a well, I'm so dry."

"Aye, that's what we need more than anything." The old man with a crooked leg peered at them, nodding his head.

"Here's what we'll do: Aisling will keep watch, I mean listen for movement from below, and I'll fill some containers from the waterfall, but first, I have to find some mugs or buckets. She started to rummage through the litter and pulled out a few stone beakers and a couple of leather buckets. The boy with fair hair helped her get the water and deliver it to the slaves.

"Are you our new leader, then?" he inquired as he sat down with his own drink.

"Looks to me as if you need one," Lena retorted. "What happened to the old one?"

"He got murdered," another slave said. "You're a right bossy one, I can see that. How did you get that way?"

"I was a school teacher. It's one of the qualifications to keep the little monsters in line." A few slaves laughed.

"Stay where you are and rest, she said. "I'll come around and give you some water." She took the beaker and dipped it into a water bag bringing out about a third of a cupful. "Here you go, brother," she said, handing it to one of the injured men. She continued among the exhausted and half-starved slaves, serving the wounded ones first. She'd had to wake up several, but she was determined that everyone would have something to drink. It would be something in their stomachs and might help them forget about being hungry for a while.

"All right," she said when she had finished. "It's time you got moving. I know you've disarmed many of them, but we don't know what they have in their stores, and they may also have eaten to reenergized themselves. On your feet; come on, you can do it. If you stay here, you could be turned into their next meal."

This got the slaves on their feet, albeit with much grumbling and gasping. They picked up their weapons and started to walk stiffly back the way they had come.

Before Lena moved on, she asked Aisling, "are you feeling all right?" Aisling nodded and turned away to watch the tunnel down which her captors had disappeared. She was so still and rigid, she looked as if she'd turned into a statue.

A mass of flying creatures with tiny sparks of light flew by above them towards the tunnel exit

26 - Caught

Aisling turned to see if Lena wanted her to keep watching and, while she was distracted, she felt hands grab her arms and start to drag her away down the sloping tunnel. Terrified, she let out a piercing scream, but the only result of that was a slap across her face from one and a kick in the leg from another, her two most vulnerable sites. The pain in her head was agonising. Every time she tried to turn her head, her neck felt as if it was being pierced by hot pokers. Her injured leg wouldn't hold her weight and gave way at the knee but that didn't bother her captors, they just dragged her. She knew they were the Family bodyguards by the tattoos of bears heads on their hands. They were taking her back to the Family for more torment. By now, she was so drained, she wouldn't be able to resist anything they did to her.

They brought her back to Momo Tilly, who welcomed her with a scowl. "You much trouble," she said, shaking her head. "My son talk you." The boy Olgon sat beside her his head bowed. He looked as miserable as Aisling felt.

It was then that she realized that the chief was standing in the shadows watching her arrival. She struggled to release herself from the grip of the guards. When Domin Cragsil nodded, they let go of her arms, allowing her to fall to the ground when her knee gave way.

Momo was angry and started ranting against the guards and her son. The son replied full force, starting one of those inevitable arguments between mother and son, which ended at a stalemate with the mother and son glaring silently at each other.

Then the chief turned to Aisling and came a bit closer. He grimaced and pinched his nose. "You stink bad," he growled. He yelled at one of the guards, who disappeared for a moment and returned with three female Korrigen, one carrying a small bucket of water. another a pile of cloth and leather. The third, who was unburdened, was a member of the family by the look of her clothes. The Domin instructed the women and then went over to the other side of the tunnel to wait. "Make you clean," he said. "Take off stinky clothes."

Aisling scuttled back to the wall. "No!" she yelled. "Don't touch me!" She kicked out with her good leg at the woman who was carrying the water and sent the bucket flying.

"I help," the chief said, strolling casually across the floor.

Aisling felt like a rabbit in a trap. As he reached out his hand to tear off her garments, she felt a power building up inside her, overwhelming her and taking control of her body. "No-o-o!" she shrieked. Then the power gave way, and everything turned black.

෨ක

Aisling woke up on a pallet with the worst headache she'd ever experienced. The pain was so bad, a wave of nausea overcame her and she released a fountain of vomit. She groaned and closed her eyes, then tried to learn more of her environment with her other senses. She could hear a barrage of sounds, people talking, children crying or squealing with laughter, someone hammering metal, and men arguing. Then she caught a whiff of the air and gagged. They must have been cooking again and the smell of pork, or *human,* overcame the stench of vomit. She buried her head under the fur blanket and realized she had no clothes on. They'd taken everything off while she was unconscious. Tears pressed against her eyes. The pain of trying to repress them was so severe, she started to sob. It was as if everything she'd suffered since she left home had been waiting to be released.

She heard someone shuffling towards her and peeked through slits of her eyelids. It was Momo Tilly with a beaker in her hand.

"What you do my son?" she asked.

"I don't know what happened," Aisling replied in a faint voice. "My head hurts too bad for me to think." She opened her eyes a bit wider and winced. Even the faint light from the torches in the tunnel hurt. She brought one of her hands out of the covers and pressed her fingertips into the hollow beside her eyes. She didn't know if it would help, but she felt instinctively that it might.

181

"My son very sick," Momo said. "You try kill him with elf magic?"

"No. I don't know what happened. I haven't got any magic." *Except far-hearing and sending*, she thought. Maybe this was a new one.

"Drink!" Momo said, holding out the beaker. "For pain."

"What's in it?" Aisling asked, sniffing at the contents.

"You trouble girl." She glared at Aisling. "It same last time." She sat down on the edge of Aisling's pallet. "You try kill son."

Aisling took a sip of the potion. It tasted the same as the others Tilly had given her, so she drank it all. *Anything to get rid of this awful pain.*

"I swear I did not do anything to your son. Something came through me because I was very frightened, but I did not control it. It just happened. It hurt me too."

She looked at the sad old woman and reached for her hand. Tilly slapped it away. "No touch!" she said sharply.

"I'm so sorry, Momo. You have been so good to me and helped me. I don't want to hurt you. I just want to go home." Her eyes filled with tears again.

The old woman stood up and looked at her. "I know," she said.

The pain was fading at last and she could open her eyes fully. She tried to sit up, but the wall behind her was too rough and hard on her bare skin. She had to pull the blanket up under her arms to hide her nakedness.

27 – Searching for Aisling
☙❧

Irial

One of the younger, hence smaller, dragons zoomed in on Irial and landed much too close for comfort. Its breath smelled of smoke and carbon almost choking the elf, so he moved back several steps. "What news, youngling?" he asked.

"We find cave," the young dragon said. "Many people inside. Lord Felivar say can we burn them?"

"Are they Korrigen?" Irial asked. He was worried that the reckless creatures might hurt those who were the victims of the Korrigen.

"I say no. Do not hurt any creature not Korrigen. Tell him the elf king will be very angry if they hurt our friends. There will be plenty of time to have fun after we rescue our people and the slaves. Do you understand?"

The youngster blew out a cloud of smoke. "Not burn friends," he said. "Have fun later?"

"Good. You may return now."

Irial grinned as the dragon flew off. "It's like trying to talk to nursery school children."

"Oh, I think they're kind of endearing," Cathal said.

"That's because you have a child," Irial replied. "They're too reckless and undisciplined for my liking." He turned and addressed the whole team of fairies and elves. "We're going up to the opening to find out who these people are, and to make sure the dragons don't get out of hand."

Before they had gone five steps, he saw Gyoka coming down the hill towards them. "Hail Gyoka," he greeted him. "Have you found them?"

Gyoka was bending over, gasping for breath. He straightened up and burped loudly and then he nodded. "Excuse me master elf. Having a bit of tummy trouble." He burped again, this time with more restraint. "Sorry about that. We found a place where we can hear voices on the other side of the wall. We think it's them, but we wanted to ask you first what you want us to do."

"That sounds promising," Irial said, relieved that they might finally be able to find the princess. "I'll send some of our warriors with you for protection while you break through the wall. Will it be difficult to get through?

"Not really. It must be a thin wall if sounds penetrate it. We'll melt the rock in no time. What do you want us to do when we break through?"

"Protect yourselves. I don't want casualties if we can help it. As you know, our goal is to rescue the princess." Irial looked down and thought for a moment. "Kill only if you are attacked and try to avoid harming children and the old ones." He looked around at his elf warriors and then addressed his second in command. "Piarus, take a dozen elves and join the dwarfs."

Gyoka led the elf warriors back into the caves. It was a long way from the entrance to the place where the other dwarfs were waiting; they'd been exploring for three days before they found anything of significance. "I've brought some elven friends to help us, not that we need any help, but we can enjoy their company for a while." The dwarfs and the elves laughed.

Gyoka nodded to his men—dwarves didn't engage women in their military activities, or in mining. "We're going in," he said. "Qurak, you and Zendo are the best burners, so get to work. The rest of you stand back."

"We know the routine, boss," one of the dwarfs quipped as he led the rush to shelter. Melting rock was serious business, so the chosen pair donned steel masks, steel mesh-reinforced leather gloves, and body armour before they started.

"I hope everyone's ready to back us up once we're through," Qurak called.

The group that had taken shelter around a bend in the tunnel put their hands on their weapons once the humming started. As the humming increased, it produced an intermittent crackling sound and the tunnel began to warm up. There was a final thump followed by Qurak's voice. "Water!" that was the signal for everyone to join in pouring buckets of water over the two workers, while keeping eyes on the opening they'd made.

The sound of chaos came from beyond the opening they'd produced: shouts and groans and screams, large objects being dragged across the floor, steel weapons

being pulled from scabbards. The cooling completed, everyone armed himself and prepared to face the enemy. The little grey men looked back at them with grimaces of shear hatred. Then a Korrigan slightly taller than the rest came forward, dragging Aisling by her arm as she struggled to cover herself with a fur blanket in the other. The Korrigan held a pointed knife against her throat.

Irial

Once the dwarven team was on its way back to the mine, Irial nodded to the rest. "Let's go and see what the dragons are up to. *I can't imagine how they can feed everybody, especially when they are barred from going outside to find game.*

Before they could set out, a cloud of nymphs appeared, accompanied by some fairies.

"What news?" Irial asked as a fairy settled beside him.

"Very bad," the fairy told him. "Everything bad."

"What about the princess?" he asked, alarmed. "Is she safe?"

The fairy chirped to the nymphs and returned to touch Irial's arm. "She lives."

It took several minutes of chirping humming and questions for Irial to get a picture of what was happening inside the caves, but the fairy was correct, it was bad. Very bad.

They weren't very far from the opening by then, so they only had to climb up a path that was not too steep. To his amusement, he found the dragons sitting on various rocks and shelves on the mountainside, all gazing hungrily at the opening to the mine. Irial looked up at them and found Lord Felivar, their leader. He bowed to him, touching his forehead with his right hand, and then turned towards the opening.

The opening was blocked with rocks which had to be removed before they could get inside. "We could get a dragon to get rid of this stuff," one of the warriors suggested.

"Better not," Irial replied. "There's no telling what sort of a mess they'd make. It might end up completely blocked with molten rock."

There were no people in sight when they finally entered the cave, but the smell coming from it was putrid, a mixture of rotting meat and human wastes. He stepped into the opening regardless of the unsavoury conditions within and called into the passage, "we are the elves. We're here to help you. You may come out. The dragons are with us to help in our search, and it was they who found this opening. They will not harm you."

Irial heard voices of people approaching. He was horrified by what he saw when they came into view. Most of them, men and women, were in filthy rags that barely covered them adequately. They were so thin their bones were visible through their skin. Several were missing limbs and had to be supported by others.

"We have brought you food," Irial said. "You may go outside; it's quite safe. We'll bring you some water from the mountain stream. Unfortunately, we don't have any spare clothes, but we do have healers. The important thing is to get you out of here and then you can tell us what happened to you." He held his hand out towards them. "Follow me."

When everyone was finally outside, the elves chose a grassy site for them to sit down. A human woman remained standing. "Are you looking for Aisling?"

"Yes, do you know where she is?"

"We were getting away, but they sneaked and grabbed her. They probably took her to the end of this tunnel. Come with me; I'll show you." She led Irial back into the cave and pointed down to the right. "I'm Lena, by the way. I spent a lot of time with her."

Bearnes

Bearnes was horrified when he saw Aisling. She had bruises on her head and neck and she could barely put her weight on her right leg. She looked half starved, her face wet with tears, and her hair was an oily matted mess. It was hard to imagine this waif was the daughter of the king and queen of Lycea. A Korrigen held her close to his body, a knife pressed against her throat.

"I Loamin Cragsil, son of Domin Cragsil, leader of Northern Korrigen." He shook Aisling's arm. "You go back. If no, I kill princess." He leered at them and pressed the knife a bit harder into her throat. Aisling cried out with shock, turning into a statue, afraid to move an iota. With a look of complete hopelessness and surrender, her legs gave way and she fell to the floor. Her pale naked body lay unmoving on the fur she had been trying to protect herself with.

Like lightening, two of the elves fired their arrows. One pierced the Korrigan's eye, and the other his throat, sending his body flying backwards. An old

Korrigan woman dashed in, wailing piteously, and fell over his body, her tears falling on his face as she stroked it affectionately. She looked around and glared at Aisling. "I good to you," she cried as she picked up the knife and darted towards the unconscious girl, but she wasn't fast enough. One of the elves jumped forward and grabbed her, pinning her arms to her sides in a tight grasp. "All right, granny, that's enough. We are sorry about him." He nodded towards Loamin Cragsil. "I could not allow him to kill our princess."

By now an elven healer was kneeling over Aisling. After wrapping her in the blanket of fur, she went to work on her injuries. The rest of the rescue team were busily engaged pacifying the Korrigen.

Irial

"How is she?" Irial asked.

"She's not doing very well, but she is alive," Lena replied. "She has seen so much horror in this place, I think it's affected her mind. She's also been hurt, her leg and her head, but the Momo has been taking care of her."

"Momo? What's that?"

"She's the mother of Domin Cragsil, their leader. She has been quite kind to Aisling and protected her whenever she could." Lena smiled. "You should have heard some of the rows Momo Tilly had with her son and grandson. She always won."

28 – The sorrows of slaves

Irial and Lena stepped out of the cave into the sunlight. Despite it being midday, the air was very chilly. The rescued slaves had built fires among the rocks, wherever there was a flat space, and now many of them were sleeping close to them. Some couldn't sleep, though, they were in too much pain from severed limbs and battle wounds. They lay on the ground moaning and cursing, waiting for the elven and fairy healers to get to them.

Ariel, the fairy healer and Euna, her elven counterpart, were working as fast as they could, but healing with magic took energy from their life forces. With such severe injuries, they had to rest periodically while their warrior colleagues recharged them or performed pain relief on the slaves with unbearable suffering.

"It's too bad we didn't think to bring clothing," Irial said. "We weren't expecting anything like this. I'd have some transported here, but it would be too heavy a load for instant transport. Let me think about it."

"There are masses of furs in the tunnels," Lena said. "They were in such a hurry to escape, they left a lot of stuff behind." The contemptuous way she said 'they' left no doubt about whom she was referring to.

191

Vicki Wootton

"Could we round up some?" he asked. "You tell us where to go, and we can bring them.

"We used to have big rooms full of clothes and furs in the old place. It was The Northern Korrigan headquarters," Lena said. "But they blew up the tunnel when we evacuated. Now everything just lies around in piles, although they carried a lot of baskets stuffed with things *they* needed. The most likely place to look would be down the tunnel in the direction they were going. I'll come with you and show you if you like."

"Aren't you getting tired?" he asked.

"A little, but not as bad as these poor devils. They were the ones doing the fighting."

Irial called a few of the elves to go with them and they started on a trek into the heart of the mountain. They had to step over bodies and body parts that were strewn all along the narrow tunnel, both slave and Korrigen. The smell of decay and excrement was nauseous.

"What brought this on?" Irial asked. He was curious about how so few slaves—about thirty in the group they'd rescued—could have wreaked so much havoc among the Korrigan masters.

"It had been building up for a long time, ever since they decided to move," Lena replied. "At the old site, they had access to the outdoors, and masses of stuff in storage, but once they blew it up, there was no way to restock. They were going to go overland to another cave system where they had stores. They were always prepared to move, but when Aisling was caught communicating, they were afraid she'd given away their hideout and they had to give up that idea."

They'd come across a ragged bundle of furs someone had abandoned but left it to be picked up on the way back.

"I see," Irial said. "What happened to Aisling while she was communicating? All I felt was a sharp pain and she was gone."

"She was communicating with you?"

"That's right. We can only communicate with someone we know; I and my partner were the ones who brought her to the Realm of Light, so she knew us quite well."

"I see. One of them must have sensed what she was doing. He punched her in the head. Her head smacked against the wall and she lost consciousness. Some of the royal family have talents."

"About the uprising," Irial wanted to hear the whole story. Now he was curious to know how much of a fight they would put up once they came into contact.

"Well, to make it short, we were starving. They were hungry too, but we never even imagined they would … would do what they did."

"Who, the slaves or the Korrigen?"

She shook her head. "*Them* of course."

Irial could see she was having trouble talking about it. Already her eyes were filling with tears. He rested a hand on her shoulder and felt she was trembling, so he sent her a little warmth. She wiped her eyes and cleared her throat. "They started killing slaves, the young ones, and eating their flesh."

Irial heard gasps from his fellow elves and could feel the revulsion radiating from them. "Cannibals!" he wiped both hands down his face. "This is the first time I've heard that about them. They truly are sons of dark forces and we are going to have to make a serious effort to drive them from the higher Realms."

"That may explain the mysterious disappearances of children throughout the Realms." The elf who'd said that clapped her hands over her mouth as if she'd uttered something foul.

Irial nodded to her. "It's getting late, we'd better continue," was all he said. In truth, he felt incapable of saying anything. Head bent, he continued down the passage.

They reached the widening of the tunnel where the slaves had made their last stand after driving the Korrigen deeper into the mountain, and where Nápla's body still lay in the middle of the floor, her blood now congealed around her.

"What happened here," Irial asked.

"That's Nápla. She was the head cook," Lena said. She shook her head sadly. "Poor Nápla. She was a good soul. She stood up for us slaves, especially for Aisling. The grandson killed her for warning Aisling not to eat the stew they were trying to persuade her to eat."

"Oh, dear God above!" Irial said. "Surely she wasn't the one who was cooking it!"

"Oh, no. She would never … she was a good woman, very spiritual. No, they were forced to cook for themselves. That's what brought the slaves' rebellion to a head. They … we started to kill them and take their weapons. Before long, they were on the run. That's why there is so much stuff littering the tunnel here. They were running for their lives and didn't have time to pick everything up."

29 – The leader of the Korrigen
ॐॐ

She hurt my son," the old woman wailed.

"Where is your son, Grandma? Is he the chief?" Piarus asked

Momo Tilly's eyes flicked to the left, then she tried to distract them by glaring at Aisling. "She bad."

He didn't really need an answer from her, he could read it from her mind. *Poor old woman,* he thought. "Why don't you go and take care of your son?" he suggested. "I know you have the healing touch."

Momo Tilly did as he suggested, limping across the cave to where he'd been hidden, grumbling as she went.

By now, most of the Korrigen had picked up their children and fled back up the tunnel, followed by some of the dwarfs and elves. The objective was not to kill women and children, but to drive them into the arms of Irial and his team.

Piarus linked to Irial to warn him of what was coming his way. *Good work,* Irial replied. *How is Princess Aisling?*

She will need a lot of healing, he replied. She's taken quite a beating and right now, she's unconscious, but Aithne is working on her. I have to take care of the Chief now. Apparently, Aisling did something to him and he's not feeling very good at the moment. We'll be on our way once we have him in custody.

Even though the old woman had gone to be with her son, she hadn't been much use to him. Whatever Aisling had done was powerful magic. Piarus and one of the dwarfs followed Aisling to the alcove where the chief lay unmoving on a pallet, his chest slowly rising and falling with each breath. His respiration was weak, but it was enough to keep him alive. He looked so pathetic lying there, emaciated limbs, and skin a pale bluish-grey with purple shadows around his eyes. His mother was sitting on the floor, tears dripping unheeded down her face as she stroked his face and murmured something in his ear.

So this is the one who has caused so much havoc in the Upper Realms. He doesn't look so powerful now.

Piarus turned to the dwarf at his side and asked him to go and get someone to help him carry the pallet. "We are going to carry him out," he said to the chief's mother. "We will not hurt him if he agrees to our terms, but that will be up to him." *But we'll execute him anyway,* he thought. He'd just wanted to give the old mother some comfort.

"Come on; let me help you up." He reached out to the old woman, but she spat at his hand and stood by herself, leaning against the wall for support. She looked so pitiful, hardly as big as an elven eight-year-old, her back bent and her legs so thin, they barely supported her. But she loved her son.

The dwarf came back with one of his cohorts. They stooped and lifted the pallet with ease. Although they were not much taller than a Korrigan male, they were a good deal sturdier. As they turned up the tunnel, his mother tried to hobble after him, but she was much too weak to keep up and gave up. She slid down the wall and buried her face in her hands, sobbing.

At that moment, Aithne appeared. "She's coming around," she reported. "but I don't think she should try to walk. Is there anything we can used to carry her?"

Piarus looked around the cavern and spotted a basket chair with handle bars. "How about that?"

"No!" the old woman screeched. "That me."

Piarus shrugged. "I guess we'll have to use a pallet," he said.

He turned to the old woman. "Who is going to carry you?" he asked.

"No care," she replied with a sob. "I die now." She curled up on the ground facing the wall. "I good to her," she murmured defiantly.

30 – The gathering
౽ఠఆ

The sun had set by the time Piarus's group arrived at the exit where Irial and the rest of the rescue team had gathered. The slaves were awake again and had been given another meal, and the dragons were still watching from the mountainside, periodically lighting up the sky with fiery puffs of smoke to remind everyone they were still there, waiting.

After giving the Korrigen food and water, they'd been left to cower inside the tunnels, guarded by dwarfs, who were not well-disposed towards them.

Piarus and Gyoka, Irial—with the fairy leader Davina leaning against his arm—sat on rocks around a bonfire to discuss their next move. Aisling, who had eaten some food and drunk an herbal concoction to aid healing, had fallen into a deep sleep on her pallet next to Lena. Lena was present to represent the slaves.

"I suppose the first thing we need to decide is what to do with the prisoners," Irial said. He glanced over his shoulder at the dragons perched above them. "I wish they'd go to sleep. I can't see leaving them to the mercy of the dragons, but how do we get around it? We did tell them they could have 'some fun'. Who favours leaving them to the dragons?"

"We'll make the dragons angry if we don't," Davina said.

Irial passed on the comment to the others, none of whom were in favour. "Any ideas?"

"We could dispose of the Korrigan leaders," Gyoka the dwarf leader suggested.

"That might satisfy the dragons, but I think we should consult the king before doing anything. First, let's see what one of their victims has to say. Lena!"

Lena had been thinking about this ever since the elves had arrived, but still hadn't come to any conclusive way of dealing with it. "May I talk about some of the things they did to us, including the princess?

Everyone nodded. "Go ahead," Irial said.

"Of course, cannibalism is the worst thing they are guilty of," she began. "We weren't aware they had such tendencies until we started to run out of food. But almost on a level with that is the fact that they took us from our homes, our families, our occupations, everything that fulfilled our lives. And they did this against our will. You cannot put a price on that. They took our lives to use as they saw fit. It didn't matter to them that we may have had children, parents, friends, in fact, they even took children." She wiped her eyes with the back of her fingers. "They must pay for that. It cannot go unpunished, But I'm not sure about giving them to the dragons. That is the sort of thing they would have no qualms about, but we are civilized people."

"Why do you think they kept her alive when the chief originally threatened to kill her to pay for the killing of his son?"

"This was Aisling's greatest fear: She thought he was going to marry her to his grandson. She was horrified. It caused a lot of consternation in his family when she rejected the boy."

Irial was horrified too. "Do you think that was their intention?"

"There is some evidence to support it. Aisling was protected by the Momo, the grandmother, and she stayed close to her. The Momo's grandson sent one of his sons to be close to Aisling. I suppose he hoped Aisling might like him, but she had a fit and demanded he leave. The poor child was devastated. When he walked away, he was in tears. It was cruel of them to use him like that."

Irial shook his head. "Unbelievable. It seems there's no limit to their nauseating ways. Thank the heavens we arrived in time to stop it." *Imagine that sweet girl being defiled by one of those unspeakable creatures.*

"Thank you, Lena. What you said is very important to all of us." He looked around at the rest of them. "I don't know about you, but I'm tired, so let's adjourn and meet again after we've rested. We still need the princess's input. I will contact the palace before I go to sleep."

After the meeting broke up, Irial went to sit under a tree where he wouldn't be distracted by the voices of others. He rested for a moment, thinking about what he would say while taking deep breaths of the bracing night air. Being in a different realm from the elven palace, he had to hope that he had not picked a bad time, although the king and queen would be happy with the news he was bringing, whatever the time was.

Queen Fenella answered. *Irial! Have you news?*

I have, your majesty, but I would like to tell you and his majesty together. I hope he is not sleeping.

No, he's right here beside me. We are just having our breakfast. Go ahead.

When he felt the king's mind join the conversation, he told them. *Your majesties, I have good news for you. We have rescued your daughter.*

He felt a change come over the royal couple. The anxiety and fear that had beleaguered their thoughts since Princess Aisling's disappearance was replaced by elation, hope, relief.

The king however, still had a touch of anxiety. *I sense a slight doubt in your mind, Irial Is she well?* he asked.

Knowing he couldn't deceive them, Irial told them. *She has been maltreated by those fiends, but she is being cared for by our healers. We expect her to be on her feet on the morrow.*

Will you bring her home then?

We hope to, your majesty, although there is something we need to decide before we can leave here.

Go ahead.

What are we going to do with the prisoners? I inadvertently promised the dragons they could have the Korrigen, but I'm having second thoughts. There are many women and children among them.

How did that come about? the king asked.

We were using them to keep their eyes on the mine entrances and report any activities to us. They are very young and reckless, and I knew they would want to blast anyone who appeared, so I sent a message to Lord Felivar telling them they should not attack anyone but Korrigen. They call it 'having fun'. I said they could have fun after.

And now you need to find a way around that? Didn't we originally say we were going to deport the Korrigen back to the underworld?

That is so, your majesty. That would not be an easy task, so I want to find a way we could satisfy all parties. The consensus here is that they must be punished one way or another. For their cannibalism, if nothing else.

Their what? He could feel the queen's horror.

Irial told them what he had learned from Lena, including the bit about them trying to force some of the cooked flesh on Aisling, and the slaughter of the slave cook who'd exposed it.

Ah, they've gone too far this time, the king said angrily. *That is an unforgivable atrocity. They must pay for that.*

What about the chief? The queen asked. *You could execute him and all the adult members of his family.*

Irial laughed. *I think your daughter has already dealt quite satisfactorily with their leader. I don't know what he did to instigate it, but it upset her so much, she blasted him. He's still unconscious, a half-day later.*

"She's your daughter all right," the king said to his wife with a smile. It was an open secret that the queen had a powerful gift of repel.

203

Vicki Wootton

"*My poor little girl,*" the queen replied. "*Under the circumstances, that's one gift I'm glad she inherited, but I'm sorry she has to suffer the aftermath on top of everything she's gone through. She must have a terrible headache. Now, about the Korrigen. I have an idea, two ideas. We could send a message to the King Jevtic asking him to withdraw his dragon children, offering a suitable reward, of course. Or, we could arm the healthy male Korrigen and let them fight it out. What do you think of that, Irial?*

Maybe we should offer them a choice.

I agree, the king said. *It would be unfair to condemn everyone without allowing them to defend themselves.*

What are we going to do with the non-combatants? Irial asked?

We'll leave you to decide that, the king replied. *Keeping in mind that we must remove them from the upper realms. And don't forget, the dwarfs have an interest in this too. They may come up with a solution.*

There's one more thing, Irial said hurriedly before they broke the link. *The slaves need clothes, and that includes the princess. They are all in rags that barely protect their dignity, let alone keep them warm. All they have now are mouldy animal skins. It's very chilly up here in the mountains. Can you send some? I estimate there are about thirty-two or so freed slaves of both sexes.*

31 – Freedom and punishment
৯৽৹

Aisling was woken by a gentle shake of her arm. Although she was wrapped in furs, her arms and ears felt cold. She opened her eyes to dazzling sunlight and realized she was out of doors, lying close to a large bonfire. Then she looked at the person who'd wakened her. "Irial!" she cried hoarsely. "What...?" her mind was still a bit foggy, and her throat was so dry, she could hardly speak.

"You're safe now, Aisling. Here, I've brought you this." He nodded to someone behind her. "Lena's going to support your head, so you can drink it."

"Does your neck still hurt?" Lena asked.

Aisling turned her head a few degrees to the side and back. "Not too bad."

"All right, I'm going to lift your head." Aisling felt her friend's arm slide under her neck and grabbed the fur cover to prevent it sliding down when her head was raised.

Irial held the cup to her lips while she drank the juice. She thought he looked tired. *Can elves get tired? Of course, silly. You get tired, don't you.*

He smiled at her. "I was up half the night talking to your parents," he said. "Drink it all. It will make you feel much better."

The drink was very refreshing and had a pleasant taste of mixed fruit and herbs. "Is this a magic elven potion?" she asked when she'd finished. Her throat was already feeling better.

"It's a fairy potion," he said. "You must be hungry. I'm going to bring you something to eat."

"I should get something to prop you up," Lena said as she gently lowered Aisling's head to the pallet.

"Don't go away," Aisling begged her. "I want to know what has happened. Did the slaves escape? Where are we now?"

"Put your arms under the furs; you're freezing. Irial has asked your parents to send clothes for everyone. They should be here soon. I don't know how they do it so fast, moving from another realm."

Aisling shuddered when she recalled the journey into the mountain. "They've got magic gates into the mountains filled with tunnels that go all over the place. Hey, I have an idea. How would you like to come with us when we go to the Realm of Light?

"What's it like? Have you been there?"

"No. I'll be a stranger there and it would be nice to have a friend with me. You're the only person I know, apart from you, is Irial." Aisling closed her eyes for a moment and sighed. "You haven't told me what's happened to everyone."

Irial arrived with the healer, Aithne. She was carrying a big cushion made of furs, and a small cloth bundle, while Irial had a glass bowl with a silver spoon resting on the edge, and a piece of white cloth. While Lena raised her head, Aithne arranged the pillow at her back. Aithne held up the cloth bundle. "I have some spare clothes here for you to wear," she said with a smile. They may be a bit big for you, but we'll manage. They are light and insulated against heat and cold." She put the bundle down beside the pallet.

"We're going to have a meeting soon," Irial said. "Do you feel up to it?"

Aisling was so hungry, she had started eating the food in the bowl, which tasted like a mixture of fruit, nuts, and seeds cooked in milk and honey, and her mouth was full. As soon as she'd swallowed, she asked, "what about?"

"We have to decide what we are going to do about the Korrigen and your input would be useful in making a decision."

Aisling swallowed another mouthful. "All right," she replied, "but I have to get cleaned up and dressed. Is there time?"

"For you, your highness, there will always be time." Irial smiled at her and then stood up and went to talk to a group of ex-slaves, leaving Aisling with her mouth open. *Your Highness? I still can't believe I'm a princess. I wish he would just call me by my name.*

Once Aisling was washed and dressed in the healer's spare outfit, a long white wool tunic and some sky-blue woollen trousers that had to be rolled up at the bottom, she hobbled over to the place where the meeting was being held. She smiled at Lena who was sitting on a thick log close to the fire, wearing some clean clothes.

"Come and sit next to me," she said. "There's plenty of room."

"Where did you get the clothes?" Aisling asked. "They look very comfortable."

"They are. Irial had them sent from Lycea. I love the colours, don't you?" Lena's tunic was pale yellow with orange trim and the trousers were dark green. She also had a little blue scarf around her neck.

"Mm, very nice." She didn't know what to say. She wasn't fond of yellow, but as long as Lena liked it.... She looked around and saw a few slaves, the injured ones. Some of them were awake, lying on pallets or furs. They were now wearing clean new clothes, mostly blue shirts and pants. They looked as if they'd bathed and had their hair trimmed too.

"Where are the other slaves?" she asked Lena.

"Oh, they've gone off into the woods to gather firewood and anything edible they can find."

All attention turned to Irial when he stood up. "We're just waiting for Gyoka ... Ah here he is." The dwarf leader bowed to everyone and sat down on one of the rocks that had been rolled close to the fire.

"Morning greetings, everyone, Irial said. "Before we start with business, I want to introduce you to Princess Aisling."

Aisling cringed. She dreaded being the center of attention. Irial went on to introduce everyone at the meeting, but Aisling was so nervous, she immediately forgot all their names. All she retained was their races and the fact that they were the leaders of their groups.

She was particularly charmed by the fairy, recalling her earlier belief that Irial and Ráona were telling her fairy stories. She smiled at the beautiful little creature who was clinging to Irial's arm. She would not forget that name, Davina. Irial bent down and whispered something to the fairy who left him and fluttered across to Aisling. She touched the princess's hand and chirped. Aisling was amazed when the chirps registered in her mind as words. "We are happy that you are free from those monsters and look forward to seeing you in the Realm of Light. Irial will tell you a signal you can use to contact us if you ever need anything, your highness."

"Thank you. I am pleased to meet you," Aisling said, looking shyly across the fire at Irial who smiled back.

Irial

Once Davina was back beside Irial, he opened the meeting. "Our purpose is to decide what we are going to do about the Korrigen prisoners. We need to decide this as a group because everyone here has been affected by them in some way. I will start by telling you about my consultation with the king and queen of Lycea. We discussed a number of possibilities which I will now put before you." He looked around the circle and continued. "One of the...."

He was interrupted by an enormous dragon flying in and casting a shadow over them. It flapped its leathery wings overhead, causing a gust of wind which demolished the fire, and then dropped to a big rock a few lengths away.

Irial wasn't fazed by the creature, although Aisling felt her heart pounding so hard she feared it would burst. Lena was squeezing her hand, almost cutting off the circulation. "A dragon!" she gasped. "I never thought I'd ever see such a thing."

"Lord Feliver," Irial said, raising a hand to his forehead. "Welcome. Do you wish to join our council?"

Feliver blew out a gust of smoke but was considerate enough to send it away from them. "I will," he replied in a husky growl. "The children are getting restless," he said, twisting his head around to look up at the mountain where the other dragons were roosting, blowing little clouds of fiery smoke at one another. I believe you promised them some fun with the foul Korrigen."

I know this would be trouble, Irial thought. *Now what am I going to tell them?*

"Your lordship, I appologise for the delay. We are trying to decide what we are going to do before we can release them. I'm sure you understand that we can't just send everyone outside. There are women, children, the old ones."

"Send bad ones," Lord Feliver replied.

"That's what we will probably decide," Irial said. "Pardon my manners. I forgot to introduce you to the princess you've helped us to rescue. There she is, the young female sitting on that log."

The dragon twisted his long neck and turned to face Aisling. "We are gratified you are safe," he rumbled. This time the smoke came towards her, making her cough.

She looks so tiny and shy, Irial thought. "Don't be afraid," he said to her. "The dragons are our allies. Say something."

Aisling lowered her head. "Thank you, your lordship," she murmured.

"I was about to tell you what the king and queen had to say about this. There are several options open to us, but one thing is essential. Those we don't punish must be sent back to the underworld, and their access points must be blocked permanently."

"Aye, we can do that," Gyoka said.

"Good. How are your people getting along controlling them?"

"We've had to knock a few heads," Gyoka replied, "but they're learning." He grinned around the circle.

"These are some of the alternatives from my discussion with the king and queen," Irial continued. "We must punish the ringleaders somehow. One way would be to arm the healthy Korrigen males and set them free outside. I think if we choose that option, we should give them a choice. Execution or face the dragons."

Feliver suddenly flapped his wings and leapt into the air. He flew around for a while and then landed again close by. "King Jevtic has recalled us," he grumbled. This time his breath had more fire in it.

He's not too pleased about it, Irial thought. "You've been an enormous help to us," he said. "We might not have succeeded in our quest were you and your young ones not here to help us." He was reluctant to say anything more for fear of sounding insincere.

Feliver grunted something, with another outpouring of fiery smoke, and took off again, making for the higher ledges of the mountainside.

"That's one problem solved," Irial said. "I really didn't want to throw the prisoners to the dragons."

"What are we going to do with them now?" Piarus asked.

"One thing we must do before anything else is send Aisling to Lycea." He smiled across at her. "But before she leaves, I want to get her opinion about the Korrigen. Would you like to comment, your highness?"

"I can't say much that's good about them," she replied. "There are a couple of people I would not want to be harmed. Momo Tilly was very good to me. She helped heal my broken leg ...."

"The Momo also protected me from the other Korrigen and let Lena stay with me."

"Who is the other person?"

Aisling drew in a deep breath and blew it out again. "It's the boy, Olgon. I was so mean to him and now I feel guilty about the way I treated him."

"What do you suggest we do with them. You realize that the granny has decided to die, don't you?"

Aisling looked shocked. "Can she do that, just decide to die?"

"I suppose it's possible. She probably has some poison potions in her baskets, or she might just refuse to eat. She's very upset about her sons."

He saw a tear leak from Aisling's eye. "I was thinking Olgon would be better off with her. I know she loves him very much."

"We can look into it," he said. "What if she's already dead?"

"Could we take him with us? Maybe we could teach him to be a better person away from his family," Aisling suggested.

"It might be a good idea, but we can't do that," he replied. "His heart is probably broken already by his father's death and losing most of the people he knows," Irial said. "I admire your tender heart, but he is better off with what remains of his family."

"Is it all right if I ask the king and queen?"

"By all means do so, but I fear they will agree with me."

"Can you talk to them now?"

"Very well, but we have to hurry."

Irial communicated with Queen Fenella for a moment, and then sighed and turned to Aisling. "Her majesty said you may bring him if he wants to go with you. You must let him decide, though." He looked up at the sky. "It's time for you to leave," he said.

"Aren't you going to take me?"

"No, I have a lot of work to do here. Euna and Piarus will take you. Euna's coming in case the pain returns. You'll be able to borrow some horses when you reach the foot of the mountain.

"Can I see Momo before I go?"

"All right, but don't be too long. Lena can take you to help you translate. You can ask the boy while you're at it."

Aisling

A space had been cleaned up for the old woman. They found her lying on a raised pallet with her eyes closed, surrounded by her family. Momo Tilly had always been small compared with humans and elves, but now she seemed to have shrunk to the size of a five-year-old human. Her hands lying across her body were curled like tiny claws.

"Is she sleeping?" Lena asked one of the women.

"What do you care?" the daughter replied.

"Princess Aisling wants to say goodbye and to thank her for taking care of her."

Momo's eyes snapped open. "Is it that girl?" she said crossly.

The woman stroked her mother's hand. "It's all right, Mamsy, I won't let her hurt you again."

Lena quickly translated the exchange for Aisling. "Tell me what you want to say to her," she said.

"Momo, I'm sorry I hurt you. I'm leaving now and before I go, I want to tell you how grateful I am to you for being kind to me and protecting me. I will never forget you." She thought for a moment. "Ask her if I can touch her."

"No touch," Momo said. "I die now." She continued in her own language for a moment.

"She says she was good to you and you betrayed her and everyone."

"I agree she was good for me, but her people almost destroyed my life. Now I am going to meet my mother and father for the first time."

After Lena translated that, the old woman closed her eyes. "Now I die."

Aisling and Lena looked for the boy after she left the old woman. They found him sitting on a pile of soiled furs in a dark part of the tunnel resting his head on his knees.

"Olgon, Aisling wants to talk to you," Lena said. The boy's head snapped up to look at Aisling with reddened eyes.

He didn't seem prepared to stand up, so Aisling knelt on the rock floor. "I'm leaving now," she said. "I'm sorry I was not nice to you, Olgon, but I can make it up to you if you like." She paused while Lena translated. When he responded with a scowl, she continued, "Would you like to come with me to live in the Realm of Light? My mother is the queen there and she said you can come with me, if you want to."

This brought Olgon to his feet, fists clenched, eyes full of rancour, and let go of his feelings about her and her idea. When he had finished his rant, he looked at her as if she was a monster, and then turned and ran down the tunnel towards his great grandmother."

"I guess the answer is no," Lena said. "Let's go back to Irial."

"But what did he say?" Aisling insisted.

"It was not very favourable to you. If you really want to know, it was basically about how he hated you and how everything that's happened is all your fault."

"No, it's their fault. I didn't offer to be kidnapped," Aisling replied. "I don't have much sympathy for any of them after what I've seen here, but I did feel sorry for Olgon."

"He's probably better off with his mother and his own friends."

Aisling sighed. "That was a waste of time," she said as they walked back outside. "I understand, though.

215

Momo Tilly loves her family just as humans do and now she's lost them and everything. She really doesn't have anything to live for, does she?"

"How did it go?" Irial asked when they returned to the meeting circle.

"Not well," Lena replied before Aisling could say anything. "He didn't want to go with Aisling and I think Momo is willing herself to die."

Irial sighed. "Well, they brought it on themselves. Are you ready to go now? "You've got a long walk ahead of you to reach the Gateway, but fortunately you can borrow some horses to take you most of the way. You want to be there before it's dark."

"I'm a bit nervous about seeing my parents," Aisling said. "What if they are disappointed when they see me?"

"It's natural to feel anxious when embarking on something so momentous, but once you meet them, you'll be very happy, and you will love them." He looked around for Piarus and Euna. "Ah, there you are. All packed, I see."

Four fairies flitted around the group and one landed on his shoulder. He listened to his chirping for a moment, and then said, "They've decided to go with you," he explained. They can fly ahead in the tunnels and scan for danger, although it should be safer now we've caught the culprits, but you never know."

"Can I give you a hug?" Aisling asked him. She was quite used to hugging people she liked, taught by the aunties, who were quite demonstrative about their affection. It used to drive her crazy when she was a toddler, always being petted and kissed, but as she grew older, she learned to take it in her stride.

Irial looked surprised, then he held out his arms.

"You next," she said to Lena. "I wish you were coming with us. I'll miss you so much." After a hug and a kiss, she parted with her friend. Maybe you can visit me when this is over," she said.

32 - Settling scores

கூ௸

Now that the Dragons had departed, the Korrigen were brought outside. It was impossible to have any kind of discussion inside the cave with such a large group. The leaders came out first, wrapped in furs against the cold. The rest sat down on the ground, looking thoroughly miserable. They didn't have the rich furs to wrap around themselves, so some of them looked around for firewood and rekindled the fire that had been lit earlier.

As Irial sat on a boulder slightly above the level where the Korrigen we seated and gazed down on them, his first thought was how pathetic they looked. But when he recalled the despicable things they had done, he felt no sympathy for them.

He turned to Lena, who was sitting nearby. "Mistress Lena will translate for us," he said. "Now that the princess is safe and on her way home, we have to decide what we are going to do with you. Before I continue, I should warn you if you are thinking of attacking us, the dragons are not far away, they just went farther back into the mountains to hunt for food, but they could be here in no time if there's trouble. They love killing creatures with their flames." *Let's hope that holds them in check.* "Here is what we've decided:

Your leader and the highest officers in your military will be executed."

This led to an outcry from the Korrigen: Shouting, cries of rage from males, and females sobbing. Many of the children started crying and clinging to their mothers.

He waved his hand at them, palm down. "That's enough," he shouted. "You must realize this is a very lenient sentence; our first idea was to turn you out for the dragons.

"If you were in our place, you would probably kill everyone who opposed you. Your chief still lives, albeit in a state of vegetation. Executing him would be an act of mercy. If anyone of you has a better idea, please bring it forward." He stopped for a while to give them time.

"Send us home," a male shouted.

"We would like to, but then someone else would take over and start attacking and abducting people from other races. Your lifestyles and philosophy are not compatible with ours, so we are going to separate you.

"We consulted King Briartach about this matter. He is a just man. He advised us to have you present at this discussion, but he left the final decision to us. Let me continue with what will happen to the rest of you. The females and children under twelve years will be sent back to the underworld from whence you came, and the exits will be sealed permanently. The remainder will be placed in the care of the dwarfs. They are constructing a prison where you will be housed for life."

Vicki Wootton

After waiting for the strident protests to end, he added. "After you have a meal, we will be moving you, starting with the children and mothers.

33 – Going home

ॐॐ

Aisling had expected the journey to find a Gateway would be the same as the last time, so she was surprised when they stopped at a farmhouse at the foot of the mountain. "Is this where we get the horses?" she asked.

"Yes," Piarus replied. "This is Davin and Ellery's place. They are our liaison with this part of the Mid-Realm."

A blond man of middle years appeared in the doorway of the barn and waved to them, then he went to the little farmhouse next to it and yelled through an open window, "Company, El! How about some tea?"

Aisling and her two companions walked towards the farmhouse, arriving just as the front door was opened by a petite woman with curly red hair.

"Welcome to our home," she said. "I've just put the kettle on. If you'd like to come inside, we'll have a cup of tea while the master," she nodded towards Davin, "readies the horses."

Davin shook hands with Piarus and said a few words, then he followed them inside.

A wave of nostalgia and yearning overcame Aisling when she crossed the threshold. The little farmhouse was so much like gran's, even down to the clucking of poultry nearby. "What's the matter love?" Ellery asked when she saw Aisling wipe her eyes.

"It's nothing," Aisling replied. "I was just remembering my grandmother. We lived in a house like this before she passed on."

"Ah, that's too bad. I'm sorry for your pain. Was it recently?"

"I think so; I've lost track of time, but it doesn't seem very long."

Ellery gave her a puzzled look and turned to the others. "Make yourselves at home," she said, offering them chairs at the table. She picked up a steaming kettle from the cookstove and poured the water into a blue teapot. "There's scones on the board, just baked this morning, and butter and honey to go with them."

As they were leaving, Euna handed Ellery a small wooden box. "These are the powders you wanted. Mix a couple of pinches in a cup of hot water. And no more than three doses a day."

"Lord bless you," Ellery said. "This should do the trick. It worked wonders for mum the last time."

Two horses and a pony stood outside the barn, saddled up and ready to go. Aisling, who was a head shorter than the two elves, got the pony. As they rode out of the yard, Davin called, "Same place as last time?"

"Same place," Piarus replied.

Even with the horses to ride, they didn't reach the Gateway until close to sundown. They left the horses tied up near a stream with plenty of grass for them to munch on. Once they were settled, Piarus uttered a few words and passed his hands through the air over them, and Aisling saw a faint light cloud fall over them.

"What was that you did?" she asked.

"I put a ward over them to protect them from predators until Davin comes for them."

"Do you move back and forth between the realms very often?"

"Not very often, only when there's a problem we can help with. There are several watchers who live over on this side who patrol the regions and inform us when they find something that needs fixing."

"What sort of trouble?" Aisling asked. "I would think that everything would be all right now that you've dealt with the Korrigen."

"They are not the only dangers that threaten the Upper Realms."

Piarus and Euna stopped climbing and started to examine the wall of rock facing them. "Ah, here it is," Euna said as her hand disappeared into the rockface. Suddenly two fairies flew past them and through the wall. "I wish you would warn us," Euna called after them as she stepped through.

When Aisling's heart stopped fluttering, she stepped through with a feeling of trepidation, recalling what they had found the first time she'd passed through one of these Gateways. She needn't have worried, everything was as it should be, warm and clean, lined with chests containing everything a traveller might need.

"Who cleans up in here and fills the chests?" she asked.

"There are maintenance teams that keep the tunnels and vestibules like this in good condition," Euna replied. "How are you feeling?" she added.

Aisling yawned, as if that would partly answer the question. "I'm hungry," she replied.

"Let's clean ourselves up first," Piarus said. "Then we can eat and rest for a while."

It didn't take long for Aisling to fall asleep despite her excitement about meeting her parents for the first time, and the horror of her recent experiences. When she awoke some time later, her two companions were already up. She sat up and rubbed her eyes.

"How was your sleep?" Euna asked.

"Perfect," she replied. "Did someone put a spell on me or something?"

Euna smiled and looked at Piarus who shrugged. "I'm glad you are rested," he said. "We'll have something to eat and be on our way. Are you excited?"

Aisling nodded. "Yes of course, and a bit scared. I hope they like me." Her face reddened when she realized how silly that sounded. To cover her embarrassment, she got up and went to the refresher cubicle.

They set off down the tunnel replete with new packs of bedding, food, and water. The fairies had gone ahead to scout the way.

"Don't they get hungry?" Aisling asked. "I've never seen them eating anything."

"Their energy requirements are different from ours," Euna replied. "They can extract energy from sunlight, the way plants do, but they do eat solid food as well. It's just that their food cannot be preserved the way ours can."

"What sort of things do they eat?"

"I'm not really sure, but I suspect it's something like nectar or plant essences."

That made sense to Aisling in a way, but she couldn't imagine how it worked, although they certainly had plenty of energy. Of course, they were not as big as humans and elves, so she imagined they wouldn't need as much food. Maybe they were like birds.

After a while Euna noticed Aisling had started limping. "Let's take a break," she said. "I don't know about you, but I'm getting hungry." She turned to Aisling. "Would you like a potion?" she asked.

Aisling thought about it for a moment before answering. Her leg was aching, and she didn't want to slow everyone down. "Yes please."

After mixing the potion and waiting for Aisling to drink it, Euna knelt on the ground in front of her and massaged the leg. Aisling felt the leg getting stronger and the pain receding immediately.

"That feels wonderful. Thank you, Euna."

"That's what I'm here for," she replied.

They sat for a while, eating the snacks and drinking fresh water, and then resumed their journey.

"How long was I with the Korrigen?" Aisling asked as they walked.

"About a season," Piarus replied.

"So, in the Mid-Realm it is the Harvesting. That means I had the sixteenth anniversary of my awakening and didn't even know it," she said mournfully. "It was impossible to measure time in those tunnels."

"Well, you're free now," Euna said, laying her arm around Aisling's shoulder in a hug. "You will have plenty of celebrating to look forward to when we get to the palace."

"Your mother will probably want to celebrate all the anniversaries she's missed with you when you return to her," Piarus said.

"Is time the same in the Realm of Light as it is in the Mid-Realm?" she asked.

"Approximately," he replied. "It's off by a few days and hours as our world seems to spin a little slower."

"To tell the truth," Euna said, "it's rather futile to make comparisons. We'd be spending too much time making calculations."

The two fairies returned, landed by the arms of Euna and Piarus, and chirped for a while. *They really are like birds,* Aisling thought.

"There's been a rockfall ahead," Piarus translated for Aisling. "We're going to have to use another tunnel."

"I wonder what caused that," Euna said. "I've never heard of that happening before."

"Yes, it does sound a bit ominous," he replied. "Maybe we should try the rapid track. It's not long since we rested so we should have enough energy. How would you like to contribute some of your energy, your highness?"

"I would if I knew what you were talking about. Is it dangerous?"

"Not really. The only risk would be running out of energy, but I think we have that covered. We don't need to go very far."

"But what happens?"

"Oh, we just get there faster. It works by focussing on a target ahead of us and willing ourselves there. It's almost instant."

Aisling still couldn't get it straight in her head. "Does that mean we go through the rock?"

"No, only open spaces. The power finds a pathway that is open to the place we want to reach. I should warn you, however, you'll become quite dizzy during the transition, but it's very fast."

"All right, I'm ready. What do I do?" *It can't be that dangerous if they want to do it*, she thought.

"Make sure your pack is secure—it's better to have it in front of you—then take our hands."

Once they were in place and ready to go, Euna and Piarus closed their eyes and murmured an incantation and suddenly, it felt as if they had been picked up by a hurricane that swerved in all directions. She almost lost consciousness from the pressure and dizziness, but it was over almost as soon as it began. They were standing together at a crossroad of tunnels, panting and weak.

Aisling took some deep breaths to relieve the nausea and leaned back against the wall. "Where are we?" she asked when she'd gained enough energy to speak.

"You see that tunnel?" he pointed to the one on the right. "In a few minutes, we will be in Lycea, not far from the palace. When we leave the Gateway, I'll contact the palace and they'll send a carriage for us."

227

34 - Dealing with the Korrigen
૭૦૯

There was much howling and wailing from the females and young Korrigen when they were taken away by the dwarfs. But this was mild compared with the rage of the older males who realized that they would never see their families again. The dwarfs knew the mountains and under levels better than anyone from the upper realms, so they were the best choice to lead the Korrigen back to where they came from. Instead of taking them outside and leading them through the outer world, they went back into the mine and down to the break in the wall they'd created during their search.

Irial was surprised by the absence of Momo Tilly and asked one of the women being led away where she was. Lena translated what she said. "She died in the night, just as she said she would. I don't blame her, really. She has lost most of her family and her son is going to be executed. She had nothing to live for."

"How did we miss that? It's a sad ending although I can't help remembering that she raised that son and must have had some influence on the way he turned out."

He turned and watched the sorry little band disappear into the mine and rubbed his hands together.

"Well, that's the first batch dealt with. Now for the second contingent."

The leaders, the ones who were going to be executed, had been moved inside the mine and taken up to a level in the opposite direction from the families. They were guarded by several of the forty dwarfs who had arrived during the night. These were the armed dwarfs who enforced the law in their communities and were a formidable group with their bristling moustaches and beards, steel armour and swords. They also carried steel-tipped pikes strapped to their backs, useful for keeping prisoners from escaping.

Once the males who had been selected for imprisonment had been led away by another team of dwarfs, it was time for the executions. This was the worst part for the elves. Killing a helpless person depleted their energy and left a lasting scar on their souls. The dwarfs had no such scruples, so they agreed to perform the executions of the nine leaders who were brought out into the open air.

The former slaves, who were sitting up the slope, jeered when they saw the prisoners.

"Now would be a good time to bring back the dragons," Qurak, the dwarf second in command said with an ironic grin.

Irial scowled at him. "Let's not get carried away," he said mildly. "I'm sure even you wouldn't want to watch a creature being burned alive."

"I was just ... I didn't mean it."

"All right let's get it over with." Icy dread was building up in Irial's stomach but he and the whole rescue team had to witness the execution.

229

Domin Cragsil, who was still unconscious, was carried out on a litter and placed on the ground. The rest of the group were forced to lie face down in a row on either side of their leader. Irial was surprised to see two more dwarfs come out of the cave, each carrying an axe. They went to stand at the two ends of the row, but Irial stopped them before they could proceed.

"I have to tell them the charges before you go on." After telling the prisoners the reason for their sentences, he nodded to the executioners.

They watched as the executioners went down the row quickly lopping off each head. The former slaves cheered as each head rolled away from its body.

"That was awful." Irial grimaced and massaged his queasy stomach. "I don't understand why they didn't put up a fight."

"We do have some compassion inside these iron-bound bodies," Qurak replied. "They were drugged."

After the bodies were burnt, no one felt like eating anything. "I just want to get out of here," Aithne the elven healer said.

"I agree, but we can't leave yet," Irial replied. "We have to repatriate all these slaves we've freed. One of the reasons we needed you to stay is that some of them are in bad shape and need our healing skills."

He beckoned to the rest of the rescuers to join him where he sat with his back to the smouldering funeral pyre, out of the path of the smoke. "Now we have to help these unfortunate souls go home. I know Lena has been interviewing them, so we can sort out where everyone comes from. Do you have the list handy? he asked Lena.

She nodded and sat down beside him. "They come from all over the place," she reported. "I don't know how we're going to get them all home, but I have an idea. Do you want to hear it?"

"Of course, especially if it will make our task easier. My people are anxious to get home, too."

"First of all, I need to know if there is a large town nearby. I don't know this region. Do you know?"

Irial shook his head. He'd been too wrapped up in the rescue to explore the vicinity. "I know," Cathal, one of the elven warriors said. "I have a liaison partner there. It's, oh, about five leagues in that direction." He pointed towards the north east. "It's called Greenway."

"Does he, or she, have far hearing and sending?"

"Yes. Her father is an elf and she inherited it. Do you want me to contact her?"

"In a while, yes, but first we have to think of how we can transfer everyone. There are more than thirty people to accommodate."

"I have another idea," Lena said. "Maybe they could bring carts or wagons to carry us. What concerns me is, how are we going to pay for it. I know from my studies that it is a market town for farmers and not very big."

"Don't concern yourself about that. We will compensate them sufficiently. They may even profit from helping you all. It's a good idea."

"All right, Cathal, contact her and see if she can talk to the town leaders about it."

It took several days to set things up because it was harvest time and most of the wagons and carts were in use, but the promise of gold spurred them to greater effort. Eventually, three wagons and a donkey cart arrived at their campsite farther down the hill from the mine. The delay had also given Irial time to have some gold coinage sent from Lycea.

One evening, Irial who was sitting near Lena eating supper, leaned towards her and asked, "How would you like to visit Lycea? I know Aisling would love to see someone she knows, and I could see the two of you were close."

"I would love to," she answered. "But I have to get back to my son. I've been away from him far too long and he'll be forgetting me if he doesn't see me soon."

"I didn't know you had a son," Irial said. "How old is he?"

Lena scratched her eyebrow. "To tell the truth, I'm not sure. He was five when I was abducted, but it's hard to keep track of time. He's probably seven or eight now."

"Who's taking care of him?"

"That I don't know either, but he usually stayed with my mother when I had to go away on school business. I hope it's her because Einar knows her best."

"What about his father?"

"I don't know where he is. He was a soldier, but he disappeared one day, and I never heard from him again. He doesn't even know he has a son, even if he's still alive. Tying myself up with him was not one of my better judgement calls, but I was young and reckless." She rubbed her cheeks with her palms. "Why am I telling you all this stuff. You must find it terribly boring."

"I'm interested," Irial protested. "It's not boring at all, and I would still like to invite you to visit Lycea. And I'm sure young Einar would be fascinated.

35 - The home she never knew
৵৵

Once they had regained some of their energy, Aisling and her companions walked along the tunnel that led to the exit. It was a cavern very similar to the one by which they had entered, and she could see no sign of an opening to the outside world. Piarus went to a spot on the wall that looked no different from the surrounding polished rock, until he walked through it with one hand out in front of him.

"How are you feeling?" Euna asked Aisling.

"Very nervous and a bit excited," she replied.

"Don't worry, everything will be wonderful; you'll love it. Shall we go?"

Aisling took a deep breath before she and Euna stepped through the Gateway together, hand in hand.

The first thing she saw was an open carriage harnessed to two white horses. A carriage driver stood by the side of the passenger box. He opened the gate in the side and helped the most beautiful woman she had ever seen step down. *Is that her?* Aisling knew she should react in some way, but she felt as if she had turned to stone. The two elves who'd accompanied her bowed, then saluted with clasped hands and said, "your majesty." Aisling imitated their bows.

When she looked up, she saw the woman's eyes sparkled with tears, and her own eyes watered in response.

"This is your true mother, Queen Fenella of Lycea," Piarus said.

The queen came towards her, holding out her arms to embrace Aisling. "My precious girl. It has been such a long time since I last held you in my arms." She laid her cheek on Aislings head. "I've missed you so much. Come on, let's go back to the castle so you can greet your father."

Aisling couldn't think of anything to say to this beautiful woman who was her mother. Everything about her was elegant and refined, her filmy mantle of turquoise over a creamy silk robe, the way her golden hair flowed in waves down her back and over her shoulders, her rings and bracelets of gold and precious stones. *How could I possibly be her daughter? She so beautiful and I'm just a nobody. I feel like an imposter.*

After riding for a few moments without talking, Fenella put her arm around Aisling's shoulders and pulled her into a hug. "Welcome home, my darling girl. What do you think of Lycea?"

Until the queen mentioned it, she hadn't paid much attention to the scenery, but now she looked and was amazed. They were passing fields of many-coloured flowers that emitted the glorious aroma of mixed fragrances. "Those are our healing and enhancing fields," Fenella said. "We have many uses for those flowers, making healing potions, home enhancements, many oils and lotions for the body, and some of them are used to flavour our food." She took Aisling's hand. "You'll love it here, I promise."

"It's so beautiful," Aisling replied. "Is it like this everywhere?"

"We try to spread the beauty of nature wherever we live, but some areas are more successful than others I'm afraid."

Flashes of colour from the sky caught Aisling's attention as a flock of green and blue birds rose from a nearby copse. The whole flock flew towards them twittering and chirping musically. She flinched when a big green bird with a crown of blue feathers on its head settled on the side of the carriage. It dipped its head from side to side as it chirped at them, when it had finished chirping, the queen made some whistling-chirping sounds in reply, the big bird moved along the back of the seat until it was closer to Aisling and chirped some more and flew back to his flock.

"He's the king of the Elaislians," Fenella explained. "He came to wish you welcome."

"That's amazing," Aisling replied. "You understand their language?"

"Of course," the queen replied. "We learn it as children. They are our neighbours and allies. They keep watch for danger and alien invasions."

"Were the Korrigen an alien invasion?"

"They were indeed and very onerous ones. They caused the most destruction and conflict we've had in centuries. I believe we've finally driven them out of the realm, both in the north and the south now, but we'll have to be alert for strays who evaded us."

After passing some farms and orchards of ripening fruit, they came to what she assumed was a residential area. Everything she'd seen so far was set amongst groves of trees and other vegetation, fruit trees, flowers, vegetable gardens. Gleaming white houses with green roofs peeked out amongst the foliage. Even the road they were on, which was paved with the smooth white rock, meandered through the woods.

Looking ahead, Aisling saw a larger building on a hill surrounded by more woodland. Most of it was hidden among the trees and only its gleaming spires were visible from the distance.

"Is that the palace?" she asked.

"It is," the queen replied. "Your true home."

As they drew closer Aisling saw that the white exterior was ornamented with turquoise and gold trim.

The carriage rolled from the paved street into a large courtyard surrounded by shrubs the like of which she had never seen before. They had green and pink lacy fronds that rose to twice the height of an elf and emitted a soothing fragrance. This shrubbery was the only separation between the palace and the outside world. Another thing she found interesting was the layers of the palace were separated from one another by slender pillars. Everything about it was light and airy, but she wondered how they got from one layer to another. "I don't see any guards or walls," she said. "I thought all kings' castles had them."

"We don't need walls or guards in the Realm of Light." The queen replied. "We have enough skills among us to be able to detect and react to danger most of the time."

After being helped from the carriage by the two drivers, they climbed some shallow steps to a pair of glass doors that stood open. They were met by a couple of elves dressed in green and white livery who bowed to them. *I'm going to have to get used to all these servants and bowing*, she thought, smiling at them nervously.

"My dear," the queen said to Aisling. "Let me introduce you to your two assistants. On the left is Opela. She will be your personal attendant, and the young man will be your..." the queen stopped for a moment to think. "...your footman I suppose. He can answer your questions, bring your meals, take messages, accompany you when you go out. All the services to help you become accustomed to living here. His name is Feorus." Fenella turned to Opela. "Let's take Princess Aisling to her suite and let her freshen up before she meets the king. You come too, Feorus."

The interior of the palace was full of light from floor-to-ceiling windows. In addition, the hallway ceilings had skylights. The walls and floors of the hallway were panelled with cream-coloured material she couldn't identify. It glowed slightly and had opalescent patterns of lighter tints, reminding her of the inside of a seashell.

They walked the length of the building and turned a corner. The inner wall of the hallway was lined with semi-opaque doors that looked like glass. Aisling noticed that the landscape outside the windows now had flower beds and fountains, and some of the windows opened to the garden.

The queen stopped at the third door and Feorus pushed it open for them to enter. The only feature of this small room was a spiral staircase in the center surrounding a white pillar. Light entered from overhead, and when they climbed above the ceiling level, she saw why. They were in a large tube of translucent glass.

They stopped at the next level so that her mother could explain how to get around. "The door on your right leads into your suite, and the one on the left is to a hallway you can use to reach other rooms and suites. Our suite is to the left at the end of this corridor" She saw Aisling's bewilderment and added, "Don't worry, Feorus and Opela can show you the way to wherever you want to go."

"This is the family residence floor. Above us is the administration level. And below are the kitchens, laundry, storerooms, and so on.

The queen led them to a wide door about halfway along the hallway and Feorus hastened to open the door for her to enter. "This is your suite," she said. "There should be everything you need, and if we've missed anything, ask Opela or Feorus. If you want to change anything, the colours or arrangement, Feorus is the one to consult. This is the sitting room, and beside it are rooms for sleeping and hygiene."

Aisling gaped. The room overlooked a garden with a fountain, its walls were pale turquoise with bands of purple and white flowers around the ceiling. The sitting room was furnished with low bamboo tables with chairs, and a sofa upholstered in lilac. She'd never seen such a lovely room. She looked at the queen—she still

239

couldn't believe this was her mother—and asked her, "All this is for me?"

Fenella drew her into a hug and kissed her cheek. "It's all yours. I hope you like it."

"I feel as if I'm in the Fields of the Ancestors. I love it."

"Good. Now look around and change into something fresh—there are some new clothes in your bedroom. Are you hungry?"

"I am a bit."

"Well, when you are ready, have Feorus bring you to the royal suite to meet your father and we'll have something to eat together. Don't be long; he's very anxious to see you."

When Queen Fenella turned to leave, a fairy fluttered in and landed by her arm. After chirping a message, she flew away. The queen laughed. "A message from your father. He's getting impatient. I'll go and sooth him, but hurry. It's you he wants to see."

Now dressed in a pale-yellow gown with a white mantle, Aisling almost felt like a princess. "These are for you," Opela said, pointing to a tray of sparkling ornaments. "Do you want to try some?"

"Not too much," Aisling said. "I'm not used to fancy things."

"Opela sorted through them and picked out an amethyst on a gold chain. "This will look good with your gown."

Feorus was waiting outside the door when they left Aisling's suite. He led them to the royal suite which was the last door down the hallway. He opened the door, bowed to the king and queen, and to her astonishment, announced her as if she was someone important. "Her Royal Highness, Princess Aisling."

She was surprised when she saw the king, her father, for the first time. She had expected an old man with a white beard, but he was tall and slender with golden hair and no beard. He didn't look much older than she was. He rose from the table and came towards her slowly, as if he wanted to prolong the moment, then he held out his arms and drew her into a tight embrace. He released her and stood for a moment with his hands on her shoulders looking at her face. "My little girl!" Tears started to roll down his face and he couldn't go on. Aisling's eyes filled as well. After wiping his face with the back of his hand, the king put his hand on her back. "Let's eat," he said.

The next few days were a whirlwind of exploring, meeting people, and becoming acquainted with her parents and the other residents of the palace. She discovered that the palace was far bigger than she'd first assumed. There were residential suites for employees and visitors, large banquet rooms and assembly halls. The service rooms, laundry, sewing rooms, and kitchens, could fill twenty Enisdale houses. There was a library, galleries for displaying works of art, a music room, an armoury, and stables that housed not only horses, but two unicorns as well. The gardens of ornamental flower compositions, orchards, gardens for growing vegetables and herbs. She realized there were no food animals like sheep, poultry and pigs.

"We don't eat animals or birds," Feorus explained.

"What about cattle?" she asked.

241

"They are raised on separate land because they use up their grazing area too rapidly, so they have to be moved frequently. We only keep them for milk products, which we buy from the farmers."

"I'm glad to hear that," Aisling said. "I would miss cheese and cream."

Irial returned on the third day and joined the royal family for dinner that evening. Everyone had questions for him, so it was a prolonged meal, followed by retirement to the sitting room for drinks.

"What happened after we left?" Aisling asked. She'd already heard about the executions and Momo Tilly's death, but she was interested in hearing about the slaves.

"There was a town nearby that agreed to take them in temporarily. We supplied some gold to help cover their expenses. Once they're fit, they'll go to their own homes," Irial informed her.

"What about Lena?"

"She went directly to her old home to look for her son."

"I didn't know she had a son," Aisling said. "I hope she finds him. She'll be a good mother."

"I agree. I invited her to bring him to visit you," Irial said.

"That would be wonderful. I'd love to see her again." She turned to her parents who were listening with smiles on their faces. "I don't know what I would have done without her," she said. "She saved my life. She'd learned their language and could speak to them for me."

"How is she going to contact us if she wants to come?" Aisling asked.

"I've given her a list of contacts who can pass on messages."

"You said she was a teacher," the queen said. "Maybe we could employ her here to teach the students about the Mid-Realms."

"That would be wonderful!" Aisling said. "I wonder what age her son is. Did she tell you?"

"He's around eight years," Irial replied.

"That's nice." Aisling was a bit disappointed. She was hoping he might be closer to her own age, which reminded her of her own anniversary day. She felt a bit confused for a moment, wondering what she would call the queen. So far, she'd avoided that dilemma, but she had to call her something. She's never had anyone she could remember to call mother, only gran.

As if she'd been tuned into Aisling's thoughts, the queen said, "Why don't you call me mother?"

Aisling blushed. "All right. Mother, can you tell me when my anniversary day is and how old I am?"

"There, that wasn't too hard was it?" her mother replied with a smile. "No mother forgets the birth of her child. You were born on the third day of Silverlight, fifteen years ago."

"What is it now?"

"It's the fifteenth day of Fallingleaves."

"Is that before or after Silverlight?"

"Before. Silverlight is the next season, so your anniversary will be in twenty days. And we will have the biggest celebration festival in living memory."

"So will I be sixteen then?"

"No, my love, you'll be fifteen."

The king yawned. "I don't know about the rest of you, but I'm getting tired." He stood up and put his hand on his wife's shoulder. "Ready, my love?"

Aisling stood up and waited. Both parents kissed and hugged her, before they left.

"Wait for me, Irial!" He was already at the door, so she hurried to catch up with him. Feorus was waiting in the hallway. Irial turned to see what she wanted. "Do you live at the palace?" she asked.

"Yes. I have rooms on the third level in the west wing, why?"

"I'll see you around sometimes; I'm glad. Good night!"

Feorus walked beside her to the door of her own suite and opened it for her. She'd noticed him stifling a yawn. "I know you're tired," she said. "It's boring just standing around waiting for someone. You don't have to do that, you know. It's not as if I have far to go to get to my room., and my parents' guards are always close by. Now, go to bed."

"That's very thoughtful of you, my lady, but it's part of my training."

They were still standing in the open doorway. "Come in for a moment, then." once they were inside, Opela joined them. "What are you training for?" Aisling asked.

"I'm going to be a guardian like Irial. He's my instructor when he's not off on a mission for the king."

"I'm sorry I've taken so much of his time lately," Aisling said. "Maybe he'll stay put for a while now. You'd better go now and get some rest."

36 – A surprise visitor

∾∾

A few days later, the king sent for her. "We have a problem and it might be something that affects you," he said. "I want you to go with Irial and Feorus to help sort it out."

"What's it about?" Aisling asked.

"They'll fill you in on the way."

Since she wore filmy lounging clothes around the palace, she had to change into something more suitable for going outside. Opela brought her an outfit with long trousers and a hip-length tunic. She found Feorus waiting outside the door.

"Do you ride, your highness?" he asked her.

"I haven't had much experience, no."

"Don't worry, we have just the mount for you. There are only two of them and they can only be ridden by female members of the royal family. Let's meet Irial at the stables."

Aisling followed him down the stairs and out through one of the floor-to-ceiling windows into the garden "I wish someone would tell me what's going on," she said as she hurried with him to the stables.

"I'm not sure myself, so I'll let Irial explain." Feorus replied.

Most of the horses were outside in one of the grassy fields, but three were standing with Irial in the courtyard outside the fence. She gasped when she saw the beautiful blue horse and saw the silver spiked horn on its forehead. Is that a unicorn?" she asked.

"She is," Irial replied. "And she's all yours. Come and meet her."

"I can't believe it," she said. "It doesn't look a bit like the ones in children's fairy tales." She stood by the creature's head and put her hand out to stroke its beautiful silver mane.

"I don't like to be called 'It' if you don't mind. I'm not a thing." A deep haughty female voice came from the direction of the unicorn, but it's mouth didn't move.

"You can talk! That's amazing. I won't say 'it' again, I promise." She felt intimidated by the creature's ability to talk and her voice sounded so assertive. "How do you talk to me?"

"I talk to your mind," she replied. "Now, let's get on with this. Climb on!"

Aisling saw Irial and Feorus smile at her.

"Her name is Hermione, by the way," Irial said. "Help her up!" he instructed Feorus.

Hermione was slightly smaller than the horses, so Aisling didn't have far to climb up into the saddle. To her surprise, the saddle was padded with what looked like lamb's wool and was very soft.

"Ready?" Hermione said.

"Yes," Aisling replied. "Where are the reins?

"You don't need reins, and you don't need to kick or poke me either. I know where I'm going and if you want to stop, just tell me. We'll get along fine as long as you follow my rules and remember I'm a person."

"Yes, Hermione," Aisling answered meekly.

They left the palace grounds by a back gate into a lane where the trees were turning multiple hues of red and gold. Berry bushes in the hedgerow looked ripe for picking and swarms of colourful birds were taking advantage of the bounty.

"This place is so lovely," Aisling said to Irial who was riding beside her on a sleek black mare. "My father said you would tell me what this is about. Is it something serious or dangerous?"

"No, It's quite funny in a way. A young Korrigan was found forlorn and lost in the tunnels. We thought you might know him."

Aisling frowned. "Don't tell me it's *the boy*," she said with a sigh.

"It might be. That's what we need to find out, and what he was doing in the tunnels all by himself."

"I don't understand their language," she replied. "So I wouldn't be much use to you."

"Don't worry about that. We have an interpreter at the confinement centre."

"What will happen to him?" she asked. "I thought he didn't want to come here."

"He seems to have changed his mind, I suppose."

"What if he wants to stay here? Will they let him?"

"As I said, we'll have to wait and see."

The confinement centre was a round brick building close to the tunnel Gateway. Like every building Aisling had seen, it was surrounded by bushes and flowerbeds.

They left their mounts in a nearby grassy field and walked to the wooden door that stood open.

Irial led them inside where he addressed a young elven woman sitting at a table braiding yarn. "Where is he?"

"Nice to see you, too, Irial," she replied, putting her handwork down on the table and standing up.

"I'm sorry, Dara, I'm becoming distracted in my old age. Let me introduce my companions, "This beautiful young lady is Princess Aisling, and this is my apprentice, Feorus." He waited until the greetings were completed and continued. "Do you want to bring him out?"

She went into another room and returned with a very downcast young Korrigan. He flicked his eyes up to look at them, focussing on Aisling, and then dropped them to look at the floor. Aisling had noticed the fleeting hope in his eyes when he looked at her.

"Shall we all sit down while we talk?" Irial suggested. "Bring him over here," he added

Dara gently took the boy's arm and led him to the seat that backed on the wall, and then arranged some more chairs in a semicircle in front of him. "Do you want me to record everything?" she asked.

"If you wouldn't mind," Irial replied. "His majesty is sure to ask me something I've forgotten."

Aisling expected the attendant to take out a notebook and pen, but she just sat down on one of the chairs and started talking to the boy in the Korrigan tongue. He replied in a barely audible voice, still not looking at anyone.

He's very scared, Aisling thought. I wish I could do something to reassure him.

"Don't worry about it," Irial said. "We're not going to harm him."

"I wish you could tell him that."

"Dara already did so, your highness." He turned to Dara. "What did you find?"

"His name is Olgon." The boy's head snapped up when he heard his name, and he stared at Aisling.

"So it is him," Aisling said. She smiled at the boy, who scowled back at her.

"Yes," Irial said. "Ask him why he was wandering around alone in the tunnels."

Another brief exchange took place. "He said the princess invited him to come here."

"But he turned down my offer," Aisling retorted.

The interview continued for a while. The result of the interchange was that Olgon had changed his mind; he didn't want to go to the underworld with the women and children of his tribe, so he managed to hide somewhere once the dwarfs took them into the tunnels. He now wanted to take up the offer her highness made to him.

"What are we going to do with him?" Aisling asked Irial.

"That's up to you and your parents," he replied. "Shall we take him back to the palace with us?"

"I suppose so. What else could we do?"

"We could leave him here or turn him over to the dwarfs." Irial said.

"No. He's scared enough already. If we go away and leave him, it will be worse. Let's take him to the palace and find somewhere to put him. Will he have to stay in confinement?" Aisling asked.

"For a while," Irial replied. "Until we know he can be trusted."

Olgon was terrified of the horses and had to be manually restrained and forcibly placed behind Feorus on his horse. He clung to Feorus's back as if his life was at stake. Once they arrived at the stables, Irial lifted him down and ordered him to "Stay!" in Korrigan tongue.

"I didn't know you could speak Korrigan," Aisling said.

"I know about three words, and that is one of them," Irial replied.

Aisling looked at Olgon who was standing perfectly still on the pavement hardly daring to move his head, although he must have been curious about his new surroundings. He held his body stiffly, but she could see he was trembling. *I know how he feels,* she thought. *That's how I felt when I saw the Korrigen.*

She wanted to do something to reassure him, but she had to take care of Hermione. She turned to look at the unicorn who hadn't moved from the place she'd dismounted.

"I wondered when you would get around to me," the unicorn said, tossing her head.

"What do you need?" Aisling asked. She was amused by Hermione's attitude, but also a bit intimidated by her.

251

Vicki Wootton

"Take me to my quarters and bring me some food and water. And make sure the water is clean and put some honey in my oats."

"Where do you live?" Aisling asked. Surely, she knows how to get to her own stable, Aisling thought.

"Follow me!" the unicorn set off around the back of the horse stables and stopped at a rather pleasant chalet. "This is my home. And don't *ever* call it a stable!"

It certainly wasn't a stable. It was built of highly varnished wooden slats with a roof of woven bamboo. Flowers and herbs grew in front of it and a fountain stood in the middle. There was another structure beside it with woven straw walls and an opening at the narrow end, and next to that was a similar chalet, but it didn't appear to be occupied at the moment.

"Your home is beautiful," Aisling commented.

"Thank you," Hermione replied. "I designed it myself. Now, what about my refreshments?"

"I'm on my way." Aisling knew that it was the time to ask for help. She headed back around the stables and bumped into Feorus.

"I was just coming to get you," he said.

"Hermione wants something to eat," Aisling told him.

Feorus shook his head. "Good old Hermione. She's training you I see. Don't pay too much attention when she gets bossy. She just wants to be assured that she has the upper hand. The stable staff will take care of it; that's their job. Your job is being the princess." He led her to the stable entrance and called one of the stable hands. "Fergus, meet Princess Aisling. She's going to be riding Hermione now. She's been throwing her weight around, trying to turn the princess into her servant. Would you take her some oats? Oh, and don't forget the honey!"

"I'll have a talk with her when I take her refreshment," Fergus replied with a laugh.

"She said she wants some clean water as well," Aisling added.

Fergus shook his head. "The fountain was put out there for her to get fresh water. She must be really impressed by you, your highness, to go to such lengths."

After Fergus went about his business, Aisling asked Feorus, "What happened to the Korrigan?"

"Irial's put him under guard in the staff dining room and they're giving him something to eat. He wants you to meet him in the royal suite."

When Aisling arrived at her parents' suite, she was surprised to see Olgon. He was sitting on the floor, rocking back and forth with his head bent. There was another elf there, an elder by the look of him. He was the first elf she'd seen with wrinkled skin and darker hair than the others.

"Come and join us, my sweet," the queen said. "Sit over here near me." She indicated a small padded chair.

Aisling dipped her knee and bowed her head to the king before she sat down. She'd seen the servants do that.

"I hear you've met Hermione," the king said with a grin.

"Yes. She's amazing."

"Don't let her boss you around; she works for you, not vice versa," he said. "Now, down to business. We must decide what to do with this young creature. Any ideas?"

"Before we get to that, may I introduce Aisling to our interpreter?" The king nodded. "Aisling, meet the Honourable Master Parthalán. He is the oldest and wisest elf in Lycea."

Aisling bowed to the elderly elf, who was sitting on a cushion on the floor. "Pleased to meet you ...." She didn't know how to address him and looked at her mother for guidance.

"We all address him as Honourable Master," the queen said. "Master Parthalán is going to help us understand the boy." She looked at her husband. "I would like to suggest something. I think the first thing we need to do is teach him how to speak our language."

"Good idea," the king said. "What's he going to do if he stays here? Can he be trusted, or will we have to keep him under guard all the time?"

Aisling noticed that the Honourable Master was talking softly to Olgon as the King spoke. Olgon mumbled a few words that made Master Parthalán smile. "He says he is going to marry the princess." This response brought on a chorus of gasps and shocked faces.

"Whatever gave him that idea?" the king asked.

"He says his grandfather promised him she would be his bride, and she invited him to come here with her." The way he expresses it is, "She's a princess, and he's a prince, so it would be proper."

"I think it should be made plain to him that is out of the question." The king shook his head. "What a nerve. Is that why they kidnapped her?"

They watched Orgon as the old man spoke to him and saw him nod his head. "Tell him, Master Parthalán, that his position here, if we allow him to stay, would be tantamount to slavery. He knows all about slavery but let him know that we are not as ruthless and cruel as his people, and we don't eat our slaves. He will have to be trained in an occupation and learn to speak the language but, until he proves himself trustworthy, he will be held under guard."

When the young Korrigan heard this, he rolled onto his face and sobbed as if his heart would break. Aisling felt so sorry for him, she knelt beside him and placed her hand on his back. "You'll be all right," she said. "This is a wonderful place to live." She looked to the old man to interpret what she's said.

The only response they got from Orgon was a shake of his head, then he got up and ran from the room.

"Shall I go after him?" Aisling asked.

"Take Feorus with you," the king said.

Feorus, who had been waiting outside the door, pointed to the garden when Aisling came out. "He went that way. Do you want me to catch him?"

"Let me go with you. Maybe he'll listen to me."

They ran through the garden, following a path that led past the stables and out onto the lane behind the palace, but there was no sign of the boy.

"Don't you have some way of sensing him?" Aisling said.

255

"Hold on, let me try." He closed his eyes for a moment. "That way," he said, pointing in the opposite direction of the one they'd taken earlier.

The trail left the lane and continued into the woods beyond. They found him lying on the ground a few steps from the lane, his yellowish blood running from a short knife piercing his neck. His face was crumpled with pain and tears streamed from his eyes, but he was alive.

Aisling rushed to him and fell to her knees beside him. "What are you trying to do Orgon?"

She reached out for the knife, but Feorus intervened before she could pull it out. "Leave it where it is, your highness" he said. "Let the healer take it out. He'll know how to do it safely. I'm going to carry him back to the palace. Would you run ahead and alert Irial?"

Aisling went directly to her parents' suite, hoping Irial was still there. She was out of breath by the time she reached the door. Holding onto the wall, she took a deep breath. "Orgon's been hurt," she said. "Feorus wants Irial to meet him out by the stables."

"What happened to him?" her father asked.

"He cut his neck," she replied. Irial was already out the door. "May I be excused?" Aisling asked.

"Go," the king said. "And take Master Parthalán to interpret."

"Let us know how it goes," her mother added.

This time, she walked instead of running to accommodate the Master, although he walked briskly. They returned to the garden and turned towards the stables, but instead of continuing to the lane, he veered off to the left into the courtyard between the two wings. "This way," he said. "They must have taken him to the healing suite." He led Aisling to one of the doors, slid the glass panel open, and stepped inside.

There were two healers standing over the bench on which Orgon lay. Aisling was glad to see that the knife had been removed from his neck and the damage was covered with a bandage.

"How is he?" she asked.

"He'll live," Irial replied.

"Do you want me to talk to him?" Master Parthalán asked.

"You can try, but he is sedated, so he might not be very responsive."

"Let me try something," the Master said. He laid his hand on Orgon's shoulder for a moment and then nodded his head. He then said a few words to Orgon.

"I told him we mean him no harm and we will not punish him. He can be happy here." He nodded towards the inner door of the room, signalling them to follow him.

After a few words with the healers, Irial followed them out. "He'll be all right there for the time being," he said. "Let's go to the guard room and talk about this."

They went a short distance down the hallway towards the front of the building and entered another room that was furnished with tables and chairs. Several guards were sitting at a table near the window that overlooked the courtyard, eating.

"I don't know about you, but I'm getting hungry," Irial said. Almost before he finished talking, several fairies flew in and started arranging food and drinks on a table for them, chirping to one another as they worked.

As she sat there with the elves, eating their strange but delightful food, Aisling realized how much her life had changed. It was beyond anything she would ever have expected. Being served by fairies, living in a palace, a unicorn that talks for her to ride, magic healing. *I hope I don't wake up and find it was all a dream.*

"How did he get hold of a dagger?" Irial asked.

"I don't know," Feorus replied. "But we do tend to leave things lying around. He could have picked it up anywhere."

"We'll have to be more careful from now on. We're lucky he didn't use it on the princess. He was obviously very upset by her rejection."

"It's more than that," the Master said. "He is in a state of complete despair. He feels he has no reason to stay alive."

"Do you think he'll try again?" Irial asked.

"I believe it is a certainty unless we can give him some hope. You must realize he's very young and young people often think everything is either black or white; perfectly good or totally bad."

"That's interesting," Irial said. "I think we need to discuss this with their majesties. Is everyone ready?"

37 – A place for the newcomer

As I see it, we have two options," King Briartach said. "We can either send the boy back to his people or find a way to make him contented."

"Could we try the second option first," Queen Fenella said. "And if that doesn't work, we could send him back. What do you think, sweetheart?" she asked Aisling.

"I think we should do what you suggest," she replied.

"And how do we make him happy?" the king asked.

"Make him feel he is welcome and give him something meaningful to do. He needs a reason to live and treating him like a prisoner or an outcast won't help," the queen added.

"We have to keep a watch on him," Irial said. "He's already shown us how far he will go."

"And we have to take more care of our weapons and tools," the king said.

"I have an idea," Aisling said. "Could you have the fairies keep an eye on him? They're all over the place. I've become so used to them, I hardly notice they're there."

"That's a good idea. Would anyone suspect that fairies are spying on us?" The queen said.

"They probably are," the king replied.

"But they have another advantage," Irial said. "They can make themselves intangible. He wouldn't even see them, if they didn't want to be seen."

࿐

The first activity they tried with Olgon was exploration. Aisling and Feorus took him sightseeing, noting the things that he seemed interested in. At the same time, he was given language lessons so that he could communicate with the elves. This was something he seemed to enjoy, although he found it difficult at first.

Aisling was delighted to have this opportunity to familiarise herself with her new home. One of the things she found remarkable about Lycea was the feeling of security she experienced. She felt safe here. She told her mother about this, and her mother replied, "It's not perfectly safe," she said. "There are always forces at our borders waiting for an opportunity to invade us."

"What sort of forces?" she asked.

"You may have noticed that there is a balance in nature. Often good is met by a corresponding evil. Our lives are spent trying to contain the evil and turn the balance in our favour. We've done that to a certain extent in Lycea, but we must be constantly on our guard to keep the dark forces out."

"Were the Korrigen one of these forces?"

"They were," the queen replied. "They brought no end of trouble to our shores. There are still remnants around. We have only dealt with one group, the

Northern Korrigen. But the Southern group may still be within our borders."

When Aisling went exploring, she was accompanied by two guards, Feorus and one of his fellow students whose name was Einri, and of course Olgon. One of the things they noticed that seemed to fascinate Olgon was the vegetation. He was constantly stopping to examine something and asking what it was called. He also liked most of the animals they encountered, particularly cats, which came in a profusion of varieties ranging from tigers to domestic and minis—tiny felines that generally lived in trees to avoid being killed by rats.

Olgon had been afraid when he first met a panther in the forest, and had tried to hide behind the two guards, but was surprised when Einri spoke as he walked towards it and stroked the big cat's head.

He looked at Feorus, screwing up his forehead as he tried to form a question while pointing at the panther.

"Friend," Feorus said.

Olgon was still unable to ask what he wanted to know, so he pointed to himself, "Friend me?"

Feorus shook his head. He didn't know what the animal's reaction would be to such an alien being, but he took Olgon by the arm and brought him closer to the big animal who was now licking its paw. It stopped its grooming and sniffed at the boy, then it growled deep in its throat. "No," Feorus said. "She is not inclined to be friendly. Maybe if she gets used to you, she will change."

Olgon didn't understand much of what Feorus said, but he did recognise 'no'. It seemed to be the most common thing he heard from everyone. "Go now," he said.

One day, they visited the Crystal Falls, a high wall of white rock with water falling in hundreds of little rivulets into a brilliant pool of blue green water. The pool, which was at least a hundred body-lengths long and about forty wide, was surrounded by white sand, willow trees and graceful reeds.

It's the most beautiful place I've ever seen," Aisling said. "What are those flowers called?" She had noticed a cluster of blue flowers at one end of the pool.

"They're water hyacinths," Einri said. "You should get closer and smell them," he added.

Aisling walked around to where she could almost touch them and was overwhelmed by the beautiful aroma emanating from the flowers.

"They call this the Fountain of Youth," Feorus said, walking up behind them.

"Is it really?" she asked.

Feorus smiled. "It's possible, but I haven't heard of anyone testing it. It is very healthy for bathing because of the minerals in the water."

Irial

Olgon's preferred occupations boiled down to two, working with animals, or gardening. When he had said he would like to learn defensive skills, the king had vetoed that idea. "We don't know what he would do if we put weapons in his hands," he said. They started him off working in the stables, but it soon became obvious that the big animals frightened him, so they decided to give him a try with smaller animals like sheep, poultry and rabbits. He was soon taken off that duty after he was caught wringing the neck of a rabbit.

"You can't go around killing livestock like that," Irial told him.

"But I hungry, and fur make nice blanket," the young Kerrigan explained.

"It will take more than one skin to make a blanket," Feorus said. "and how did you intend to eat it?"

"I make fire over there," he replied nodding towards the woods across the lane.

"Let's go and take a look," Irial said, taking the boy's arm.

What he found in the woods took him by surprise. Apart from a firepit surrounded with stones and animal bones, there was a bag hanging from a tree branch filled with feathers and animal skins. "You can't do this," he told the boy. "From now on, we are going to have you watched." *Why had the fairies not reported it?*

"I'm afraid we'll have to put you to work on the farm. You seem to have an affinity for plants, so you can help the gardeners and harvesters. And no more killing. Don't we give you enough to eat?"

Olgon looked down at the ground, scuffing the soil and ashes with his bare foot. He did not look very pleased with this new turn of events. "It not my food," he mumbled.

38 – Leán
❧

One afternoon Aisling was returning to her suite after her magic class when a woman coming towards her caught her attention. She looked familiar. Aislings stopped, her forehead wrinkling. *Where have I seen her before?* It was the red hair that made her memorable.

The woman came closer and stopped in front of her. "Aisling?"

I know that voice. "Have I met you?" she asked.

"I didn't think you'd remember. Walk with me and I'll explain," the woman replied.

They went out into the garden and stopped near the fountain. "I'm Leán," she said. "I was your mother when we were in the Mid-Realm."

Aisling's heart jumped, and her eyes filled with tears. She sniffed and wiped her face with the back of her hand. "I remember you," she said. "Why did you leave me?"

"I couldn't help it, love. I was ordered to return to the Realm of Light." She put her hand out to comfort Aisling, but she flinched and stepped back. "I'm sorry, Aisling. I didn't want to leave, but there were fears that our identity might be discovered. The Korrigen had been seen in the Mid-Realm, and it was becoming more difficult to hide that I was an elf with so many strangers coming and going. My cousin thought you would be safer with gran, who was not an elf. Believe me, I didn't want to leave you, my precious."

Aisling pondered this for a moment, trying to sort out her feelings. "How did they find you? Did you get in trouble for taking me away?"

"Oh, it was not hard for them to trace me. We have contacts all over the Mid-Realm who send reports of unusual happenings in their areas. One of them must have sensed magic somewhere close." She sighed. "As for punishment, the answer is yes I was punished, stripped of some of my powers."

"Is that bad?"

"It's devastating," Leán said. "It's like losing a part of your body, but I had no right to make such a decision. I suppose I was too young to judge the wisdom of what I was doing. I'm also banished from the palace," she added.

"So how did you get in here?"

"I asked my cousin to allow me to tell you how sorry I am for what has happened to you, and she agreed."

"Who's your cousin?"

"Queen Fenella," she replied.

"So you are my, what?"

"Cousin, I suppose. Shall we go back inside?" she said. "I think your parents would like us to join them for the midday meal."

Vicki Wootton

39 – The search
꙳

Aisling woke with a start. It was still dark outside, and the only sound was the wind in the trees near her window. She snapped her fingers to bring on some light and looked around her room, but there was nothing there. It did not feel right, but she couldn't place what was causing the feeling, except that something seemed to be missing. *Oh, well, nothing I can do about it.* She snapped off the light and went back to sleep.

Later that morning, Irial stuck his head through the door of Aisling's classroom. "Has anyone seen Olgon?" he asked. "He didn't turn up for his language class, and he isn't in the fields."

"No," Aisling replied. Her instructor and the other students shook their heads. It's strange, but I woke up in the night with a funny feeling, as if something was missing."

"That might mean something," Steofán, the instructor, said. "Come in, Irial, we might be able to help you."

"How so?" Irial said, closing the door behind him.

"I was about to start teaching these young people how to use their roving senses to find something lost. I think maybe we could use to locate the Korrigan," he said.

266

"I've scanned the area, already along with some of my colleagues," Irial said. "I came back to get a tracking dog to follow his scent."

"We can take the search farther afield," Steofán said. "Anyone up for some horseback riding?"

All three students stood, enlivened by the thought of going somewhere outside the classroom.

They made their way to the stables where some horses were already saddled. Aisling went over to Hermione. "Good morning," she said, stroking the unicorn's mane.

"It's about time we went for a ride. I need exercise, you know." Hermione replied.

"Can't the stable hands take you out?" Aisling asked.

"It's not the same," the unicorn said. "I can only be ridden by females of royal blood."

"I forgot about that," Aisling said. "I'm sorry I've neglected you, Hermione. I'll try to take you out more often. Maybe my mother could go with us on her unicorn."

"We'll see. Get on or they'll leave without us."

They followed the other riders out into the lane where Hermione immediately moved to the front of the column.

"I'm sorry to inconvenience you, Hermione, but I'm afraid we'll have to allow the dog to lead us because he's going to track the scent and show us where to go,"

Hermione tossed her head and snorted. "Very well, if I must, but you realize it's humiliating for me to have to follow a mere dog."

Vicki Wootton

Before they started the search, Irial took out one of Olgon's skirts. He held it out and let the dog sniff it. "Good girl, Flancy. Find him."

Flancy sniffed the skirt and gave a little bark and a tail wag, looking up adoringly at Irial. She was a beautiful dog, tall with long golden hair and a noble head with a white patch on her forehead. She went slowly at first, carefully scanning the area before giving a little woof and setting off in an easterly direction, her nose to the ground.

"What puzzles me," Irial said as they rode out the gate, "I don't sense his life force. I think we have to prepare for the worst, I'm afraid."

"You mean he's dead?" Aisling said.

"Maybe," Irial replied. "It's either that or he's moved to another realm."

"How could he do that without going through the tunnels?"

"He might be able to if he met some of his own people and they took him. They can move through the mountain caves where there's a portal. They got into our portal, so they must have some ability to pass through."

Flancy went slowly in a meandering path. After a time, she barked and took off into the woods beside the lane. "I think she's found something," Irial said, dismounting. Everyone else followed suit.

"Does anyone sense anything?" Steofán asked the students.

One of the boys shrugged, the other shook his head. "I don't," Aisling said.

"Nor me," Steofán added. "That means he may not be alive. Let's wait here and see what Irial finds.

Irial came back, shaking his head. "It looks as if he stopped here to rest and cook something to eat." he said. "There were signs of a struggle, so he may have been captured by someone or something. Let's see where she takes us." He patted the dog on her head and gave her a piece of dried meat. "Good girl. Go!"

She continued her meandering path for a few more lengths and once more took to the woods. There were scrape marks along the path as if something had been dragged along.

"This isn't getting me any exercise at all," Hermione complained. "If we have to keep stopping all the time, I might as well have stayed at home."

"I'm sorry, Hermione. I'll take you out tomorrow, I promise." She knew the unicorn was bullying her, but she didn't know how to respond." *Maybe mother can show me how she handles it.* The unicorn snorted and shook her head.

As they followed Flancy into the woods, Aisling realized that the feeling of trepidation was back. Something was wrong, but she couldn't identify what it was. "Does anyone else feel something bad?" she asked.

Irial, who was directly behind her answered, "you mean like anxiety? Yes, I feel it, and it's not a good sign."

The dog started barking ahead of them on the path, then she whined.

"I smell blood," Hermione said. She started to trot a little faster, despite Aisling's trying to hold her back.

"Hermione stay where you are!" Irial said sharply. "Let me go and find out what's happened first."

He dismounted and went ahead, but returned a moment later, shaking his head. "Something was killed back there, but there's no way to tell what it was," he said.

"A doe," Hermione said.

"Thank you, Hermione. Let's continue," Irial said. "How are the students doing?"

"They're doing well in spite of the stress they're undergoing," Steofán said. "We have that ominous feeling that something bad is about to happen."

"We'll take a break when we come to a stream," Irial said. "I brought some honey cakes in case anyone is feeling hungry."

"I love honey cakes," Hermione said. "Let's hurry!"

"Who said you were getting any?" Irial said.

Hermione snorted. *Don't worry, he doesn't mean it. I'll get one for you,* Aisling mind-sent to her.

After the break, Flancy led them to higher ground where there were fewer trees and the soil over the rocky base became thinner. They were at the foot of the mountain.

Irial looked at the sky. "I think we should turn back now if we want to be home before sundown," he said to the others.

"But what if he's lying hurt somewhere?" Aisling objected.

"I don't sense any life apart from that of the wild creatures," Irial said. "Does anyone else?"

Nobody did, so Irial continued, "We can return on the morrow if you feel it is necessary, your highness. It's my job to get you home safely and I think it is time to give up. Remember, he brought this on himself and we can't keep wasting our time looking for him when he is either departed or has been abducted." Flancy was lying on the ground with her head resting on her paws, panting. "I think Flancy is ready for a rest, and she still has to walk all the way back."

"All right," Aisling said. "I'm getting tired too."

"How do you think I feel?" Hermione said. "Traipsing all over the place going nowhere."

Aisling stroked her mane. "I know and I'm sorry to put you through this." She turned to Irial, who was carrying their supplies. "Are there any honey cakes left?"

Irial rummaged through his satchel and came up with one that had been squashed under other things. He handed it to her and watched her give it to the unicorn. "You're going to spoil her, you know," he said with a grin. "There'll be no living with her before long."

Hermione swallowed the morsel in one gulp, looking at him scornfully, and then snorted. "Well, let's go if we're going. You're the one who was in such a hurry."

40 – Aisling meets a dragon
❧

The next day, Aisling, Irial, and Feorus left at dawn and returned to the mountain. This time they brought a wheeled basket that could be hitched behind a horse so that Flancy would be able to rest when she got tired. Before they left the stables, Aisling asked Hermione if she would like to stay home and she'd take a horse instead. This resulted in a display of foot stamping, snorting, and head tossing. Hermione was insulted. "I will go," she said. "You are mine, not some frowsy horse." That settled it.

They moved a lot faster now that they were retracing the route from the day before. They arrived at the mountain foothill and set Flancy tracking. "It's a good thing there was no rain last night to wash away the scent, but it will be fainter today," Irial commented.

Flancy continued from where she'd left off the day before and made her meandering way towards higher ground. They stopped at a mountain stream to water the animals, and then continued. The path took them around the mountain to a shelf that looked down into a wide valley where water fell from cliffs into a great pool bordered by rocks and trees. It then escaped through a narrow gap to become a river that foamed its way through more rocks and disappeared out of sight below the rapids.

"It's beautiful," Aisling said. "This is the sort of place I imagine dragons would live."

"Look over there," Feorus said, pointing to a steep ledge across the valley.

Once she saw the puffs of flame-tinged smoke, she realized she'd been right. "Is this their home?" she asked.

"This is where the blue dragons live," Irial replied. "They dwell mostly in that valley but they're never still; always on the lookout for game or enemies. They've been at odds with the red dragons for over a hundred years and sometimes still raid each other's domains."

"Are they the same ones who came to help you find me?"

"Yes. These are the ones closest to Lycea."

"Oh, look," Aisling cried. "It looks as if it's coming here. Should we hide?"

"No, there's nothing to be afraid of. We have a treaty of mutual respect with them. He's probably curious."

The horses were not reassured by this and started to back away, shivering and tossing their heads. Even Hermione danced around restlessly. "We'd better get them to a safe place," Feorus said. I'll take them down around the bend and find a place to hide them."

Irial dismounted and handed his reins to Feorus. Aisling jumped down from Hermione's back. "Do you want to go with them?"

Hermione blew out her lips. "I'm not some puny snivelling horse," she said disdainfully. "Besides, if that's Felivar, I have a bone to pick with him."

Feorus had just disappeared around the edge of the mountain when a massive shadow fell over them. Aisling moved to Irial's side and clung to his arm. "Are you sure...?"

Before she could finish, the huge, terrifying creature was over them, flapping its leathery blue wings, preparing to land. Irial put his arm around Aisling while Hermione backed away as far as she could go against the mountainside. The dragon blew out a fiery breath over his back and dropped onto the shelf close to them. Too close for Aisling's liking. She clung to Irial's hand as if her life depended on it. Irial bowed. "Lord Felivar, well met."

"What are you doing here?" the dragon growled hoarsely, emitting small puffs of warm smoke.

"We are searching for a friend who has disappeared. We followed his trail to this area. I don't suppose you've seen any strangers in this vicinity, have you?"

The dragon stretched his neck and looked back over his shoulder to blow out a streak of flame, then he turned back to face them. "Aren't you going to introduce me to this sweet young creature?"

"Oh, I beg your pardon, my lord. This is Princess Aisling whom you recently helped us to rescue from the Korrigen." He bent and whispered in Aisling's ear, "thank him." at the same time conveying the thought, *don't want to upset him.*

Aisling gazed up into the huge blue eyes of the dragon feeling her knees weaken. She bowed. "Thank you for helping to rescue me, my lord," she said in a shaky voice.

"Yes, well." He turned and released another puff of fire. "About this friend you've lost. What race is it?"

"It's a young Korrigan boy. He was staying at the palace, but he disappeared suddenly."

Lord Felivar closed his eyes and shook his head. "Korrigan, eh? Well ... to tell you the truth, some of my boys found a group of them coming up here. Well, you know how they are, reckless and impulsive as always. I'm afraid they ate them."

No!" Aisling screeched and threw herself into Irial's arms, sobbing.

"She's upset," the dragon said, surprised. "I thought she would be happy about it after what they did to her." He looked over his shoulder again. "Well, I'll be off then, unless there's anything else."

Hermione immerged from her hiding place. "There certainly is," she said haughtily. "I haven't been compensated yet for the damage your boys did to my father's home. I put a lot of work and gold into constructing it for his retirement and now he's having to live in an old shack."

"Oh, it must have slipped my mind," the dragon answered. "I'll look into it immediately. As soon as I get back to the cave."

"You'd better," the unicorn said. "You can send the gold to the palace. That's where I live now." She tossed her head for emphasis, making her blue mane fly up around her face.

"Well, it was a pleasure to meet you all, especially you, princess," the dragon lord said. "I'm sorry about your friend. I will punish the boys for what they did." He hopped a few lengths down the ledge and took off across the valley leaving a trail of smoke behind him.

"Lot of good that will do," Hermione grumbled. "It won't bring him back. Let's go home!"

"All right, Hermione, we're on our way," Irial replied. He looked down at Aisling, who was still clinging to him, then raised his hand to stroke her head. She seemed to be frozen in place and he had to remove her arms gently from around his body. "Come on, Aisling, let's go back to the palace."

"What?"

"We have to go home. We know what happened to the boy and there's nothing we can do to change that, so we might as well give up and leave this place."

"I know," she murmured, looking around as if she'd lost something. "Where are the others?"

"Feorus took the horses down around the bend, and I don't know where...." A bark interrupted him. "Ah here she is," Flancy trotted up, tail wagging and tongue lolling. "He patted her neck and gently pushed her away to keep her from slobbering on him. "You're a good girl. Here, I have a treat for you." He dipped in his pack and came out with a crunchy meat biscuit. She snatched it from his hand and started to gnaw, still wagging her tail.

"Are we going to sit here all day," Hermione said tapping her front hoof on the ground.

"Be nice to Aisling. She's very upset and she doesn't need to hear your complaining."

The unicorn sidled closer to Aisling and nuzzled her arm. "I'm sorry about your friend. Are you ready to go now?"

Aisling rode home in a fog, what-ifs and if-onlies reeling though her mind. She went through necessary motions like an automaton.

"It's over," Irial said at one point. "There's nothing you could have done, so you don't have to feel guilty about what happened to Olgon. He chose his own path, made his own decisions. I'm not saying don't mourn his loss, but don't blame yourself."

"But if only I...."

"No!" Irial said a bit more sharply than he intended. "You can't change the past, Aisling."

Aisling went to bed early that night and woke the next morning feeling rested and refreshed. To her surprise, she had slept well. *Maybe someone put a spell on me*, she thought as she sat up and put her feet on the floor.

"Did you have a good sleep?" Opela asked, entering the room and pulling back the window curtains.

"I did," Aisling replied.

"It must be all that fresh air and exercise you've been getting recently."

It still hurts though, Aisling thought

"Your mother and father would like you to join them for breakfast," Opela said, looking through Aisling's wardrobe for a suitable outfit.

When Aisling arrived at the king and queen's dining room, she was surprised to see Irial was there too.

"Come in my love," Queen Fenella said, hugging her. "I'm glad to see you are well-rested. Irial has some good news for you."

Aisling's heart skipped a beat. She looked at him curiously and saw he was smiling. "What news?" she asked him.

I received a message last night from one of my contacts in the Mid-Realm. Lena and her son want to visit you."

Aisling was overjoyed. *Just the person I need right now*, she thought.

"Do you think we could get her to stay, mother?" she asked. "She's a school teacher; maybe she could teach elven children about the Mid-Realm."

"Sit down, Aisling. Have something to eat." Aisling sat next to the queen, across from Irial. "Now, let's get her here first and see how she feels. We could certainly use someone with her skills."

Aisling smiled and looked across at Irial through her eyelashes. "How soon could she get here?" she asked.

41 The boy's adventure

ॐ~ॐ

When he'd met the other Korrigen in the woods, Olgon had decided to join them. He had little hope of making a life here with the elves after Aisling had rejected him. The two Korrigen men had told him they had a settlement on the other side of the mountains that could be reached through a tunnel that started high up the mountainside.

"We have to watch out for dragons up there," one of them had warned him, "so keep your eyes open."

"What were you doing so far from home?" Olgon had asked.

"What do you think? We are watching them. We need to know if they are planning to attack us. What are you doing here?"

"I was a prisoner," Olgon had said. "I just escaped." He'd been too embarrassed to tell them the truth.

He went on and told them about how the Elves had destroyed his tribe and killed all the leaders. He'd claimed they'd taken him as a hostage but had omitted mentioning his relationship to the Loamin and Domin.

The trek through the forest and up the mountain had been exhausting. They'd kept themselves alive by killing animals along the way, sheep being their favourite. By the time they arrived at the entrance to the cave, they'd been hungry and exhausted.

The attention of one of the Korrigen was alerted by a deer he'd noticed as it emerged from a cluster of trees to drink at a mountain stream. He'd nudged his companion and the pair of them had gone after it, while Olgon sat down inside the cave entrance.

They had been so intent upon the deer, they hadn't noticed the creature with the large leathery wings that was swooping down on them until they felt the heat of its breath.

Olgon had retreated into the cave, hoping he wouldn't be noticed. The cries of his companions and the scent of roasting flesh had filled him with nausea as he backed deeper into the tunnel.

At first, he'd tried to find his way through the maze of tunnels to the Korrigen tribe's settlement but had become hopelessly lost. It had taken him several days to find his way out of the tunnel maze. He'd been close to despair, killing rats for food and drinking from little pools of water that trickled down the walls. When he'd finally found an exit, he wasn't sure where he was or what to do next.

Olgon had sat for a while outside the cave opening, looking at the scenery spread before him, the green of the trees and fields, the occasional white structures that were probably elven homes. Olgon's aesthetic senses had been developed in twilit caverns and had not been refined by the beauty of external landscapes, although he was starting to be drawn to some of the scenery he'd been exposed to recently.

He'd decided to just follow a trail no matter where it led him, although he'd still felt the urge to scan the sky for dragons every few steps he took. *What does it matter?* he'd asked himself. *I might just as well be dead, anyway.* The one thought that had kept him going was that there'd be more to eat now that he was in the open.

After walking for three days and sleeping under trees, he'd met a group of elves, two females and three males.

At the palace

Aisling and her parents were eating their evening meal by the open window of the royal dining room when a page arrived.

"Pardon me for interrupting your meal your highnesses," she said, addressing all three of them. "A messenger has arrived. He says he has some important information for you."

"Ask him to wait in the anteroom," the king replied. "We'll attend him there when we finish eating. We're almost done."

When the family emerged from the dining room, a young elf stood up and bowed to them. "Pardon me for disturbing your meal, your highnesses."

"You're forgiven," the king said with a smile. He and the queen sat down and picked up the drinks the fairies had left for them. "Here, help yourself to a refreshment. The king indicated the tray of glasses on the table in front of him. "Now, what is it you want to report, son?" the king asked.

The elf bowed again. "Everling, your highness. We heard about the search for the missing Korrigan boy. My colleagues and I may have found him."

"You ... he's alive?" Aisling said. "Where is he? Is he all right?"

"We brought him to the palace. He's now in the care of your guards. You see, we thought he might be an escaped prisoner. I hope I did the right thing," the young elf added.

"You did, Everling, you did," the king said. "We are grateful and thank you. Now, do you require accommodation for the night?"

When the messenger had departed with the page, Aisling asked, "what are we going to do about him?"

"I don't know about you, but I'm going to bed," her father replied. "We'll talk some more about it at daybreak."

On her way back to her suite, Aisling told Feorus she wanted to go to the guard room. When they arrived, she was surprised to see Irial was there with a very remorseful Olgon. The boy was sitting at a table opposite Irial, his head down, his fingers rolling a piece of bread into a hard pellet on the table.

"Greetings, your highness," Irial said, smiling at her. "Look who's come back to us!"

Aisling nodded to him and walked around the table to sit down adjacent to them. "Welcome back, Olgon," she said. He flicked his eyes up to glance at her and quickly refocused them back on the table. "We thought ... feared really ... that you'd been taken by the dragons. I'm so glad to see you are alive. How do you feel? Are you happy to be back?"

He seemed to be reluctant to speak. Aisling looked at Irial who shrugged. "I was asking him what he wanted to do now, but he isn't very forthcoming, I'm afraid."

"Hate me," Olgon muttered.

"We don't hate you," Aisling said.

"Not want me."

Aisling sighed. "I don't want to wed you, but there's no reason we can't be friends."

"Korrigan and elf not friends,"

"Has anyone here in the Realm of Light done anything to hurt you?" Irial asked him.

"Not like me," the boy repeated stubbornly.

Now it was Irial's turn to sigh. "You have to make yourself likeable," he said.

"How I do that?"

"Act friendly," Irial said. "Smile at people, greet them, remove that chip from your shoulder."

"What that mean?"

"Stop feeling sorry for yourself."

Olgon pushed his stool back, stood up and turned his back on them. She saw his shoulders shaking, and she heard his sniffling. Aisling's heart filled with pity for the poor boy. She wanted to comfort him, hug him, but she wasn't sure that would be appropriate. She sent a thought to Irial, asking his opinion. *Go ahead*, he replied.

Aisling stood up and put her arm across his shoulder. She felt him stiffen, but she squeezed his shoulders. He felt so thin and fragile. "I'm sorry," she said. "It's been a terrible experience for you, losing everything you loved, but I want to make it up to you. If we could be friends...."

Olgon shrugged her off angrily. "No friends." He wiped his nose on his sleeve and elbowed her away.

"If it's me you don't like," Aisling said. "I'll leave you alone, but don't make it difficult for yourself by alienating everyone else. They won't harm you; they want to help you, so give them a chance. Who knows? You might have a wonderful future ahead of you."

She nodded to Feorus and he opened the door. "Happy dreams, everyone!"

42 - Four seasons later
ôôôô

Aisling took Hermione out every day to look around and give her some exercise. She was learning quite a lot about the Realm with Hermione's guidance. The Unicorn and Aisling had settled into a comfortable relationship. Once Hermione had agreed that Aisling was in charge, she had become less domineering—*pushy*, as her mother called it—and demanding. Their relationship was now more of a friendship between a young adult and an older woman.

"Where shall we go today?" Aisling asked as they left the stables and went out to the footpath.

"There's something I want to show you," Hermione replied. "This way."

Aisling was curious, but she knew the unicorn liked to spring surprises on her, so she didn't ask where they were going. They rode slowly along the path through the awakening woodlands, past some farmland, and meadows with new-born lambs and calves, until they came to a small lake, surrounded by a glorious flower garden.

"That is so beautiful," Aisling cried. "Does it have a name?"

"Let us go and ask the gardener." Hermione replied. She turned onto a narrow path that led to a small shack on the lakeshore. It was then she noticed a small figure busily hoeing one of the beds. "Is that Olgon?" she asked.

"Why don't you go and ask him?" The unicorn stopped for her to dismount.

Aisling walked slowly along a narrower path towards the gardener. He must have heard her because he suddenly looked up and stopped working while he waited for her to reach him. He looked almost afraid as she got closer.

I'll have to reassure him, she thought. *He might feel I have a grudge against him after the last time.* She hadn't seen Olgon in two seasons, and the last time they'd met, he'd been surly and uncommunicative.

"This is beautiful, Olgon," she said with a smile as she reached him. "Did you do all this yourself?"

He rested his hands on the hoe and looked at her, still a bit anxious. He nodded and almost smiled, at least his lips twitched as if he wanted to smile.

"It's amazing. I've never seen such a beautiful garden. Does it have a name?"

"I call it Friendship Garden. I make it for you." He started fidgeting with the hoe, tapping off a clod of soil. "You like?"

Tears filled her eyes. "I love it! Does this mean we can be friends now?"

Olgon nodded, looking pleased at last. He dropped the hoe on the ground.

"I want to hug you," Aisling said. "Is that all right?"

"I not clean," he said, brushing his clothes with his hands.

She sensed that he was discomforted by her suggestion and it might embarrass him. "That's all right," Aisling replied. "At least we can shake hands."

He wiped his hand on his shorts and held it out to her. She realized his head was level with her shoulders now. He'd grown a bit since they'd last met.

"We are friends now," she said. "Do you live nearby?"

He pointed to the wooden shack by the lake. "That my house. I build, but elf help me. I eat fish from lake."

"It looks very cosy. Are you happy?" she asked.

A shadow passed over his face as he looked away into the distance. "I miss my people, but this is good place. I got friends, little animals, and sometimes elves visit me."

"I'm glad you've found something that you enjoy doing. You seem to have a natural talent for growing things. You must get that from Momo Tilly," Aisling said. "I will never forget her and what she did for me."

"She die," Olgon said. He suddenly looked quite miserable.

"I'm sorry, Olgon, I shouldn't have reminded you. May I come and visit you again?"

Olgon nodded. "Wait! I give you flowers."

&~& End &~&

Appendix

A – Characters

Elves

Aisling (pronounced _Eye-sling_)- Elven Princess

Queen Fenella of Lycea – Aisling's Elven mother

King Briartach (pronounced Bree-**art**ak) of Lycea – Aisling's Elven father

Irial (pronounced Eerial) - Elven leader

Ráona (pronounced Rayona) – female elf

Róisín (pronounced (Royshin) elf (F) – interspecies diplomat

Andrel – court healer

Cathal (pronounced Kathal)– elven warrior

Euna (pronounced _yu-na_)- elven healer

Piarus - (pronounced _Pee-arus_) - elven warrior, 2nd in command

Aithne - (pronounced _Ethne_) elven healer

Feorus - (pronounced _Feeorus_) Aisling's footman

Opela – Aisling's body servant

Parthalán – the honourable master, elder and wise man

Hermione (pronounced _Her-me-ony_) – the unicorn

Einri - (pronounced _Eyenry_) one of Aisling's guards

Leán - (pronounced Lee-an) Aisling's Mid-Realm mother, Queen Fenella's cousin.

Steofán – (pronounced Steyfan) Aisling's teacher.

Flancy – Palace tracking dog

Everling - Messenger

Humans

Gran - Muirne Mac Roibín
Gran's friend - Aunty Patsy
Lena (pronounced *Layna*) - Slave

Korrigen

Domin (father/chief) Cragsil – leader of the northern Korrigen
Loamin (son) Cragsil – son of the Domin
Momo (grandmother) Tilly – healer – mother of the Domin
Olgon – "the boy" son of Loamin Cragsil

Fairies

Innes - (m) King's councillor
Queen Máire (pronounced Ma-**ee**ray) - queen of the fairies
Davina – (F) fairy leader
Areilt – (F) (pronounced *Arayilt)* - fairy healer
Bearnes (pronounced Bee-**arn**es) - (M) fairy warrior, second in command

Slaves

Lena – slave, Aisling's friend
Master Gobrum – the slave master
Nápla – slave head cook

Dwarfs

Gyoka - leader of the dwarf warriors

Qurak – dwarf second in command

Dragons

Lord Felivar (Pronounced Fell-**ee**var) – dragon leader

Jevtic (pronounced Yevtix) – dragon monarch

Korrigan singular
Korrigen plural (Pronounced "Korrighen)
Dwarfs
Fairies – Small winged creatures
Elves – Aisling's people.

Human world – Mid-Realm

World of magic – Realm of Light

Underworld – Dark-Realm

Distant lands – Far-Realms

Fields of the Ancestors - Home of the departed

Enisdale – Mid-Realm village where Aisling grew up

Lycea – Aisling's Realm of Light ancestral home

Glendonia – Nápla's homeland

About the Author

Vicki Wootton was born and educated in England but has spent most of her adult life in North America. She currently resides in British Columbia.

Among her many occupations, she has been a mother, galley girl on a fishing boat, law office accountant, and a government contractor. She is now a full-time writer and book designer.

She is a vegetarian and a Jesusonian and enjoys balcony gardening. To wind down, she does online jigsaw puzzles.

෨෬

It would mean a great deal to the author (me) if you could find a moment to leave a *review* on amazon. Thank you so much!

෨෬

www.ingramcontent.com/pod-product-compliance
Lightning Source LLC
Chambersburg PA
CBHW020343180626
46812CB00001B/315